HELLO HEARTBREAKER

KELSIE HOSS

Editing by Tricia Harden of Emerald Eyes Editing.

Proofreading by Jordan Truex, Hannah Bryant, and Elizabeth Thompson.

Cover design by Najla Qamber of Najla Qamber Designs.

Have questions? Email kelsie@kelsiehoss.com.

Readers can visit kelsiehoss.com/sensitive to learn about potentially triggering content.

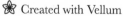 Created with Vellum

For the lovely stylists I've had throughout my life. Thank you for making me feel beautiful every time I sat in your chair.
Angela Salazar & Michelle Jerles & Nikki Popp & Virgie Popp

CONTENTS

1

MAGNOLIA

I STEPPED over a box in the kitchen to get to the coffee pot, already full of golden-brown liquid. "Cam, you are a lifesaver," I said to my best friend, who was already sitting at the table and eating breakfast in her scrubs.

She sent a cheeky wink my way. "Knew you'd need it for your first day at work!"

"And every other day too," I said, pouring myself a cup. "I don't understand you early birds, but my inner night owl salutes you." I held up the mug in cheers to her before bringing it to my lips. The aromatic liquid burned and brought me to life simultaneously.

"How'd you sleep?" she asked as I rummaged through the fridge for some yogurt and then dug through a cardboard box to find a spoon.

"Like shit," I admitted. With a clatter of stainless steel, I finally found a spoon and sat across from her. "I'm so nervous."

She brushed aside her blond fringe and looked up at me. "Don't be."

I arched an eyebrow. "Right. Because I didn't just quit my job and move back to my hometown for a *chance* to prove I'm worthy of owning the salon."

"You know Rhonda. She never had kids. That place is like her baby. A baby we both know you're going to take amazing care of." Cam was so confident in me. Until she frowned. "Do you think you'll see him today?"

"Who?" I asked, even though we both knew who she was talking about.

She gave me a look.

I let out a sigh and set my spoon in the yogurt container. "I'm sure he cuts his own hair, and I have no plans to visit the diner until news of us moving back has died down. I swear, everywhere I go it's like a family reunion with all my long-lost relatives dying to tell me how happy they are I'm home. And asking why I'm still single."

Cam winked. "I don't mind the attention."

Of course she didn't. She had been the one always getting me out of the house when we moved to Austin after graduation. She made tons of friends in nursing school while I was more focused on work and tending to my broken heart. "You can have all the attention," I said, finishing my yogurt and getting up from the table. "Don't want to be late."

"I'll see you after my shift," she said. "Remember, your dad's coming over to help us put the furniture together and my mom's helping us decorate after."

"Please be careful with my—"

"Precious metal art," she finished with a smile. "I know; we will."

I put my hands together and shook them in the air. "Thank you."

I started walking toward the door, and Cam said, "Keys!" She lifted a flap of a box near the table and pulled out my key chain with the wire art sunflower.

"How did they get in there?" I asked.

She shrugged, tossing them my way.

"The retirement home is lucky to have you," I said with a grin.

"Don't I know it. Good luck today!"

With a wave, I was out the door, driving from our little rental house to Rhonda's, the only salon in Cottonwood Falls. It was a cute brick building on Main Street with painted teal trim and a sign overhead with swirling cursive font.

Rhonda's Salon

My heart swelled at the sight, realizing I could be mere months away from reaching my dream of owning my own salon. After a dozen years working in the city but getting nowhere with my ultimate goal, Rhonda called like an answered prayer. She said she wanted to retire, but she wouldn't be letting go of her salon unless she could pass it to someone she trusted to take care of this town's needs. If I could work there for six months and treat her clients well, I could buy it for myself. Make my own stamp on this town.

The place that built me.

The place where I'd first fallen in love.

And the place where my heart had been so broken, I never thought I'd recover or even want to come back.

I could see young me all over this town, cruising Main Street with him. Wearing his jersey to football games.

Getting shakes at the diner for our very first date. Holding hands in the movie theater. Giving him all of my firsts, all of myself... And I remember the small-town skyline in my rear-view mirror as I drove away.

I took a breath. I could handle being here. I wasn't the eighteen-year-old me with her faith shaken and tears in her eyes anymore. I was a grown woman with hopes, dreams, notches in her bedpost and a future ahead of her. I could own a business, live closer to my dad, enjoy time with my friends. Finally reach my dreams.

Getting out of my car, I walked to the front door of the salon, just in time to see Rhonda flip the sign from "Sorry, we're closed" to "Come in, we're open!"

She waved at me through the glass, her eyes crinkling with her smile. Her permed brown hair was piled atop her head with a clip, and her lips were painted with bright red lipstick to compliment her cheetah print blouse and teal-blue glasses frames. She always did have flair.

The bell on the door jingled as she opened it and said, "Come here, you!" She pulled me into her arms, and I grinned, hugging her back and basking in the familiar smell of her perfume.

Rhonda was like a second mom to me after my own mom left Dad and me, giving me work at the salon to sweep up hair, stock products, make sure everyone had what they needed. The money had been helpful, but the work gave me a much-needed distraction while it felt like my world was falling apart.

"It's so good to see you," I said into her shoulder.

"You too." Her smile turned to a scowl as she pulled away. "It's been too long since you've been home. A phone call every month wasn't near enough Maggie time for me."

I gave her a guilty shrug along with a smile. "Guess I'll have to make up for lost time."

She put her arm around me, pulling me close. "Good girl. Now let me show you around."

For the next half hour, she showed me how she'd rearranged and updated the shop over the years, made sure I was familiar with the payment system and scheduling software, and then glanced at the windows. "Oh, it looks like your first appointment is here."

I followed her gaze, expecting to see an older woman from the community.

Instead, I saw *him*.

Rhett Griffen walked down the sidewalk toward the salon in all his six-foot, two-inch glory. His jeans hugged his legs like God himself painted them there. His T-shirt wrapped around thick biceps and hung loose around his waist. But best, or possibly worst, of all were his hazel eyes, staring right at me, stealing all the breath from my lungs.

"Oh, hell no," I said.

Rhonda turned and stared at me like I'd kicked a kitten. "Language, dear."

"Sorry, it's just—you know our history. Are you sure you don't want to take him?" I asked.

With a knowing look, she said, "This is a test, Maggie. Can you take care of every client in this town the way I would? If not, I'm afraid I'm not sure what you're doing here."

I gritted my teeth together. This six-month trial

period wasn't going to be a walk in the park. Rhonda was going to make me work for this opportunity.

I took a deep breath as he approached the door.

"Of course I can take care of him."

Scissors would help.

2

RHETT

IF LOOKS COULD KILL, I'd be a pile of ash blowing down the sidewalk.

But even with that stink on her face, Magnolia Ray Gibson was beautiful as always.

She had her dark brown hair pulled back off her neck, showing earrings shaped like a pair of saguaros. Soft pink lipstick made her lips that much more appealing. And years had curved and shaped her body in a way that had my hands itching to reach out and hold her.

Knowing I couldn't, I pushed my way through the door and then kept my hands hooked to my pockets just in case. "Rhonda, Mags, aren't you a sight for sore eyes."

Rhonda fanned her face. "Aren't you the charmer."

I smiled back at her, but my eyes quickly slid over to Maggie. The passing years hadn't changed my attraction to her, and just like back then, I felt like a planet spinning around her, just begging for an ounce of sunlight.

But seconds passed as I waited for Maggie to say

something. Acknowledge the fact that we were seeing each other, talking face to face, for the first time in years.

Instead, she said, "My chair's this way."

Right. She was still pissed.

I couldn't say I blamed her.

Rhonda gave me a knowing smirk as I followed Mags back to her chair, trying to keep my eyes above the sway of her ass.

"Sit," Maggie commanded.

"Yes, ma'am," I said, lowering into the chair in front of her.

She scoffed but didn't comment, instead getting a cape, flaring it out angrily like she was showing down a bull in Spain, and put it around my neck just a little too tight.

"How's that?" she asked, her voice dripping with syrup.

"If you want to choke me, you need to buy me dinner first," I replied.

Her cheeks heated bright red, and I held back a grin as she loosened the collar.

"What do you want me to do?" she asked.

"Now that you mention it, I'm thinking you and me at dinner sounds good. I could pick you up after work today."

She gave me her signature glare in the mirror, and even though we'd both aged, it was the same Mags I remembered. The one who appeared in my dreams night after night no matter how much time went by. Fire in her eyes, passion in her heart, and she looked cute as hell all the while. She blinked at me innocently. "I'm sorry, I've never heard of that hairstyle. But then again, I've never been to the state of Delusion."

I smirked. "Guess you're the professional. Whatever you say is alright with me."

"Right." She turned my chair and then pushed on the foot lever so I slid down abruptly. And within two seconds, she had the clippers at the back of my head, slicing a path through my hair.

"Whoa!" I said, jerking forward. "Don't you have a guard on that?"

She looked innocently at her clippers. "I'm sorry, I thought you said I could do what I wanted."

"I didn't want you to scalp me!"

She shrugged. "Sorry, I guess I figured I would give you whatever cut kept you out of my chair the longest."

From the other side of the salon, Rhonda cleared her throat loudly.

Maggie's voice was strained as she said, "I'm sorry, sir. I'll do my best to clean up that cut."

"Sir?" I asked. I hated to admit the places that word took my mind.

She glared at me.

And even I knew when to stop. Especially when the one doing the glaring had an assortment of sharp and pointy scissors sitting on the counter.

I kept my lips pressed together as I watched her work in the mirror. She wore a pink apron tied around the back that only accentuated her curves. When she dipped her head, the curls that hung loose from her hairdo draped along her face, sometimes obscuring my favorite part of her.

She had these eyes that were like ocean tides,

changing color by the day. Today, they were more green than blue because of the olive toned V-neck T-shirt she wore, and I knew at night they'd turn the color of dark denim.

"I can feel you staring at me," she said without looking up.

Busted. "Just making sure you don't massacre the rest of my hair."

"What's left of it," she muttered.

My jaw dropped, and I had to feel my head just to check. "I'm not even close to going bald."

"Mhmm."

"Now you're just being cruel."

"What? I *am* the professional." She wore a pleased smile.

I would have shaken my head at her, but she was too busy working for me to risk it. She did some scissor work along the top of my hair, used the clippers around the swath she'd already mowed down, and I crossed my fingers in my lap. Just a couple minutes later, she set the scissors down and was spraying me with ice cold water.

"Jeez," I said, "You're worse than Mom on Sunday mornings."

"I'll tell her you said that," Mags said, just a hint of warmth to her voice. She and my mom had always gotten on well.

"You wouldn't dare."

She arched a brow. "Don't test me."

I smiled at her in the mirror. "Going to let me look at the cut?"

Cringing, she said, "I think it's best if you don't."

I let out a small laugh, breathing a huff of air out my nose. "I'll take your word for it."

She reached for the cape, removing it and the small towel from my neck. But then her fingers caught my skin, sending fire down my spine. "What is this from?"

Realizing she had touched the surgical scar, I jumped out of the chair like I'd had an ice cube put down my shirt. "Nothing. How much is it?"

Her dark eyebrows drew together as she studied me. "It's on the house. First customer is free. Congratulations."

I shook my head, reaching into my wallet, and took out a hundred-dollar bill, pressing it into her hands. "A tip."

"You don't owe me anything," she said uncomfortably. "The back really didn't turn out all that well..."

I lifted a corner of my lips. "I think I owe you more than that bill could cover."

Her mouth moved, but no words came out.

And I already knew I'd overstayed my welcome. So I put on my hat to cover up at least part of the haircut and left the salon, waving to Rhonda on my way out.

As I walked down the sidewalk, one thing was clear. Mags hadn't forgotten what happened between us, and it was going to take a lot more than a botched haircut and a tip to win her back.

3

MAGNOLIA

I TRIED to focus on work for the rest of the day, not sure whether I was more upset about seeing Rhett or getting off on such bad footing my first day at the salon.

But Rhonda didn't say much about the incident while we worked alongside each other. Her calendar was booked, and I was able to help with walk-ins and take a few extra appointments while she worked. I could see in the way she moved that she was hurting. She took ibuprofen twice in the ten-hour day and walked like her hips or back were aching.

At the end of the day, she bent to get something from the cabinet under the register and sucked in a sharp breath.

"Let me get that," I said quickly, reaching for a fresh roll of receipt paper. She gave me a grateful smile. "Thank you. I'm not as young as I once was."

Still concerned, I asked, "Is it arthritis?" I knew standing on your feet all day was hard on the body. One of the reasons I wanted to own a salon instead of counting on a job that only paid if I was there, doing hair.

With a frown, she said, "My hip's been giving me trouble. My doctor thinks I need a hip replacement, but I haven't been able to take off work, or afford the surgery if I'm being honest."

My lips parted. "Rhonda... that's awful."

She nodded and continued closing up the register. "Some people have a retirement plan. I have this salon. Raleigh and I have put everything into this place over the years." After a moment, she said, "We all do the best we can, don't we, Maggie girl?"

I lifted a corner of my lips. "I probably should have done better for Rhett this morning."

She let out a laugh, then walked out the front door with me. "Rough start, but we made it through," she commented as we walked toward our cars parked along Main Street.

My cheeks heated at the strip of too-short hair I'd left at the back of Rhett's head. "I promise it won't happen again," I said. "I was just a little caught off guard. I didn't expect to run into him quite so soon."

She stopped at the curb in front of the old Ford pickup she'd been driving for years. "Arnie Weston."

I raised my eyebrows. "That name sounds familiar."

She smiled, her eyes crinkling at the corners. "We broke up when I was twenty-two, and he still drives to the next town over for his haircuts because I told him I'd impale him if he came by here again."

My jaw dropped open. "Sweet Rhonda, threatening violence?"

"Oh hush," she batted my arm. "We all have our

moments of weakness. Just don't make it a habit, sweetie. A town this size, you can't afford to make enemies. Especially when they're as well-loved as Rhett Griffen."

I nodded in understanding. "I promise, I won't."

She gave me a short hug and a kiss on the cheek. "See you tomorrow morning, darlin'."

"See you," I replied.

We went separate ways to our cars, and when I pulled up to my house, Dad's truck was already out front and he was sitting on the front porch steps. My heart warmed at the sight of him and his sweet three-legged rescue dog.

"You're early, Daddy," I said.

He smiled at me before struggling to get up. He cringed with pain, pushing on his thighs to stand up straight.

"Daddy?" I asked. "Are you okay? I thought your back was getting better." At this rate, everyone around me was hurting.

He shook his head. "I'm okay. Just acts up sometimes."

Still not convinced, I said, "Okay, let's get inside." I went to the door, unlocking it for us, and stepped inside the house, mostly covered in boxes. Cam's parents had helped us unload everything, and it was a hot mess.

"Oh, honey," Dad said, taking off his hat and wiping his forehead.

"I know," I said with a sigh.

Eileen nudged her head under my hand so I'd scratch her ears. "Good thing we have you here, sweet girl," I said to her. "We're going to need all the emotional support we can get."

She bumped her wet nose against my hand like she understood.

"Better get to work," Dad said, readjusting his Gibson Trucking ball cap. When he bought his own semi-truck, I'd had it made for him to celebrate his new business.

We went back to my bedroom, and he started piecing together my bed while I unpacked my clothes, sorting them into my dresser and closet.

"Have you ever thought about downsizing?" he teased.

"No way." I laughed. "I have thought about the nursing home for you and your stuff, though."

"Hey now," he said with a chuckle. "I won't say another word about all your junk."

"How was work today?" I asked him.

"Great, until I got home and found out none of the wiring in the house is up to code."

I stalled on the shirt I was hanging up. "What?"

He nodded, focusing on the screw he was twisting into the bed frame. "I got home from work, and the lights wouldn't work on one side of the house. Called an electrician, and he said it's a miracle the house hasn't gone down in an electrical fire."

My heart skipped. "Seriously?"

"Yep." He set the part aside and moved on to connecting the slats. "Wipes out all my savings to have it replaced and then some, but I'd rather that than a house fire."

I frowned. "I'm sorry, Daddy." I wished I could help, but all my money was being saved for the salon.

"It's okay," he said. "I'm just glad you're back. I know

we talked on the phone almost every day, but I still missed you all these years while you were busy in the big city."

"I know. It was just hard to come back here after... and then with work..." I didn't finish the sentence, and he didn't ask me to. "How did you stay in that house after Mom left?"

He shrugged. "At the time, I was trying not to think about myself. It seemed like it would be harder on you to lose your mom and your house. So I focused on the good times instead of the bad and hoped it would get better."

"Did it?" I asked. Because seeing Rhett today had brought back all those feelings I thought I'd buried years ago. I'd been beside myself, so angry with him and hurt all over again.

"It did." He smiled. "Sometimes you can't go somewhere new. You have to create new memories right over the top of the old."

The front door opened, and Cam called, "Honeyyy, I'm hoooome."

Dad and I exchanged a grin. She used to say the same thing when she came over to our house to visit when we were teens. "Been a while since I heard that," Dad called back.

She came into the room, still wearing her scrubs from work, and bent to give Dad a hug. "Good to see you, Ray."

"You too, sweetie," Dad said.

Cam said, "I'm going to get changed. Come tell me about your first day, Mags."

I followed her back to her room, and while she dressed, I relayed my run-in with Rhett and his new, terrible haircut.

She covered her mouth, laughing. "Talk about payback."

I laughed. "I'm just lucky Rhonda didn't fire me on the spot."

"She could never. So when are you seeing him for dinner?"

I raised my eyebrows. "I'm not going to dinner with him. The last thing we need is the two of us in a room with steak knives."

Cam turned, pulling on one of her old volleyball shirts. After ten years, the fabric was thinning and had holes in some places, but she never stopped wearing it.

"What?" I asked, knowing her silence meant something.

"I mean..." She turned back to me, adjusting the hem of her shirt. "It *has* been fifteen years."

"Fourteen," I corrected.

"Over a decade." She reached in her closet for the flip-flops she wore around the house and slid them on. "It's a small town, and we're going to be here for a while. Don't you think it's time to bury the hatchet?"

"In his back?"

She snorted. "Think about it, okay? If nothing else, it's a free meal."

"Hasn't anyone ever told you? There's no such thing as a free lunch."

Laughing, she patted my shoulder. "I think you should do it. Besides... what could go wrong?"

4

RHETT

I GOT in my shower after work, rinsing off the dirt and grime of the day, thinking about seeing Mags for the first time in years.

It was great to see her, even if she was pissed at me. I might sound crazy, considering the butchered haircut and all, but being around her just confirmed that I wanted there to be more between us. This was my chance, the one I'd prayed for over the years, to make things right with her.

But I couldn't do that if she wouldn't so much as look me in the eye without wanting me to combust. And since I was better at hooking up than relationships, I knew I needed advice from the two most in love people I knew.

After I got dressed in fresh clothes, I texted to make sure it was okay and then I was on my way to Fletcher and Liv's house. My brother-in-law was my best friend in the world aside from Cooper, but Coop didn't know my history with Maggie like Liv and Fletcher did.

Their big white house appeared at the end of the dirt road, and I pulled into the driveway, getting out and walking around to the backyard, where I could hear Maya and Liv laughing together as chains clattered and creaked on the swing set. When I rounded the corner, Maya yelled, "Uncle Rhett!"

She rocketed out of the swing and ran up to me, hugging me tight, and I made a show of stumbling back. "Watch it, killer! Where did all those muscles come from?"

"Swim lessons of course." Her dog, Graham, came bounding behind her, and she said, "Heel."

He sat at her feet, pink tongue lolling out of his mouth as he looked at me. I scratched his brown and white fur and said, "I know your dad thinks he's a mutt, but I'm pretty sure he's a hundred percent good boy."

Maya got to her knees, caramel hair falling over her face as she hugged his furry neck. "Yes, you are a good boy, Graham! Yes, you are!"

Liv walked up to us. As she tucked her short brown hair behind her ear, her wedding ring caught the light. "Hope you're okay with hot dogs. I've been craving them like crazy lately." I noticed her stomach just starting to show with the pregnancy.

I snorted, just as Fletcher came out of the house. "Tell your wife to stop talking about her hot dog cravings in front of me."

Fletch rolled his dark brown eyes while Liv's cheeks got pink. She hit me. "Grow up."

Maya seemed confused but shrugged. "I'm gonna go swing."

"Good idea," Liv said with a smile. "Want a beer, Rhett?"

I nodded, going to the seating area near the grill while Fletcher started the food cooking.

"Holy hell," he said when my back was to him. "What happened to your hair?"

I cringed. "It's not that bad, is it?"

"No."

I let out a sigh of relief.

"Just like my mullet wasn't bad," Fletcher added.

"Shit," I muttered.

From the swing set, Maya sang, "Dad's gonna wash your mouth out with soap."

"Bullshit," I said, "it wouldn't work."

"We could test it out," Fletcher suggested with a laugh.

Liv passed me a beer and said, "My parents tried it on him years ago. I'm pretty sure he burped and farted bubbles all of fourth grade."

Maya laughed, but I shuddered at the memory. "I didn't come here to be retraumatized."

Fletcher shut the lid on the grill and walked toward us, taking a beer from Liv. "What is it? Not that we're not happy to have you, but usually you don't come over on a Monday night."

I sipped my beer and set it on the wooden patio table. "I saw Magnolia today."

Liv nearly choked on her lemonade. "Why didn't you say that earlier?"

Fletcher said, "She the one who gave you the haircut?"

"Yep." I popped the P.

"Show me," Liv demanded.

I turned so she could spot the bald patch at the back of my head, and when I turned back, she was covering her mouth, holding back laughter.

"Well now I see who's side you're on," I retorted, taking another drink.

She pressed her lips together, but they peeled open with her smile. "Sorry. What happened?"

"I went into the salon to see her, and I had to get a haircut because I couldn't just show up."

"Brave choice," Fletcher said. "How did you know she'd be there?"

I jerked my thumb at Liv. "She told me last Wednesday that Mags was coming back to town, so I called Rhonda and made an appointment."

"That worked out real well," Fletcher deadpanned.

I sent him a look, and he looked away to hide his laugh.

Liv said, "So she gave you a haircut, and then what?"

"I asked her out to eat, and she said no."

The two of them exchanged looks. It was annoying seeing my best friend do that with my sister, communicating without words. "What?" I asked.

Liv said, "Well... that's it?"

"What the hell else was I supposed to do?"

She laughed. "If you think Mags is going to go out with you just because you surprised her at work after fourteen years apart and then asked her to dinner one time, you're off your game."

I scrubbed my chin. Maybe she had a point. I could

put in a little more effort, show her that I was ready to do things differently this time...

"While you think about that..." Fletcher said like there was more to his sentence.

I raised my eyebrows. "Need help on the grill?"

"Actually... Maya has a question for you." He waved over his daughter. "Come ask Uncle Rhett."

Suspicious, I pinned Fletcher with a stare. "What is this about?"

Maya came to stand in front of me, her hands clasped in front of her.

Liv nodded. "Just like we practiced."

"What?" I asked, staring between my sister and her husband. But then I looked at Maya and saw big puppy dog eyes staring back at me.

"Oh hell no," I said, getting up from my chair and backing away. "No, no, no."

She stepped closer, eyes still wide and begging. "Uncle Rhett?"

I continued backing away, but Graham flounced up to me and nudged my leg.

Grumbling, I stopped, "What is it?"

She smiled sweetly. "Will you coach my Little League team?"

I stared from her to her parents. "Me with a dozen ten-year-old girls? You gotta be out of your fucking minds."

Liv stood beside Maya, her hand on her stepdaughter's shoulder. "Look, I'm pregnant and don't need the extra stress. Fletcher is on call during a lot of the games on the schedule, and none of the other parents will do it. Please? It would mean a lot to us. And Maya."

I shook my head, kneeling in front of Maya. "I'm sorry, sugar, but I would be a terrible coach. Surely there's some other person you can con into it. Maybe Uncle Tyler? Or Grandpa Jack?"

She looked down, her bottom lip sticking out.

"Don't do that to me," I said, my chest physically aching from saying no. "I'm not going to fall for it."

She sniffed. "If we can't find a coach, it'll be cancelled."

Graham came to stand beside her, nuzzling his head under her hand. She held him, saying, "It's okay. Maybe I can play softball next year."

I glared up at Liv and Fletcher. Fletch shrugged, while Liv tilted her head.

"Fine, *fine*, I'll do it," I said.

Maya looked up, grinning. I *knew* those were crocodile tears.

"On one condition," I added.

"Anything," Liv answered. "It really means a lot."

I looked between Maya's parents. "I don't know what it is yet, but when I need a favor, I'm calling on y'all. Anytime, anywhere, anything."

"You've got it," Fletcher answered, shaking my hand. "Maya, go get him his jersey."

"My jersey?" I fumbled for words. "Shit, you already knew I'd cave!"

Liv's smile told all as Maya ran inside.

When she came back out, she was holding a pink baseball jersey with UNICORNS pasted across the chest in silver sparkle letters.

I held it up, staring in abject horror. She turned it over to show a sparkling appliqued unicorn bucking on the back. My balls were practically shrinking back just looking at the damn thing.

"What do you think? Isn't it pretty?" Maya asked.

"I think..." Liv pinned me with a stare that made me hold back. "I think... Go, Unicorns."

5

MAGNOLIA

I PACED BACK and forth across our living room Tuesday night while *Love Wins* played on the TV.

Cam sat on the couch, eating popcorn from the bag. "This season is so messy, and I love it."

I would have laughed. Except my life felt even messier than the show. Reality TV just didn't hit the same when you couldn't say you were doing better than the people on the screen.

Our house was looking so much better since we'd unpacked most of our things yesterday, and Cam used her day off to clean with her mom. They'd even hung up all my favorite wire art pieces on the wall.

But I couldn't get Rhett off my mind.

I'd done so well for myself in Austin, rebuilding my life, my heart, piece by piece. At first it was hard, but then I realized I'd gone a day without thinking about him, and then a month. And I was able to have other relationships.

But ten minutes in a room with him, and thoughts of him were plaguing my mind.

I felt stupid, still unable to let him go.

Cam sighed. "You're thinking about him, aren't you?"

I nodded and dropped onto the couch across from her. "I feel so pathetic."

"Give me your phone," Cam said.

I raised my eyebrows. "Why?"

She wiggled her fingers, and I passed her the device. Within seconds, she held it to her ear. "It's ringing."

"Who are you calling?"

She gave me a look like I should already know.

"Holy shit!" I said, my heart already beating fast. "I didn't think you'd call him!"

She held the phone out. "Better say hello."

My mouth fell open.

She shook the phone for me to take it.

Finally I did and squeaked out, "Hello?"

"Mags?" Rhett's voice was rough but honey at the same time. Equal parts hopeful and bashful. Hearing him say my name only brought back memories and stirred feelings in my heart that should be long since gone.

"Yeah, it's me. Um. You still have the same number."

"I couldn't change it," he said. "Not when I was hoping you'd call."

My heart somersaulted in my chest. I shoved the excitement down. This had to be just another one of his lines. "Um, I was thinking about that dinner you offered."

"Yeah?" The hope in his voice slayed me.

I bit my lip, feeling Cam's eyes on me. "Is it still on the table?"

"Definitely. Want to meet at the diner tomorrow night? Shit, I can't tomorrow. Thursday at six?"

"Thursday's fine," I said. The silence between us felt

so heavy, especially knowing the past versions of us were as close as two people could be.

"Goodbye, Mags." The way he said my name lay heavy on my heart.

"Bye." I lowered my phone to my side, and Cam munched popcorn, staring up at me. "What happened?" she asked. "I swear you're better than the show."

I rolled my eyes at her, then took a deep breath. "Rhett and I are having dinner Thursday night."

When I tell you she screamed.

I covered my ears. "Cam! The neighbors are going to call the cops on us!"

"Let them!" she cried, jumping out of her chair and setting the popcorn on our thrifted coffee table. "Oh my gosh! We have to find you an outfit. Now."

"Now?" I asked, following as she ran to my room. "It's not until Thursday!"

"You're going to look so damn good." She went into my closet, digging through the clothes. "He's going to rue the day he was born."

"Because I look good?"

She paused, in thought. "Rue the day he let you go? That's it." She continued searching.

I sat on my bed, knowing it was hopeless to try and stop her when she got like this. "I mean, we were just high school sweethearts. Like seventy-five percent of those relationships end in divorce. My stupid heart needs to let him go."

"That just means twenty-five percent of high school sweethearts make it," she said. She came out of the closet, holding up a sundress with a stretchy, ruched top that showed off the girls. "This is it."

I smiled from her to the dress. "Am I making a mistake? Maybe it's better to let sleeping dogs lie."

"You're two adults going to dinner. It's been so long since everything happened. Maybe it will be nice to get to know the adult version of him, so you can let the younger version go. Either you'll see he's exactly the same or you'll find out he's different and can get to know the new Rhett." She gestured at the sundress. "And you'll look damn good doing it."

I nodded, taking a deep breath. "What about you? Dating prospects aren't exactly amazing here."

"I know." She flopped back on the bed. "I got on a dating app just for the fun of it, and there were like three people in a sixty-mile radius."

I lay back beside her. "That sucks."

She rolled her head toward me. "But I have a plan."

I raised my eyebrows.

"We're going to the rodeo this weekend."

"You're kidding," I said. "You know Rhett rides bulls!"

She shrugged. "Another way for you to prove you're totally fine now, showing up looking hot and flirting with some country boys. *And* a way for both of us to scout—I mean, meet—every cute cowboy in the tri-county area. Win-win."

I grinned, holding out my hand. "Evil genius."

She gave me a high five and held it. "Those boys won't know what hit 'em."

♥

RHONDA and I sat in the waiting area chairs during an empty appointment slot, drinking coffee from her pride and joy—a teal one-cup coffee maker with a million different flavor cups to choose from.

"I'm glad we have some time to chat," Rhonda said as she retrieved her matcha latte.

I nodded, sipping my hot coffee doctored with cream and sugar. "For such a small town, you keep your schedule pretty full."

With a smile, she said, "Everyone's got hair. Well, mostly everyone."

"True." I laughed. "I know because I dump half of it out of my bra every night."

She chuckled. "Raleigh leaves a nozzle attached to the air compressor in the garage so I can blow the hair off after work."

My eyes widened. "Oh my gosh, that's brilliant. I need to see if my dad has an extra air compressor I could use."

She winked. "Look at you go."

I smiled, taking another sip.

"So a big part of this salon for me is community outreach," she said, setting her coffee cup on the table. "Over the years, I've found my favorite things to support." She held up her fingers, ticking them off. "I always sponsor a Little League team in the summer and serve as the assistant coach. It's so cute to see those girls tear it up on the field."

I nodded, remembering playing for a team sponsored by Rhonda's Salon. "I still have my little pink jersey in my memory box."

"I love that." Rhonda worked her fingers through her

hair, adjusting the curls. "Some other things we do are care for a few of the flower baskets on Main Street, give pro-bono services for foster children in the community, and I'll care for some of our elderly clients in their homes if they can't get out. But I know once you take over, you'll get to decide which projects matter to you and make them your own. Over these next six months, I'd like you to find projects around town where you can volunteer and show me that you're invested in this community."

"I love your heart, Rhonda," I said, reaching out and touching her hand. "You've always been so giving. The way you were there for me when I got the stress-induced alopecia after my mom left..." My voice broke.

"Don't mention it, honey," she said. She squeezed my hand. "It's what family does." She glanced toward the window. "There's our next appointment."

For the rest of the day, I focused on work, trying to think of what types of service projects I could do and trying not to worry about my dinner with Rhett tonight. Before I knew it, I was at home, swapping my black clothes for the dress Cam and I picked out.

Since she was at work, I sent her a picture of me in my outfit. She usually couldn't text much, but a few minutes later, my phone pinged with her reply.

Cam: HAWT *fire emoji*

I smiled at the phone.

Maggie: Thank you *heart emoji* wish me luck *fingers crossed emoji*

Cam: Good luck *four leaf clover emoji*

I tucked my phone in my purse, slid on a pair of sandals, and then walked out the door... to see Rhett already waiting in his truck.

6

RHETT

THE EARLY EVENING sun caught all the gold in Mag's dark hair as she stepped out of the house. A breeze added movement to her dress, making her curves that much more apparent. I had to press my lips together to keep my jaw from dropping.

But her lips fell into a frown when she saw me. She walked up to my truck, spinning her finger in a circle so I'd roll down the window.

When I obliged, she said, "How do you know where I live?"

"There was like one rental house in town." He nodded toward my car. "And your car's your favorite color. *Cerulean.* Wasn't too hard to guess."

But then my eyes caught the wind chime hanging by the door. My lips parted as I took it in, remembering where it came from...

"Gosh, I missed living in a small town," she said drily, oblivious to my distraction. "Anyway, I'll be driving myself to the diner."

I raised my eyebrows. "Do you have no concern for the environment?"

She rolled her eyes at me.

"It's not funny. *Think of the fossil fuels.*"

"If that's your concern, we should be taking my car instead of your big-ass truck."

I laughed slightly at her attitude. That was the Mags I knew. I hit the button to turn off my truck, making her eyes widen.

"I didn't mean to invite you to ride with me!" she said.

I shook my head. "Do it for the environment."

With a huff, she turned and said, "Get in."

I followed her to her little Fiat and opened the door. This had been a really bad idea. I felt like a clown getting in, my knees almost to my chest before I pulled the lever to make room for myself. My head was still brushing the ceiling.

"Comfy?" she asked, a smug smile on her lips.

"Could fall asleep right here," I replied, despite the way my heart picked up in this car. It smelled so much like her. I was surrounded by the scent of honeysuckle and getting lost in the past. In what I wished our future could be.

She put the car in reverse, pulling onto the street and starting the short drive toward the diner.

"How's Ray?" I asked.

Her dad was her favorite person, and it instantly showed in the relaxation of her shoulders. "He's doing well. Just had to have a bunch of electrical updated at his house, which sucks."

"That's the worst," I agreed. "I saw him the other day at the grain elevator, picking up a load."

"He tries to stay busy ever since he bought his own semi and started working on contract," she said.

"I saw a flyer for his services in the gas station," I said. "Sounds better than driving to Rutlage before driving all day for work." Her dad always used to leave so early in the morning to get to work. I knew because I used to be the one picking Mags up for school. Having her in my passenger seat, singing along to whatever was on the radio, was always the best part of my day.

"He likes doing his own thing," she agreed. "And your parents? I haven't seen them around town yet."

"They're good. Dad's busy on the ranch, and Mom's having fun this summer, hanging out with all her grand-children."

"I saw online that Gage got married. And Liv," she said.

I nodded. "Tyler did too a couple years ago. I'm the last one standing." The words came out of my mouth roughly, knowing that life could have been so much different if only I'd made a few better choices when it came to us.

"Here we are," she replied, parking in front of Woody's. It was like déjà vu, being with her at this place again. But we were both older. I could actually grow a full beard now, if I wanted to. She'd filled out since then too, making her even more womanly than before.

Before I got too distracted by her curves, I got out of the car, hurrying to her side to open her door.

She got out, her chest inches from me, and gave me a look. "You didn't need to do that."

I put my hand on the hood of the car, my voice low as

I said, "I've learned a few things about how to treat a woman since we broke up."

Color flooded her cheeks. "Let's go inside."

We walked through the diner, and I could feel everyone's eyes on us. No one commented on it, though, until we got back to the booth and Agatha approached with her ticket book.

"Imagine that, Rhett and Mags here together again," she said, her grin deepening the smile lines on her face. She pulled a pencil from behind her ear. "Last time you two were here in the same booth, you couldn't keep your hands off each other."

Now Mags was blushing even harder, but I said, "Can you blame me? I mean, look at her."

Agatha tossed her head back, laughing. "Quite the charmer. What can I get you two to drink?"

We ordered sodas, and as Agatha walked away, Mags looked around the diner from the black and white checkered tiles to the businesses advertised on the laminate tabletop. "Things really haven't changed around here, have they?"

"That's not true." I gestured toward the tabletop. "CJ owns the garage now. And Fletcher owns the doctor's office. It's Madigan Medical now. Tyler opened boutique apartments for seniors. And thanks to Gage, the school has turf for the kids to play football on now."

"And you? Same old Rhett?"

I shook my head. "I'm hoping to show you that I've changed too."

She raised her eyebrows. "Is that so?"

I leaned forward to reply, but Agatha came back, setting down our drinks, taking our orders and distracting us from our conversation. Maggie sipped from her straw, not quite looking at me. But I had to make her see.

"Look, Mags. I know I have no right to ask for a second chance since I messed up the first chance so badly, but I want us to get to know each other again. Not the Rhett and Maggie who were high school sweethearts and thought they were invincible. The us now. Because the truth is fourteen years is a long time, but you've always been in the back of my mind. And even though this diner looks the same, I'm not that guy you knew, and I want to get to know the woman you've become."

7

MAGNOLIA

I LOOKED at this man across from me. He did look so much like the boy I used to love. Bright hazel eyes. Dimples in his cheeks that only showed with the slightest quirk of his lips. Strong arms and calloused hands. A smile that could melt gold.

But he was different too. I could see the color of five o'clock shadow under his skin. His hair was still full, but his widow's peak was more distinct. And instead of being wiry, he had thick arms and legs with muscles formed from years of hard work.

I'd loved Rhett with all my heart back then. What if he had grown out of all the parts that hurt me? Could my life with him be better than I dreamed it through the idealistic eyes of a young woman? Could I forget the pain he caused me?

I didn't know.

"Rhett, you proposed to me."

He lowered his gaze. "I did."

"And an hour later you were sleeping with another

woman," I reminded him, that wound coming up, buried in scar tissue but painful nonetheless.

His eyes begged me to understand. "You said no. I thought we were over, Mags. I didn't know how to cope."

"So what happens next time we have a fight? Next time you're upset?" I asked, my voice shaking. "I come home from work and see you with someone else?" The pain was growing, transforming, slicing through my chest. I pressed my hand over my heart, trying to soothe myself. "I can't do that again, Rhett. Do you know how bad it hurt, knowing I was going to come back and say yes to you, only to see you'd already moved on just that fast?"

"But that's the thing, Mags. *I hadn't moved on.* I still haven't."

I scoffed at him. "It's been over a decade, Rhett. And your reputation isn't exactly a secret. People have told me you've *moved on* with plenty of other women."

"I fucked plenty of other women," he said roughly. "I've only ever made love to you."

His words pulled at the last stich covering the old wound, and now my eyes were stinging with tears. "I loved you, Rhett. I loved you with everything I had, but we were young, and I was *afraid*. That's why I said no. I didn't want something happening to us like what happened with my mom and my dad. But when I came to my senses and wanted to say yes..." I shook my head, pressing at the corners of my eyes to stem the flow of tears. "It's been so long. I don't want to go back there. I don't want to hurt like that again."

He reached across the table, holding my hand. "Please," he breathed.

And that word, his touch, was my undoing. I looked into his hazel eyes, unable to look away. "Okay."

His lips spread into a happy grin. "Okay?"

I nodded, sniffing back moisture, but his smile was contagious. "I will get to know you again. Platonically. But we're taking it *slow*. I mean a snail's pace."

He held up his hands. "Slow down, killer. We haven't even had dinner yet."

Agatha approached our table with two dishes of food. "Let's change that."

The plate in front of me with a chicken bacon ranch sandwich and fries looked so freaking good. "No one in Austin makes a CBR like Woody's."

"Eat up," he replied, and it didn't take long for me to indulge in a mouthwatering bite.

"Oh my gosh," I said, wiping at the corners of my mouth. "So good."

He laughed. "I wish I liked any kind of food as much as you like that sandwich."

I finished chewing and stuck out my tongue.

He only smiled, eyes crinkling as he did.

I couldn't deny that old familiarity trying to creep back. So I leaned in, trying to set aside my old assumptions. "Are you still riding bulls?" I asked.

He nodded. "Coop and I go to rodeos once or twice a month all summer."

"Coop?" I asked. I didn't recognize the name.

"He works out at Finnigans with me," Rhett explained. "Pretty much my best friend aside from Fletcher. He rides saddle broncs."

"Oh, nice... How is Fletcher? I haven't heard from him in forever." One of the casualties of our breakup.

Fletcher and Rhett were inseparable in high school, which meant when Rhett and I broke up, my friendship with Fletcher ended too.

Rhett's features softened when he talked about his friend. "He married Liv, has a ten-year-old little girl with his first wife and then he and Liv have a baby on the way. Due in six months now. Owns the practice, like I said earlier. Living the American Dream as far as I'm concerned."

"Good for him." I smiled. "I always thought he and Liv had a thing."

"You did not," he replied.

I nodded fervently. "I did! Remember them dancing together at prom? You were so pissed because you thought he was moving in on your sister."

"I guess I didn't know the feelings went both ways," I said. "But they're good for each other. She helps him move forward, and he keeps her grounded, you know?"

I smiled at his description. "I miss Liv too."

"I'm sure we can all hang out sometime."

My chest tightened at the hope that sentence brought. "Maybe someday." I needed to protect myself. Keep things moving slowly.

He seemed to understand what I was saying and glanced down at his plate. "I need to use the restroom. Excuse me?"

I nodded. "Go ahead."

He walked toward the back of the restaurant, and as he went, a blond woman called, "Rhett. Rhett!" Giving up, she stopped by our table. She shook her head, blond curls swinging about her face. "I swear that man has a one-track mind."

My lips parted as I realized who she was. "Lola." She'd changed her hair from the red it used to be, and she must have spent less time in a tanning booth now than she did in high school, but I'd recognize her anywhere. Especially when she was seared in my mind, wrapped in a sheet and standing behind Rhett at his door. Cheeks red, her hair a mess.

Her lips parted. "Oh. My. God. Magnolia! I didn't know you were back in town." If she felt any awkwardness, she didn't show it.

"I'm working at Rhonda's," I said, trying to fight the nausea in my stomach.

"Good for you." She gave me a patronizing smile. "Will you tell Rhett I'll be by around eight?"

"By where?" I asked, my vision growing hazy.

"His place, silly." She giggled and turned to walk away. "Good to see you, Magnolia. Welcome back to town."

I couldn't find the words to speak. Not over the rush of blood pounding in my head. Lola, of all people, was going to his place tonight? On the night he was begging me to make up with him? On the night I was ready to set aside all that pain and try to turn over a new leaf?

I heard Rhett's voice before I saw him. "Miss me?"

I glanced up, seeing that grin on his face. It made me want to puke. "So, *Lola* wanted me to pass on the message that she'll be at your place tonight at eight."

His lips parted. "Mags, it's not like that. I—"

I shook my head at him. "I don't want to hear it." I stood up, grabbing my purse. "God, I can't believe I almost got sucked back in. Our relationship is in the past, and that's where we need to leave it. Have a nice life." I turned away from the table, and he moved to follow me.

"Mags, let me explain."

I turned to face him. "Save your breath. I'm sure Lola will give you a ride to your truck. And probably another one at eight."

8

RHETT

LIV LISTENED to my sob story as I got all the shit for Little League out of the bed of my truck. She came early to help me sort everything. The parks and rec lady had given me bags of softballs, a bundle of bats, the world's oldest catcher's get up, and a handful of gloves in case any of the girls forgot theirs.

"It was awful," I finished, having told her all about my disastrous get-to-know-you dinner with Maggie.

She cringed, rubbing her stomach as she walked beside me. "Yeah, I don't know how you're coming back from that one."

"Liv," I said, frustrated. "A little help might be nice."

We rounded the metal bleachers, going through the gap in the chain link fence by the dugout.

Liv questioned, "I mean, I have to know... Why the hell was Lola coming over anyway?"

I set the bats in the dugout and continued toward home plate. "She had to pick up a piece I made, and that was the only time I could do it because I had that dinner with Mags."

"Ah." Liv frowned. "I mean, surely Maggie's cooled down a little since yesterday. Maybe you can explain it to her tonight."

I stopped at home plate, dropping the bag of softballs. "I'm supposed to show up at her house again?"

Her eyes widened, and her lips parted. "No one told you?"

"Told me what?" I asked, worry settling in my gut. Had she decided to move out of town already?

Several yards away, I heard Maggie's voice. "Oh, hell no."

Through the chain link fence, I saw Maggie standing next to Rhonda. My eyebrows drew together as I looked from them to Liv. "What are they doing here?"

"Rhonda sponsors the team," Liv said as Maggie and Rhonda drew near.

Rhonda added, "And we provide an assistant coach." She put her arm around Maggie's shoulders. "Maggie offered to do it this year."

Maggie's face was pale and her lips were pinched into a smile, but that just frustrated me more. I didn't want her to spend time with me because she had to. I wanted her to spend time with me because she was open to giving me an actual chance.

"I don't need an assistant coach," I said. "I can handle it on my own."

"What?" Liv said at the same time Rhonda replied, "Don't be silly. Twelve preteen girls is a lot for two people to manage, let along one. Maggie will be great help, won't you, dear?" She gave Maggie a pointed look.

Mags pinned a fake smile on her lips. "Absolutely."

Liv gestured toward the bleachers. "There's Fletcher with the snacks."

"Brilliant." Rhonda rubbed her hands together. "Do you want to talk to all the parents and players at the bleachers?"

I nodded grimly. I knew coaching was a bad idea.

I approached the bench, noticing Maggie following as far behind me as she could while we passed through the gap in the fence and stood in front of all the parents and players.

Maya ran up to me, jumping into my arms for a hug.

"Hey, sweet girl," I said, spinning her around. She was why I was here, and I'd do anything for that girl. Time to remember that. "Ready to obliterate the competition?"

I set her down, and she banged her fist into her palm. "We're going to crush them."

Raising her eyebrows, Liv said, "Isn't this supposed to be *fun*?"

Maya and I both turned to her, giving each other and then Liv skeptical looks. "What's the fun of playing if you can't win?" Maya asked.

I nodded in agreement. "I ain't coaching no losing team."

"Yeah!" Maya pumped her fist.

I heard my friend's chuckle and saw Fletcher walking up with Graham on his leash.

"No dogs at practice," I told him.

Maya went to Graham, putting her arms around his neck. "We need a mascot, don't we, Uncle Rhett?"

"That's coach to you," I said. "And no."

Mags made a sound.

I turned to stare at her. "Don't tell me you're already undermining my authority."

She seemed way too pleased by that prospect. "Only saying a mascot could boost team spirit. And that dog would look awfully cute in a unicorn horn." She glanced toward the stand where Rhonda was now perched, looking like she was already watching a game. Maybe she was.

Rhonda gave a thumbs-up.

Fletcher chuckled. "Looks like you're outvoted, Rhett." He walked to Mags, outstretching his arms for a hug. "It's good to see you, Maggie."

Seeming pleasantly surprised, she gave him a hug back, and I hated how jealous I was of my friend.

"Good to see you too," she said warmly, rubbing his back. "And you too, Liv," she said to my sister. "Pregnancy suits you. You're glowing, and I'm having some serious hair envy."

Liv smiled, rubbing her stomach instinctively. "Pregnancy might suit me, but morning sickness does not."

Mags chuckled, and I hated that my sister was the cause of that sound.

I wanted to make Maggie laugh.

I wanted to make her smile.

But now was not that time. I pulled the roster from the pocket of my shorts and glanced over all the names. "I need to make sure everyone's here," I said loudly, and everyone stopped talking. "When I call your name, say here. Loud enough for me to hear you. Got it?"

There was some mumbling.

"I need you to say, 'Yes, Coach.'"

Maggie mumbled, "They're little girls."

I gave her a look, then faced the bleachers again. "When I call your name, say here. Got it?"

The girls chorused, "Yes, Coach."

"Good," I said. Then I held up the paper, reading down the list. In a few minutes, we'd determined all the girls were, in fact, present. Then, I said, "Any questions?"

One of the girls, Dahlia, raised her hand.

"Yes?" I pointed at her.

"What happened to your hair?"

From the center row, Rhonda cackled. "Sorry!" she quickly said, covering her mouth. "Sorry."

I shot Maggie a glance and said, "Better behave with this one. She'll get you with the clippers."

The girls' eyes widened, and they suddenly got quiet.

"Now here are the rules. Rule number one, I make the rules."

Maggie cleared her throat.

"Rule number two"—I jerked my thumb toward Maggie—"she actually makes the rules."

That earned me a chuckle, even from Maggie.

"Rule number three, you're going to give it your all. Every practice, every game. Understand?"

The girls nodded and mumbled.

"I said, do you understand?"

The girls said, "Yes, Coach."

"Rule number four. Arguably the most important one. Don't be a shithead."

Liv's eyes bugged out, and Mandy Green, one of the moms, glared at me. Maggie whispered, "Curse words..."

The tips of my ears grew hot. I knew I would fuck this up. "I mean. Don't be a... well, there's not another good word for that. Just don't do it. Okay?"

The girls were giggling as they said, "Yes, Coach."

"Players, to the field," I said. "Coach Maggie, can you please pass out the practice and game schedule?"

Maggie nodded.

I went to the first row of bleachers where I'd stacked the packets and put a rock on top to keep them from blowing away. I got them and went to hand them to Maggie.

Our fingers brushed and heat spread from the contact. I held my breath, trying to shove back the feeling.

If she felt the same, she didn't show it. She simply took the stack and began passing out the papers. It made me embarrassed, knowing I had all these one-sided feelings.

I turned my back, adjusting my ball cap and going to join the girls on the field. If I couldn't make things right with Mags, this was going to be one *long* summer.

9

MAGNOLIA

ON SATURDAY AFTERNOON, Cam sat in the chair in front of me as I curled her hair for our evening of scouting eligible men at the rodeo. Upbeat music played on the radio, and it felt like one of those nights when I could see our lives behind us and before us. The pair of us doing hair before prom... doing hair for a night out... doing hair for our weddings... getting ready for our children's graduations... in a nursing home...

"I'm so glad we're going out," I said. "I feel like it's been forever since we've had a good night on the town."

She bit off one of those massive Sweet Tarts, chewing through the sour candy. "We're not in our twenties anymore."

"Thank God," I replied.

She laughed. "Right? I can't help but think these are the days, you know? Like these could be some of our last times just you and me, living together, watching trashy reality TV on the weekends... hanging up another one of those wire art pieces you're obsessed with..."

"Don't make fun. And don't make me sad. Are you sure we can't just be single besties forever and live on a commune or something?"

"It's a possibility." She winked at me in the mirror.

But I knew she was right. She broke up with her last boyfriend in Austin because he didn't want to have children someday like she did. Which meant she had a certain kind of future on her mind. And one thing I loved about Cam? She always went after what she wanted, no matter what anyone else thought.

"Maybe you'll meet the one tonight," I said.

"The one, or the one for the weekend. Either way is fine with me," she replied.

I smiled. "Maybe that's what I need too. A casual hookup to break me in to this new dating scene. Rhett's crawled under my skin, and I need to get him off my mind."

She shook the Sweet Tart wrapper to get another disc out. "Or you can bang one out with him."

I nearly dropped the curling iron. "Shit." I fumbled with it and pulled it away from her head.

"You almost burned me, you bitch!" she yelled.

I laughed. "You surprised me!" I set the curling iron on the table, just in case.

"With my fabulous idea?" She turned in the chair, resting her forearm on the back and her chin on her forearm.

"The guy is like a drug, Cam. One second around him and I'm sucked back in and he's all I can think about! What do you think sex would do to me?"

She got a cheeky smile, and I said, "Don't answer that."

Letting out a laugh, she replied, "I mean, handling all those balls at practice didn't get you fired up?"

I covered my face with my hands. "You're incorrigible."

"It is my middle name," she replied. "Camryn Incorrigible Childers."

"Has a nice ring to it."

She nodded, turning back in the chair, and I picked up the curling iron, continuing to work my way through her hair. She had the prettiest natural sandy-blond hair with just enough wave to hold a curl.

When I finished, she had this cute curly do that went perfectly with her long-sleeve cotton dress. I wore a dress too with my cowboy boots and paired it with some silver jewelry.

We took a few pictures together, and I smiled at the images, hearing her words echo in my mind. *These could be some of our last days together as single girls.*

THE COTTONWOOD FALLS county fairgrounds were busier than I'd ever seen them, the grass lot lined with pickups and trailers. Cam and I got out of my car and walked toward the dirt arena, where we could already hear the announcer booming and the crowd cheering.

"I forgot how much I loved this," Cam said, her eyes lighting up.

There was a feeling of electricity in the air, excitement and community too.

That was the one thing I'd missed most about Cottonwood Falls, knowing, despite all its flaws, you couldn't turn around without seeing someone who you knew would have your back.

Cam and I had a friend group I loved in Austin, but it was never quite the same.

The smell of food from the concession stand hit my nose, and I breathed deeply. "I have to get the nachos here."

"I'm dying for some popcorn," she said.

We began walking around the arena toward the white shed where they sold concessions every year at the rodeo. On the way, we ran into our old high school English teacher, one of Cam's dad's coworkers at the conservation office, and a former classmate with her three kids.

But then I heard his voice.

"Didn't think I'd see you here," Rhett said.

I turned my gaze toward him, connecting with his darkened eyes shaded by a black cowboy hat. Holy fucking hell.

He looked like hot incarnate in a dark green shirt with the top three buttons undone and starched dark blue jeans.

My mouth went dry as I looked back at him, trying to come up with words. Trying to remind myself of reasons why banging it out with him would be an exceptionally terrible idea. I didn't even notice the guy beside him until Cam said, "Hey, trouble. Long time, no see. Who's your friend?"

"This is Cooper. And Cooper, this is Camryn."

Now my eyes landed on Cooper as he shook my friend's hand. He had dark blond hair that curled under his cowboy hat, a strong build like Rhett's and warm blue eyes. His hand was so big it nearly enveloped Cam's.

"H-hi," Cam said, her usual confidence nowhere to be seen.

Rhett and I met eyes, sharing a small smile.

"Nice to meet you, Camryn," Cooper said, his voice low.

Hello, Josh Turner, what are you doing in Cottonwood Falls?

Over the speakers, the announcer called, "That's it for our barrel racers! Up next, the steer roping!"

Rhett nudged Cooper, who was still holding my friend's hand. "That's our cue."

Cam seemed to come to, giving Cooper a small smile, and then waved goodbye.

"Will you be at the bar after?" Cooper asked.

"Maybe," Cam replied casually. "Depends on how you do."

He chuckled and walked away. After we got out of earshot, I said, "Nice recovery."

Cam's eyes were wide as she turned to face me. "I think I blacked out. What the hell just happened?"

I chuckled. "I think you just met the one."

Cam shook her head as she walked beside me toward the concessions stand. "We are *definitely* going to that bar."

10

MAGNOLIA

CAM and I made our way to the bleachers, sitting about halfway up as people in the arena rode horses and chased down steers with their lassos.

I dipped a chip in nacho cheese, savoring the flavor. "I swear, food in Cottonwood Falls just hits different."

Cam laughed. "You're such an easy date. This and a chicken bacon ranch is all you need."

"True," I said with a smile. "It brings back so many memories—being here."

She nodded, looking around us wistfully. "You remember what Rhett used to do after every ride?"

I covered my face, my cheeks warming at the memory. "That's so embarrassing."

She dragged another piece of popcorn through my cheese and brought it to her mouth. "No way. It was adorable, seeing him get off that bull and point to you in the stands, like it was you who gave him the bravery to do it in the first place."

My heart warmed, because that was exactly how it

felt. And to be acknowledged by him, deemed special by him when so many girls in the area crushed on him? It meant the world to me as a teenage girl with stars in my eyes.

"Things have changed since then," I reminded myself, reaching for a chip.

She nodded. "Have you decided on your service project yet?"

I shook my head and wiped a bit of cheese from the corner of my mouth. "I like the idea of free haircuts for foster children, so I'll definitely continue that, but I've been trying to come up with something new too. Do you have any ideas?"

"Actually, there are some ladies at the nursing home who I think you could help. The CNAs clip their nails and help with hygiene, but you know it's not the same as being pampered."

"Oh my gosh, you're so right. Maybe we could do a beauty day every month and paint their toes or curl their hair so they feel pretty."

"You'd really be making a difference," Cam said. She booped my nose with a piece of popcorn, then popped it in her mouth.

Rubbing my nose, I laughed. "You're so weird."

"Back atcha."

The announcer came over the radio, saying, "Up next, we have our saddle bronc riders! Are you ready to see some guys hit the ground?"

Cheering erupted around us, and I laughed, joining in.

"Up first is our very own Cooper Lawson. He's a big

guy, coming in well over six feet, but still smaller than a two-thousand-pound horse! Let's give it up for him!"

Cam cheered loudly, and I smiled over at her. "You've got it bad."

"Oh shush," she said, still clapping with her cheeks gaining color.

My eyes turned toward the gate holding back the horse which Cooper sat atop. Next to him, in the corner, was Rhett among the guys holding the horse and helping Cooper prepare.

The countdown timers sounded and then the gate flew open, the horse instantly bucking into the arena.

Cooper held one hand in the air, his other gripping a rope over the horse's shoulders.

"Oh my God," Cam whispered as we watched.

I totally agreed. I held my breath, the seconds passing feeling so much longer than usual. The buzzer went off, Cooper still on the horse, and a couple of other guys on horses rode alongside him. One pulled Cooper onto his horse, and the other guy lead the bucking bronc out of the arena.

Everyone in the crowd went wild, shouting, "COOPER! COOPER! COOPER!"

Cam's grin was so big as she cheered and clapped along.

We watched the rest of the bronc riding, and then it was time for the bull riding.

"Rhett's turn," she said.

I nodded. He'd been riding bulls since we were sixteen years old. I remembered going to his first rodeo and cheering for him from the stands, so proud that he was my boyfriend. He'd ridden his bull for eight seconds that night.

He said I made him feel invincible.

Neither of us knew then that what we had could break.

Things were different now, but when the announcer called Rhett's name and I saw him in the chute, on the back of that massive, horned animal, my heart still leapt to my throat.

I still held my breath as it bucked, him holding on to the back.

The seconds seemed to drag by until the buzzer went off, signaling he'd made the entire ride. He flew off, rolling on the ground and then easily springing to his feet as a rodeo clown sprinted out and distracted the bull.

Rhett ran to the fence and stood at the top rung.

And, in front of everyone in the audience, he pointed right at me.

All the people around me turned to take me in, and my cheeks flushed bright red as I lifted my hand to wave. The cheering got louder, and I realized Rhett was egging them on, clapping, waving his hands.

The announcer joined in on the fanfare. "Looks like Rhett Griffen wants to give the praise to a special little lady in the stands. Let's make some noise!" A sound effect of clapping and cheering joined the deafening ruckus around me.

As Rhett met my gaze across the space between us, I mouthed, *I hate you.*

His grin only got bigger.

11

RHETT

IT WAS dark outside when Cooper and I rolled up to the township hall where the town's events board was throwing a post-rodeo "barn dance."

"Think she's gonna kill you?" he asked.

I smirked, turning off the engine to my truck. It was old enough I still had to use a key in the ignition. "Mags never minded the attention before. But it has been a long time since then." Shit. Now I was second guessing myself.

"What the hell happened between you two anyway?" he asked. "I swear I've never seen you put in this much effort for a chick before."

I let out a sigh, looking out my window even though I could only see the truck parked next to me. "I don't like to talk about it."

"That's obvious."

Why hadn't I told him? Probably because it was one of the dumbest things I'd ever done, and thinking about it still hurt like hell. Time didn't heal all wounds; it just taught you how to live with it. "I was twenty years old, and Mags had just graduated high school. She was about to go study cosmetology, and I'd just graduated from a diesel mechanic program. I had this idea that I could follow her to Austin, work there while she got her degree, and then we could move back to Cottonwood Falls together."

Cooper gave me a teasing smile. "Quite the romantic."

I rolled my eyes at him.

"I don't see the problem."

"The problem is I thought we could do it all as man and wife. Several couples from the years before us had gotten married straight out of high school, and I thought we could make it too. I proposed, and she wasn't ready. She turned me down, I freaked out. I was hurting so bad I did the only thing I thought I could to make it through the night and hooked up with a girl to try and cover up the hurt. Then Maggie showed up at my place to say she was ready to say yes now that the shock had worn off... while the girl was there."

Cooper winced.

I nodded. "It was the worst mistake of my life."

With a frown, Cooper said, "We're all dumbasses at twenty. Some of us stay dumbasses our whole life." He gave me a pointed look.

A smile tipped my lips, and I got out of the truck. Then I looked across the hood at my friend straightening his cowboy hat. "Hopefully after tonight, she'll give me a chance."

We looked both ways, then crossed Main Street to the building with people going in. "Speaking of tonight..." he said.

"Yeah?"

"Can I borrow your place?"

I stopped on the curb. "What the hell?"

"I wanna bring Camryn home, and my place is a mess."

"Never seemed to stop you before," I said, pinning him with a falsely curious stare. We both knew he liked her, but I kinda liked watching him squirm.

He shoved my arm. "She's different and you know it."

"You've known her for two seconds. How do you know she's special?"

He glanced down and then back toward me. "It's a feeling, okay? I just looked in her eyes and..." The tips of his ears were growing redder by the second. "Don't make me say it."

"Okay." I chuckled. "And you think my place is clean?"

"You're weird about shit like that," he muttered, adjusting his hat again.

"Only because my mom could pop by at any moment, and I don't want to catch any grief," I replied. "But yeah, you can take my place. As long as you agree to do early feed duty for the next month."

"Fuck," he said, looking over his shoulder like he really had to consider it. And I didn't blame him. The cows were not the kind of ladies you wanted to see when you woke up at four a.m. "Fine." He stuck his hand out for me to shake. "I'll do it."

I shook his hand, grinning. "Let's get in there and seal the deal."

We walked up the stairs, saying hi to a fourth of the county on the way in and half the guys we knew from rodeos in the surrounding area. When we finally got into the big area set up like a dance floor surrounded by folding tables, Cooper said, "Do you see them?"

I scanned the room, seeing a lot of girls but none of them like Maggie and Cam. "Not yet."

"Let's get a drink," he said, nodding toward the cash bar.

We made our way over to the set up in the corner of the room, standing in line to wait, when a gal named Mindy came up to me, giving me a tight hug that had her tits pressing against my middle. "Rhett, you did so great out there tonight!"

I smiled at her, stepping back to put some space between us. No way in hell would Mags see another girl on me tonight. "How ya doing, Min?"

"I'll be better after a drink and a spin around the dance floor?" She batted her wide green eyes at me, and it struck me how different life already was.

A month ago, hell a week ago, I would have spun her around to whatever country song blared through the speakers, taken her home, and showed us both a good time. But now the idea of going home with anyone but Mags...

My dick didn't like it. It would feel like fucking my hand—I'd get off, but it wouldn't be anywhere near satisfying.

My heart didn't like the idea either. Not that it usually had a lot of say in what I did.

"I think I'll take a rain check," I finally told her. "Have fun tonight for me, yeah?"

She pouted her full lips. "I'd rather have fun *with* you."

I chuckled. "Give a guy a chance, Min."

She shook her head, waving her hand at me, and sauntered off.

Cooper watched with me as she went. "Shit, you have it bad."

"Yep."

The people in line ahead of us walked off, and we went to the bartender, ordering a couple drinks and handing him cash.

Cooper muttered something about highway robbery, and I couldn't say I disagreed. We found a table toward the edge of the room, and Coop sat on the side that would let him watch people walk in. His eyes tracked the entrance.

"Shit, dude, could you be more obvious?" I asked.

But he got up, beelining toward the open double doors.

He'd seen Cam.

And I saw *her*.

Mags walked into the dance hall, her head held high. The dress she wore left her shoulders bare, and the ends of her curls danced over the bare skin I wished I could touch. Her lush hips swayed with each step forward, and her breasts filled out the top like no one's business. The slight curve to her lips made me feel like she hid a secret, and the spark in her eyes made me want to find out exactly what it was.

Cooper intercepted Camryn, and Mags smiled, stepping back to give those two space while they were lost in their own little world. She caught me staring at her then, and her lips lifted into a slight smile. Like even though she may have held a grudge against me, her body held a muscle memory of what we used to have.

But instead of continuing toward me, she gave me a small wave and changed direction, going to the cash bar in the corner.

I decided to follow because I was done messing around. Especially when it came to Mags. I knew what I wanted, and I wasn't giving up until I got it. I met her as she reached the front of the line. "Whatever she wants is on me," I told the bartender, reaching into my back pocket for my wallet.

Mags arched an eyebrow. "In that case, I'll have two shots of whiskey."

The thought of sweet brown liquid burning its way down my throat made me smile. As I passed the bartender the money, I said, "How did you know I was in the mood for a shot?"

Mags picked up the shot glasses. "These aren't for you." She downed one, her thick throat moving, and then she immediately took the other. Didn't even flinch. It was so fucking hot. She passed the glasses back to the bartender, thanking him, and then started walking toward the tables skirting the dance floor.

"How about a dance?" I asked. "For old time's sake."

She looked over her shoulder at me. "If it's for old time's sake, then maybe you should dance with someone else."

"Hey now," I said, her words like a punch to the gut.

Giving me a guilty look, she placed her hand in mine. "One dance."

My heart buoyed as I led her to the brawl of dancers. I took her hand, spinning her away and then spinning her back to me. The song was faster paced, so we made quick moves in our two-step, keeping up with the people around us.

She was breathless as she said, "It's been a long time since I danced like this."

I was just trying to think with her chest pressed against mine, her hand warm in mine, her blue eyes looking up at me.

But I couldn't think. So I spun her away from me, leading her in a pretzel and then spinning her around to the music. The song was nearing the end, slowing down as I dipped her back, hair falling from her shoulders, nearly brushing the ground.

Her eyes were wide as she looked up at me, our faces inches apart. My chest moved with my breath, with emotion.

The last note faded to silence, and I picked her back up as the next song began playing.

"Another dance?" I asked.

She shook her head, walking off the dance floor.

I followed, embarrassment and disappointment battling for my attention. "Maggie, why are you always *walking away*?"

She turned on me, arms folded across her chest. "I don't know how to tell you this, Rhett, but every time I look at you all I can see is *her!* I'm trying. I'm trying so fucking hard, but I don't know how to stop."

I reached for her hand, and when our skin connected, it was... everything. "Every time I see you... I see my future walking away."

Her eyes filled with emotion, moisture brimming at her lashes.

"Why do we have to stay stuck in the past?" I asked. "I don't live there anymore, and neither should you. We can make new memories so those old ones aren't so damn fresh!"

She folded her arms across her chest. "You want me to see that you're different?"

I nodded. "Fuck, Mags, I'd do anything."

"Then tell me what you were doing with Lola at eight that night."

I bit the inside of my cheek. Showing her that would... show her more than I was ready for. But I might not have a choice.

She shook her head, blinking quickly. "I knew it." She turned to walk away again, but I took her hand. The warmth was better than any whiskey.

"I'll show you. But you have to come with me."

She scoffed. "Is this just a way to get me in your bed?"

"Baby girl, when I get you in my bed, it's not going to be a trick. You're going to be begging for me to take you there."

12

MAGNOLIA

MY STOMACH SWOOPED at his words, and my thighs clenched instinctively.

Fuck, did this man have a hold on me. Especially with two shots of whiskey heating my insides and making my cheeks warm.

I knew it was a bad idea to go with him to his house because getting close to him had torn me apart so badly the last time. But now I didn't have college in another town to escape to. I'd own Rhonda's Salon if I had my way, and she needed me to buy it and take care of it. I could never betray her by buying it and selling it just to get away from Rhett.

Which left me here. Standing across from him. Country music blaring from the speakers. His hazel eyes watched me, waiting for an answer.

And I couldn't say no, even if it was the smart option. Because my heart was in control. And it was clearly fucking stupid. And desperate to know he wasn't still sleeping with the woman who was there on the worst night of my life.

"I'll go with you," I said.

He tilted his head toward the door. "Let's go."

I stopped by Cam on the dance floor, and she barely said hello as I gave her the keys to my car. She clearly wasn't going to be my DD tonight, so I was glad that I could at least ask Rhett for a ride home after we went wherever we were going.

Rhett was waiting for me at the bottom of the stairs outside the building. Standing there framed by the dark night outside, his cowboy hat guarding his eyes, his jeans showing off his body like no one's business... It was hard not to be that girl falling for him all over again, swept away in the excitement of it all.

I squared my shoulders and took a deep breath, because this man's cologne paired with his heart-melting smile was my personal kryptonite. When I met him at the bottom of the stairs and went to cross the street with him, he placed his hand on the small of my waist.

Just that contact sent heat spreading to every corner of my body.

That simple touch.

And I knew what he said was right. I'd be begging for him. And the question wasn't if, but how long I could hold myself back.

We walked across the street to his pickup, and he held the door open for me.

I gave him a look.

He arched an eyebrow. "I have to."

"Why is that?" I asked.

"When you have a woman you care about, you do the little things for her. Not because you're putting on an act, but because every part of you wants to make her life easier, better, in any way you can."

My heart fluttered, but I held back. Rhett had been a natural at sweeping me off my feet back in the day, and he'd had a lot of practice with women over the years. My heart might be gullible, but my brain knew to look out, at least a little bit.

I got into his truck, sitting in the passenger seat, and he waited until I was buckled in to shut the door. I looked around the cab, noticing a leather cord with a ring hanging from the rearview mirror.

Tears sprang to my eyes as I reached for it, taking the metal in my hand.

Rhett opened the door and got in, looking between me and the ring in my hand. The metal was rugged, just like it had been all those years ago when he got on his knees after my high school graduation and asked me to marry him with a ring he'd made himself. The one hanging from that very mirror.

"You still have this?" I breathed, my voice hoarse.

His gaze was heavy when he met my eyes. "I meant it when I said I've never forgotten you, Maggie Ray."

Tears pooled along my bottom lash. "I think I need you to take me home."

"Mags?"

I brushed away the tears sliding down my cheeks. "I'm sorry, it's just a lot to see it."

"I'll take it down," he offered quickly. "It's been there so long, I didn't think about it upsetting you."

I shook my head, my hand falling from the ring. The symbol of our past and our broken future. With a sniff, I said, "Leave it there. But take me home."

"I want you to know I didn't sleep with Lola."

Maybe it was the look on his face or the ring in front of me, but... "I believe you."

His expression softened to a smile. "Let's get you home."

We drove toward my house, and after a few minutes, he stopped in the driveway, putting his truck in park. We both looked at my house, the wire wind chime illuminated by his headlights.

I looked at the metal design and took a deep breath. "There's this thrift store in Austin near the house Cam and I used to rent. I'd go in there from time to time and find wire art, like the kind you used to make... I guess I didn't want to let go of *all* the parts of our past. There were good memories there too."

He tilted his head, eyes illuminated by the dash lights. Even with a serious expression, there was a ghost of a smile on his lips. "I hope there will be new ones too."

I lifted the corner of my lips. "Are you going back to the dance?"

He dropped his head back. "Shit."

"What?" I asked.

He ran his thumb over his lip. "I told Coop he could stay in my house with Cam tonight."

I laughed. "You're just supposed to sleep in your truck? You're a good wingman."

"I can sleep in Coop's place." He cringed. "Maybe my truck would be better."

I shook my head. "I'm sure my couch is better."

Raising his eyebrows, he replied, "Are you sure you're okay with that?"

I nodded, then sent him a wink. "But I'm not going to beg."

13

RHETT

I FOLLOWED Mags into her house, still in disbelief she'd let me get this close. But when she opened the door and showed me inside, it was hard to stand up straight.

That wind chime wasn't the only wire art she had. There were twisting wire coffee cups in the kitchen. Wire birds on the wall of the living room. A stand in the center of the table with wire flowers sticking up.

She wrapped her arms around her middle. "It's not much, but it's home."

I swallowed to clear the emotion from my throat. "It's great, Mags."

Seeming to relax, she gave me a short tour, showing me the kitchen, the couch, and the bathroom. Then she took some sheets and a blanket from the end of the hall and told me good night.

From the other side of the house, I heard the sink turn on, the splash of water over porcelain. She was getting ready for bed, and I was here, hearing it all...

The light switch flipped, and then the bathroom door

shut. Her footsteps were soft over the creaking wood floors, and then the bedroom door closed.

I spread the sheet out on her couch, slipped out of my boots and jeans so I was in my boxers and a T-shirt, and then lay on her couch. I was tall enough I had to bend my knees to fit. But I could smell her perfume in the sheets, the cushions, and I stared up at the ceiling, feeling more at home than I ever did in my own bed.

14

MAGNOLIA

I WOKE in the morning to the most delicious smell. And then it hit me. Rhett was in my house. He'd slept here all night. In fact, after I did my skincare routine and went to my room to put on my pajamas, I lay in bed, hearing his soft snores coming from the living room.

I'd tiptoed down the hallway to see him asleep on the couch, lying on his side, one olive-toned hand up on his pillow near his face. He looked younger in his sleep, and for a moment, I could picture what life would have looked like if I'd said yes right away all those years ago.

Figuring out life together.

Laughing over cooking fails.

Raising children and eating dinners with his family on Wednesday nights and seeing my dad be a grandpa on the weekends.

But instead, we were in our early thirties, living separate lives, and wondering if, somehow, we could come back together again.

I got out of bed, my heart feeling heavy as I got

dressed for the day in a pair of shorts and a buttery soft T-shirt. I slipped on a pair of Birkenstocks I'd had for years and then walked out to find Rhett in my kitchen, wearing his jeans from the night before with a white T-shirt that hugged his tanned biceps.

His back muscles moved as he bent over the pan sizzling with the food he was cooking.

At the sound of my footsteps, he turn his shoulders and head, sending me a smile that made me weak in the knees. There were those phantom memories again, or rather ghosts of what could have been.

"Good morning," he said, his voice bright enough to match his smile.

"Morning," I replied, shuffling into the kitchen. "What are you making?"

He turned just enough so I could see brown balls cooking in oil. "Doughnuts."

"You can make those at home?" I asked, impressed.

He nodded. "It's easy. You take some biscuit dough and fry it. I made some glaze too." He lifted up a bowl and dragged the spoon through the thick white mixture.

"We had ingredients for that in our house?" I asked, going to the coffee pot. He already had some brewed.

As I poured myself a cup, he said, "I made a quick trip to the store. I got you some flowers. They're on the table."

I turned, finding a vase of sunflowers already clipped and setting in water. "You remembered these are my favorite," I breathed, walking my cup to the table and running my fingers over the delicate yellow petals.

"How could I forget?" he asked, already back to cooking.

My heart was swelling in my chest, conflicted but tired of holding back. I sat at the table, taking a sip of my coffee. The sunflowers in front of me brightened the entire house, even my heart.

"I wonder when Cam will be home," I said absent-mindedly.

Rhett brought a plate with little round doughnuts and the container of homemade glaze, setting them beside the flower vase. "Knowing Cooper, it could be a while."

I reached for a doughnut and dipped it in the glaze. When I popped it in my mouth and chewed, I couldn't help letting out a contented sigh. "Oh my gosh, these are so good."

Rhett smiled across the table at me. "As good as a chicken bacon ranch?"

I smirked. "Don't get ahead of yourself, cowboy."

He chuckled, eating a doughnut too. "What are you up to today?"

I shrugged. "I might go hang out at my dad's for a little while. You?"

"My parents are having a little anniversary party, if you want to come along."

I cringed at the idea of being around his entire family. "I'm sure they'd love to have your ex hanging around."

He finished chewing his bite and said, "They've always loved you. I swear to God I hear your name come up every Christmas."

"Why's that?" I asked.

"Because they know that you're the one who got away." He finished up his food and stood up.

I looked up at him. "Are you leaving now?"

He reached out, brushing some hair behind my ear, and cupped my chin. "I'll see you at practice Tuesday?"

I nodded. "And for dinner Wednesday night." I was going out on a limb, hoping he'd be okay with another fresh start.

He cringed, and my stomach immediately turned.

"You don't want to," I said, looking down. God, I felt so stupid. This was just a game, and now that he had me...

His hand fell to his side. "Of course I want to, but I always have dinner with my family on Wednesdays," he said. "How about we do something Thursday? I have a spot I'd love to show you."

I lifted my lips, nodding. "That sounds good. Unless you're wanting to show me your bedroom."

He tossed his head back, laughing. "Sounds like something I'd do, doesn't it?"

I shook my head at him.

"I'll see you then."

AFTER RHETT LEFT, I called my dad to see if he wanted to hang out, but he said he'd picked up a few extra loads to haul. I frowned, wondering how often he worked on Sundays.

But since he was busy, I occupied myself in the house, meal prepping for the coming week, sorting through my things, sweeping and mopping.

It was late when Cam came home wearing a big plaid button-down shirt like a dress along with her cowboy boots from the night before. Her blond hair was pulled into a high ponytail, and her cheeks were glowing.

"Oh. My. Gosh." I said, taking her in. "Tell me *everything*."

She grinned, coming to sit with me at the table. I went to the fridge, getting out a couple sparkling waters for us, and passed her one.

"I'm assuming you need to hydrate," I teased.

"You have no idea."

I laughed. "Was it good?"

"Which time? The first or the fifth?"

My jaw dropped open. "You slore," I said.

Laughing, she said, "Tell me what happened with Rhett. We saw him leave the dance with you and noticed his truck didn't come back to the ranch all night."

I nodded toward the couch. "He slept on the couch, made me breakfast, and brought me flowers."

She covered her chest with her hands. "That is so sweet."

"Enough about me!"

"Okay, here goes..." She told me they stayed at the dance, spinning on the dance floor until they realized almost everyone was gone. Then Cooper took her to the water tower, and they sat up top, taking in the lights of our small hometown, talking about everything from how they grew up to what they wanted for their futures. She said she'd never met someone who saw life in the same way as her.

And then they went back to his truck and made love for the first time. When the sun started coming up, they went back to Rhett's house, making use of his kitchen... his bedroom... his living room.

And then Cooper braved showing her his messy place.

I thought I might be sick when Cam told me about his toilet, but she had so many stars in her eyes, she didn't seem to mind.

And to be fair, a toilet could be cleaned. A bad personality was harder to fix.

"I think he's the one," Cam said, sighing happily.

My eyes stung with emotion. "The one?"

She nodded and rested her chin in her hand. "Dad said he saw Mom walking by at college and knew it was her from that second. Maybe it's in my genes to have a knowing in my soul."

"I'm so happy for you," I replied with a smile. All those years ago, I'd felt like Rhett was the one, and I hadn't gotten that feeling since. Maybe it was just getting older and jaded. But Cam always lived with her heart wide open.

"So I need to ask you a favor," she said.

I raised my eyebrows. "You're not moving in with him, are you?"

She laughed. "No. But he did ask me to go with him and Rhett to an out-of-town rodeo a few weeks from now. And we don't want Rhett to feel like a third wheel, so I was wondering if..."

"If I'd come along?" I asked.

She cringed, nodding.

I may have made some progress with Rhett last night, but an entire weekend with him? I wasn't so sure how well that would go. "I don't know."

"Please?" she asked. "I promise I won't abandon you. And if it's terrible, we'll just hole up in the camper and make them sleep in the truck."

"Camper?" I asked.

She nodded. "Apparently, they drive this camper to out-of-town rodeos to save money on hotels when they can't drive back the same night." She chuckled. "But if you're uncomfortable, we can get a hotel too. Please?" She linked her hands together, pleading. "Pretty please? With cherries on top?"

I laughed, pushing her prayer hands away. "Fine, I'll go."

"Yes! We're going to have a great time. I feel like Cooper and Rhett are so fun together. And this camper sounds like a trip. They call it the—" She trailed off mid-sentence, seeming to decide against it.

"What do they call it?" I pressed.

She winced. "The Stabbin' Wagon."

What on earth had I gotten myself into?

15

RHETT

"HUSTLE, HUSTLE!" I yelled at the girls as they ran around the bases during practice on Tuesday night.

Going around third base, Maya huffed, "Do. We. Have. To?"

"Extra lap for you, baby girl!" I said, grinning.

I glanced toward the stands to see Liv shaking her head at me as that dog lay beside her on the bleachers.

I only shrugged.

"You girls want to win the league championship? We gotta be fast! We gotta be strong!"

Maya fell to her knees by home base, theatrically saying, "We gotta take a break."

All the other girls finishing their laps stopped beside her, laughing despite their red faces.

I blew my whistle. I was having way too damn much fun with this thing. "Maya Madigan, I have a deal for you."

She peeled herself up from the ground and looked at me. "Anything."

"Anything?"

She nodded. I smirked.

"No more running this practice if you can beat me around the bases," I said.

Maya put her hands on her hips. "You're wearing cowboy boots."

"And?" I said.

Mags giggled from where she stood at the water cooler, pulling out waters to pass out.

"Anything to add, Coach?" I asked her.

Maggie nodded. "Kick his butt, Maya."

Maya let out a battle cry, and soon all the girls were shouting, "KICK HIS BUTT. KICK HIS BUTT."

I swear to God, some parents were joining in, Ms. Rhonda cheering louder than anyone else.

Maya wore a smug smirk as she said, "Put your money where your mouth is, Uncle Rhett."

I laughed, loving her feisty spirit. "Let's go. Mags, can you call it?"

She nodded, and the two of us went to home plate while everyone continued cheering for Maya. She waved her hands, making everyone yell louder. I gave Liv an incredulous look where she sat up front in the stands. This girl was going to rule the world or burn it down one day; there was no in-between.

Liv arched an eyebrow like I should know exactly where Maya learned to act like this.

Mags came up, lifting one hand, then another, and when she waved her hands down, Maya and I took off around the bases. I usually worked out in my tennis shoes, but my boots were just fine since I worked in them all day long.

I let her get a little ahead of me after we rounded first, and the cheers from her teammates got exponentially louder.

As we rounded second, I let the lead get wider, but at third base, I picked up speed, pumping my arms and getting even with her. She glanced my way, and I met her gaze as we got closer to home.

A look of pure determination in her face, she leapt forward, sliding to home base and crossing it with her fingers in a cloud of dust.

She got up, cheering, shouting, pumping her fist. "I BEAT YOU, UNCLE RHETT!"

I hung my head, pretending to be all tore up as her teammates rushed her and picked her up, carrying her and celebrating.

Mags came and patted my shoulder. "Think you'll survive the defeat, Coach?"

I sent her a wink. "I still got her to run the extra lap. And now the girls are bonding as a team. Far as I'm concerned, I won."

She smiled at me, the late evening sun catching in her pretty blue eyes.

"Have I told you how pretty your smile is?" I asked.

"Not in a long time."

"I'm changing that," I said. "It's very beautiful, and I could tell you about it all night. But I got a little girl to congratulate."

Her smile was a little softer, a little warmer.

I turned away from Maggie to find the girls letting Maya off their shoulders. I walked up to her, extending my hand for her to shake.

She held out her hand, but the second we were about

to touch, she pulled her hand back and ran it over her ponytail. All the girls started laughing, but I picked her up and tickled her side, making her laugh.

"Fine! Fine!" she yelled, "I'll shake your hand!"

Chuckling, I set her down for a do-over.

"Good job, Uncle Rhett," she said.

I grinned and shook her hand. "Good job, Maya. Now, everyone, head to the dugout! Get a drink and then line up. We're taking turns at bat!"

For the rest of practice, Maggie and I traded off pitching and catching while everyone on the team took turns batting. A few of them had been playing since T-ball, but this was the first year for others. It was fun to help them get their swings down, see the pride on their faces when the bat connected with the softball and their teammates cheered for them.

At the end of practice, we huddled up and Maya said, "Uncle Rhett, a few of the girls and I came up with a team cheer at swimming lessons this week."

I raised my eyebrows. "Is that so?"

She nodded proudly.

"Let's see it."

Maya yelled, "One, two, three!"

Everyone on the team pointed a finger from their forehead and held their other hand at their side like a hoof. Then they dragged their feet across the ground and shouted, "UNICORN ROAR!"

I held back a laugh. "I love it."

"Now you do it, Coach," Maya's friend Tessa said.

"Oh, I don't think that's necessary," I said.

Mags patted my back. "Come on, Coach. Gotta lead by example, right?"

Maya grinned and yelled, "One, two, three!"

I closed my eyes before copying them and yelling, "UNICORN ROAR!"

Everyone had a laugh as my cheeks and the tips of my ears got hot as hell. I walked over to the parents, several telling me good job on the way, but when I got to Liv, she was still shaking with laughter.

"You put her up to that," I said.

Liv shook her head. "Maggie did. She gave Maya a haircut this week."

I turned to stare at Maggie by the water cooler, wiggling her fingers in a little wave.

I hate you, I mouthed.

She put her pointer finger on her forehead like a unicorn horn.

I'd get her back for that at our dinner Thursday night.

16

MAGNOLIA

I WENT in the bathroom at work to freshen up. Rhett was supposed to pick me up from the salon, and I still had no idea where we were going to eat. Not that there were a lot of options to choose from in Cottonwood Falls.

Opening my makeup bag, I pulled out a mini deodorant and perfume, spritzing a little all over. When we were younger, he always used to compliment how I smelled. I wondered if he remembered my perfume like I remembered his cologne.

Then I touched up my mascara and lipstick and brushed away stray hairs that had gotten on my clothes over the day. Releasing my hair from the claw that held it up made my curls fall around my shoulders. I tousled them with my fingertips and sprayed in a little extra hair spray.

Even though I was physically ready, I had to pause and look at myself in the mirror.

All those years ago, I promised myself I would never go back to him. If younger me could see me now, nervous for a date with Rhett, she'd shake me. Tell me to run as far and fast as possible. Part of me felt guilty for letting her down, even though she was me and I was her. Probably something to ask a therapist about later.

But right now, I didn't have time. Rhonda had left early for a dentist appointment, so I needed to finish locking up the shop.

I left the bathroom, crossing off the list of end-of-day duties, and then stepped outside the store, into the warm evening air.

Just as warm was Rhett's voice, saying, "You look beautiful tonight."

I turned to find him leaning against one of the large planters lining Main Street. He had on a pair of light washed jeans and a dark blue button-down shirt, rolled at the sleeves, the top couple buttons undone to show the tanned skin and short hair of his muscled chest.

Fuck me.

My mouth went dry at the sight of him, and I had trouble finding the right words. Even one as simple as hello.

He grinned, getting off the planter and walking toward me with so much swagger it should be outlawed. "Ready for our date?"

I wet my lips, finally finding my voice. "Did we say it was a date?"

He tilted his head. "You, me, dinner? That math equals date."

"I think you need to go back to school," I teased.

"They wouldn't take me back," he replied, his heart-melting smile on full display. "Come on, let's get going."

I followed him toward his truck parked along Main

Street, the diesel engine still running. I remembered him telling me all those years ago that it took more fuel to turn the truck off and on than it did just to let it run a few minutes. It was funny, the memories that Rhett brought with him.

He held the door open for me, and I got in. The smell of chicken bacon ranch instantly filled my nostrils and made my mouth water. When he walked around the opposite side, I asked, "I thought we were going out to eat?"

"We are, just not in the diner, where it'll feel like sitting in a fishbowl," he replied.

"Good idea," I said.

"But I did get you an appetizer," he said, reaching into the back seat. He leaned forward again with a black velvet bag in his hands.

My eyebrows drew together. "The food's in that?"

He nodded, passing it to me. The insides felt a little hard in my hand. Maybe pretzels? He watched as I pulled the drawstring open and reached inside, pulling out...

A little pink magnetic dick.

"What is this?" I glared at Rhett.

His face was already red with repressed laughter. "It's a bag of dicks. For that stupid unicorn roar."

I wanted to roll my eyes at him, to tell him he was stupid, but his laughter was so contagious that soon I was laughing too. I held one up, turning it over in my fingers. "How did you get them to make an exact replica of your penis?"

"Ohhh." He held his hands to his chest like he'd been wounded. "Why would you do me like that?"

I giggled, setting the bag of dicks between us. "Does this mean we're even?"

"For now." He tipped his hat and then put his hand on my seat while he looked over his shoulder to back out. His fingertips brushed my shoulder, making goosebumps rise on my arm. But he kept his eyes on the road like he barely noticed.

I hated how strongly my body reacted to him, how it craved his touch, even after all these years. It was like he was imprinted on my cells and never left.

"How was work?" he asked as he drove south on Main Street.

I shrugged. "It was good. I'll be happy when all the regulars see me because I feel like we have the same conversation about me being back in town about five times a day. I'm ready to talk about something else."

He chuckled. "You always did like to talk."

"You were just as bad," I popped off. "Remember Mrs. Leitner separating you and Fletcher? And then you and James? And then you and Jarrod?"

Pretending to pout, he said, "Don't make fun. My desk was in the corner the rest of the year after that!"

I laughed at the memory. "You know she retired after she had our class." She taught current events, and that class had all ages in it because one year the administration thought it would reduce bullying between seniors and freshmen. What it actually did was ensure the teachers had to deal with all different levels at once.

"Can't say I blame her."

I glanced over at Rhett. He had a hand resting atop the steering wheel and the other leaning on the center console. I was so distracted by him, I almost didn't notice we were leaving town.

I pointed over my shoulder. "You know town is that way, right?"

He pretended to be confused. "It is?"

I rolled my eyes. "You're not kidnapping me, are you?"

He glanced my way, his gaze slowly sliding over my body. "Could you blame me?"

My cheeks grew hot. "Where *are* we going then?"

"Just a few more minutes. I want it to be a surprise."

The earnestness behind his tone had me looking around at our surroundings. He turned off the blacktop onto a dirt road. In the side mirror, I saw dust billowing behind us, contrasting the green ditches. The sky was big and blue, broken up with white puffy clouds. With all the early summer rains, the pastures were green, dotted every so often with cattle and horses.

The tension in my chest automatically eased. "It's beautiful out here."

He glanced my way, more gravity in his gaze than usual. "It really is."

Something about the way he said it made me glance at my hands in my lap.

The vehicle slowed, and I looked back up, seeing we were crossing through an open gate. Rhett guided the pickup over a trail worn in the ground from years of travel. When we crested the hill, a soft gasp escaped my lips.

We must have been at the highest elevation in the county. From here, I could see our little hometown of Cottonwood Falls, a stream passing by with dozens of old established trees lining the water. Every little homestead for miles.

"This is amazing," I said. "How did you find this?"

He was looking out the windshield too, hazel eyes more green than brown at the moment. "My grandpa owns this land. He bought it as an investment several years back, and he's been renting it out for cattle to graze. I'm saving to buy it from him so I can build a house right there." He pointed at a spot not too far from where we were parked.

I looked at the tree near where he pointed, taking in the leathery green leaves and open white flowers. "Is that..."

"A magnolia," he said, meeting my gaze.

"They don't grow wild here."

"I planted it twelve years ago." His lips twitched before he looked my way again. "Something about you always felt like home."

My heart pulled and tugged at his words, at what it meant that he planted this tree twelve years ago and never took it down. I swallowed, glancing down at my lap. "Should we eat?"

His lips twitched to the side. "Wouldn't want it getting cold."

17

RHETT

I BACKED my truck to the view and got out, pulling out the picnic blanket from the back seat. While Maggie held the takeout containers, I lowered the tailgate and spread the blanket out for us to sit. Then she opened one of the containers as I set my favorite playlist to play on my phone and pushed it back on the truck bed.

I leaned on one side of the back while she rested her back against the other, sitting cross-legged. Something about having her here, in this place that held all my wishes for the future—it set my heart at ease.

Chewing her sandwich, Maggie said, "This is so freaking good."

I chuckled. "I almost forgot..." I reached for the cooler on the bed of the pickup and dug through the ice. "Gatorade? Beer? Lemonade?"

"Lemonade," she replied.

I rubbed the bottle on my jeans to dry it off and cracked the seal on the lid before passing it her way.

"Thanks." She took a drink and then set it down

beside her. "So tell me. What have you been up to all these years?"

I laughed. "That answer might take a while."

She gestured around us. "I'm kidnapped. I think I have time for the villain's monologue."

I smiled, shaking my head at her. I loved her sense of humor. Lord knew she'd need it to be with me. "After—well, after." I reached into the cooler and took a drink of lemonade, imagining tasting it on her lips. "I moved back here and got a job as a tractor mechanic. Hated every fucking second."

She laughed. "Really?"

I nodded. "You try working in a tin shop all day with farmers breathing down your neck about their shit not getting done fast enough."

"Way worse than an air-conditioned salon," she agreed.

"Although, tractors can't talk back or complain about their paint job."

She laughed, and the sound made music with the wind rustling through the grass. "Good point."

"It was good money," I said, "but I only lasted there a couple years. Then I got a job farming with the Gremleys. That was alright, except I like ranching better. So after a few years, when the Finnigans needed a hired hand on their ranch, I jumped on the opportunity. I still have to farm sometimes, but mostly it's working with cattle. Been there for almost nine years now."

She smiled. "You left out the part where you coach your niece's softball team."

I waved my hands in the air, shutting down that idea. "This is a one-time thing," I said. "I'm shit with little kids.

You know Tessa's mom told me she started calling her little brother 'shithead' after the first practice? I only said it once!"

She giggled. "Tessa's mom asked me to talk with you too."

I shook my head. "I know I shouldn't cuss so much, but not a lot of words feel as good as 'fuck' does."

Her cheeks warmed, and suddenly I realized what I said. Fuck happened to be my favorite word and the activity I most wanted to do with Maggie. But I had to keep it in my pants if I wanted a chance with her. I needed to prove I was different than I used to be.

"Anyway. I'd rather just hang out with my nieces and nephews at Wednesday night dinners or family vacations and not fuck up in front of their friends too."

"And the rodeos?" she asked. "Ever thought about bull riding professionally?"

"Fuck no." I laughed. "I know I act all tough, but I think I'd miss Cottonwood Falls too much."

She smiled, glancing around as she chewed on a French fry. "There really is no place like home." When she looked back my way, she said, "You never did tell me about that scar on your neck."

"Story for another day," I said, picking up my sandwich to eat. "I've been talking about myself too long. What about you? I'm surprised no one's married you up." Even if it would have hurt me like hell, I knew she was a girl worth holding on to.

She smiled slightly. "I've come close a couple times."

"Yeah?"

She nodded. "I didn't date for a while after—" She caught herself. "After I left home. I just focused on work and hanging out with friends. Cam was in a sorority in school, so there were always lots of girls in and out of our house."

I stopped myself from making the joke I wanted to.

But Mags caught me anyway. "Impressive self-control."

I tipped my hat. "Not all heroes wear capes."

She laughed. "I got a lot of certifications while I was working, and that kept me pretty busy."

"What kind?" I asked.

She glanced up, like she was thinking, and it was so damn cute. "I learned how to do afro-textured hair, became a licensed hair braider, got my esthetician license, trained in massage and body work, got a certification on working with children... I think that's it."

"Wait, back up. Body work?" I wagged my eyebrows.

She threw a French fry at me.

I caught it, laughing, and ate it. "That's impressive, Mags. You always were determined."

She smiled, pride clear in her eyes. "It's made me a better stylist, even if I don't use all the certifications all the time."

"That's awesome," I said. "How'd you have time to almost get married with all that?"

She shook her head at me. "I dated a few guys. One proposed, and I said yes, but he didn't really take my career seriously. He wanted me to quit when we got married, or at least when we had kids, so he could keep working full-time. I knew I'd never be able to own a salon when my partner and his family acted like my job was a distraction or a hobby. I ended up breaking things off before we ever set a date."

I hated that for Mags. But also... "I feel like an asshole," I admitted.

"Why's that?"

"Because. I'm happy you're here. That it didn't work out with him."

She smiled, the sun catching her pretty blue eyes. "Surprisingly? I am too."

It was like all that sun landed on my chest, the way her words made me feel. I held back a smile as I ate the rest of my sandwich. Closing up the box, I said, "So I could take you back into town."

There was a small smile on her lips. "Or?"

"Or I could get you dessert at my place. And that's not a euphemism for anything else. Cross my heart."

She laughed, then rolled her lips between her teeth and nodded. "Dessert sounds nice."

18

MAGNOLIA

THE SUN WAS STARTING to go down as we cleaned up dinner and got back into Rhett's pickup. He started the engine, and when I saw it was nearly eight, I realized I hadn't even thought about texting anyone or wanting to leave for over two hours. I was having fun talking with him, getting to know him again.

There were still some similarities that existed between him and the Rhett I used to know, like the spark of mischief in his eyes or his heart-melting smile and the warmth in his laugh. But there was some new maturity there too, some depth and a clear sense of what he did and didn't want. It was like having the boy I loved back but also the man I wished he could be.

And I realized I didn't want this night with him to end, not when I saw the magnolia tree he planted in his dream plot of land, reminding him of me for the last fifteen years. In the span of seconds, I hadn't felt dumb or weak for thinking about him all this time.

He'd been thinking of me too.

Soon, we were driving under the Finnigan Farms sign and down a dirt path to a site with a few homes spaced out and a bigger shop and barn toward the corner of the property.

Rhett pointed out a stucco white house with brown trim. "Cooper lives in that house over there. Art and his family are in that big tan house over there." He pulled in front of a small white clapboard house with a short cut lawn and a bed of sunflowers out front. "And this is mine."

I took in the house, my heart tugging at the sight. A million different lifetimes ran before my eyes, one where this would have been the house we shared, both of us working toward our dreams.

"It's cute," I said.

"Cute," he echoed, getting out of the truck.

When he came to get my door, I said, "What? What's wrong with cute?"

"Nothing—when you're describing a baby bird or one of those regular-sized things made into a really tiny version. But a grown man's house?"

I laughed, following him down the weathered sidewalk. "My apologies. This house sure is *swole*."

"'Swole'?" He laughed. "What does that mean?"

I raised my eyebrows. "It means buff. Ripped. Tough."

"That's the best you could do?"

"It's the first masculine thing that came to mind!" I laughed, not adding that his muscular shoulders may have influenced me.

He chuckled, going to the front door and pulling it open. I was still getting used to being back in Cottonwood

Falls, where no one ever locked anything. The thought made me smile, like his door was always open. Even to me.

We got inside, and I looked around, poorly veiling my curiosity. The front area was similarly laid out to mine, with a living room and a kitchen that had a little ledge between the cooktop and the dining area. His furniture didn't look new, but it was clean and free of rips or tears. A hand-crocheted afghan he used to keep in his bedroom now rested over the sofa.

There weren't many decorations on the walls, but a copy of Van Gogh's *Sunflowers* hung in the dining area.

"It's not much," he said softly. "I've been saving most of my money for the land."

Then it struck me, confident-bordering-on-cocky Rhett Griffen was... nervous for me to see his place.

I turned back toward him and smiled. "It's great."

His smile made me feel like I'd found gold. "I'm glad you think so."

In fact, I was having a hard time remembering why I had to stay away. "Do you mind if I use your bathroom?" Maybe if it looked like Cooper's, I could douse this flame my heart was building for him.

"Sure," he said. "I'll start on the cookies."

"You're baking them?"

He smiled. "Better than store bought."

"True." I walked toward the door on the other side of the living room to use the bathroom, but he rushed to block the door. "This is the garage. Bathroom's over there."

I raised my eyebrows at him pressed against the door. "You don't want me in there?"

"You said you weren't ready the other day after seeing the ring."

His words sobered me, but my curiosity was getting to me. "And what if I'm ready now?"

"Then let's wait until we have dessert so I can give you a proper tour."

"Of your garage?" I asked, skeptical.

He nodded.

"You're not going to tell me, are you?"

He smirked. "And here I thought you'd forgotten me."

I shook my head at him, giving up and walking to the bathroom. But my mind was still on his garage. He'd told me after the rodeo he would show me something in there that proved he was different. And now he didn't want me to see?

This man was a bundle of contradictions, and I hated that it made me even more curious about what mysteries he kept about his life. I got into his bathroom and shut the door behind me, looking around.

The fixtures weren't extravagant, but they were clean. I even pulled back the blue shower curtain to find the drain clear of hair and the tiles free of mold or mildew. Even the toilet had clearly been regularly scrubbed.

There went that plan.

I used the bathroom and washed my hands. When I opened the door, I could hear the sound of a sheet pan, the beep of oven controls. Rhett's boots on the floor as he moved about.

I held my hand over my heart. There was something soothing about the sounds, about him cooking for me and caring enough that I had homemade dessert instead of store bought that made my heart melt.

After a second of listening, I walked back into the kitchen to see him wrapping up the end on a tube of cookie dough.

"I thought you were making homemade!" I said.

"I am," he replied, putting the dough back in his refrigerator.

I raised my eyebrows. "Here I thought you were in here cracking eggs and measuring flour."

He leaned back against the counter, folding his arms across his chest. The way his pectoral muscles moved through the gap in his shirt was distracting. "Why would I make all that mess when these taste just as good?"

"If your mom heard you say that, she'd have you disowned."

He cocked an eyebrow. "It'll be our secret."

I laughed, noticing how easy it was to laugh when I was around him. I was starting to let down my guard. Something that excited and scared me at the same time.

He reached into his cupboard, pulling down mismatched coffee mugs. One had clearly been painted and designed by one of his nieces or nephews, and the other had our high school mascot on the front. "Do you still drink milk? I know it's trendy to cut dairy nowadays."

"Nowadays? How old are you?" I teased.

He rolled his eyes at me. "I don't have any almond, soy, whatever bullshit milk. Seems wrong to me. You can't milk a nut."

Maybe he was wearing off on me, because my mind instantly went to the gutter. "You sure about that?"

His lips curled into a salacious smile. "We could test it out, if you want."

My pulse quickened at the images forming in my mind. "Dairy is fine."

He reached into the fridge, getting out a gallon of whole milk. Because of course he could stay fit and muscular like that without worrying about the extra calories. His forearms flexed as if showing off while he filled both our mugs, then put the milk back in the fridge.

He passed me a cup and took a drink from his.

"So 'The Stabbin' Wagon'?" I asked him.

He laughed, spitting out his milk. The stunned look on his face and milk dribbling down his chin had me in stitches.

"Shut up," he laughed, turning to the sink and getting a rag to wipe his face. "You caught me off guard is all."

I was still grinning when he turned back to me and resolutely set his milk on the counter.

"How did you know about that?"

"How else," I replied. "Cooper told Cam and Cam told me."

He shrugged. "We take the camper to rodeos when they're too far out of town to drive back home. Saves us a shit ton of money on hotels."

"And girls are okay with you bringing them back to something called The Stabbin' Wagon?" I asked.

He smirked and opened his mouth to answer.

"Okay, I don't want to know," I said quickly.

The timer on the oven went off, and he turned, getting a worn blue oven mitt out of a drawer. He used it to pull out the pan, the smell of freshly baked chocolate chip cookies intoxicating.

He set the pan on the stove and said, "Go sit down. I'll bring you some."

I went to his table with the cups of milk and sat at one of the wooden chairs while he plated us a few cookies each. He brought them over, and I picked up a piece, bringing the warm and gooey bite to my mouth. The sweet flavor flooded my taste buds, and it took all I had not to moan. "Okay, don't tell your mom, but I think I agree with you."

He laughed, dunking his cookie in milk and then eating it. "I won't say 'I told you so.'" He glanced over at me. "You have a little... on your cheek."

I reached to wipe it, but he shook his head. "A little to the right. Other right."

I moved my hand again.

"You made it worse," he said, chuckling.

"Help me," I cried, laughing too.

He reached out, and I could feel the warmth of his hand before he cupped my cheek. His callouses were rough on my skin as the pad of his thumb swept over my bottom lip.

I suppressed a shudder as he drew his thumb back and brought it to his lips. I looked from his mouth to his captivating hazel eyes. We were only inches apart. If I leaned in closer, tilted my head...

The doorbell rang, startling me back from Rhett. My heart raced as he rose from his chair. "Sorry, one second."

He wiped his hands on his jeans as he walked to the door, and I tried to compose myself. I couldn't believe I'd been about to kiss Rhett Griffen.

And I wondered if the opportunity would still be there when whoever was here went on their way. If I wanted a chance to taste his lips after all these years.

That was until I heard Rhett stumbling over his words, footsteps into his living room.

I turned to see a woman a few years younger than us dressed in short denim shorts and a pink crop top. She had a toned body, perky breasts, tanned skin, perfectly smooth blond hair pulled into a ponytail.

"I've been wanting to see you so bad," she said in a cutesy, whiney voice.

Everything I'd eaten that night threatened to come up.

She saw me and stopped on her path to what I assumed was his bedroom. "Oh. I'm totally down for a threesome."

Feeling sicker than before, I got up and said, "Excuse me. I was just leaving."

I walked past them, going out the door as Rhett said, "Mags, wait."

Tears were already building along my bottom lash, and I fought to keep them at bay. I didn't want him to see how much he still affected me. How shitty it felt to know women were still showing up at his door, even while I was there.

I was so stupid, letting my heart get carried away, letting him drive me out to the country, where I didn't have my own car to get away. I pushed out his front door, walking down the sidewalk to the dirt road.

I pulled my phone from my pocket, fumbled with it to call Camryn for a ride.

"Mags, wait!" He jogged after me and put his hand on my arm to stop me.

I turned, facing him, and snapped, "Don't touch me!"

He immediately raised his hands in surrender. "Magnolia, I promise you, I did not invite her over. I didn't know she was coming, and I'm sending her home right now. Please, just come inside. We were having a good time before she showed up."

I stared at him incredulously. "You want me to come back into your house, knowing that women feel comfortable showing up any hour of the day, walking back to your bedroom right in front of me?"

"That was my life before you came home," he said.

"And now all of a sudden it's different?" I demanded? "Why?"

"It's been different, ever since—" He cut himself off.

My eyebrows drew together. "Ever since what?"

"Things changed last year, Maggie."

I shook my head. "And yet they're still coming around." I gestured toward the house, where the woman stood awkwardly on the porch.

His eyes darkened. "Damn it, Maggie, you weren't even in town for over a decade! I was dead to you. Was I supposed to live like a fucking monk hoping you'd come around someday? You wrote me off just like you wrote off this town the second we broke up."

The tears were really falling now, and I wiped them away, acutely aware of the girl getting in her car and pulling away.

"She moved out of town last year and must have come back for a visit, assuming things were the same ol' same ol'."

I shook my head and wrapped my arms around myself. I felt so small. So pathetic.

"Please," he said.

"How am I supposed to know someone else isn't

going to show up the second I leave, or text you for a booty call, or call you to set up another date?"

He stepped away, wringing his hands together. "You know what?" He pulled his phone out of his pocket and threw it to the ground. The heel of his boot stomped against the screen, shattering it to pieces, then he picked it up and bent it with his hands, fracturing it further. "I'm done with the past. I'm getting a new number, and the only people who will know it are you and my family, and maybe Cooper."

I let out a tearful laugh. "*Maybe* Cooper?"

"I love him, but man, he's a mess."

I shook my head at Rhett. "I can't believe you did that."

He reached out, gently taking my shoulders in his hands. "This means something to me, Maggie. You and me."

This time, I didn't fight as he pulled me closer to him and held me to his chest. Because maybe it meant something to me too.

I didn't trust him fully, not yet. But I could feel the walls around my heart crumbling, brick by brick that he took away.

19

RHETT

SO I MIGHT HAVE FUCKED up by tearing up my phone without telling anyone. I went into Cottonwood Falls to get a new phone from the store, but they were out of the smart kind. I didn't want a dumb one, so then I had to drive half an hour to Rutlage and sit around in the store while I waited for them to let me spend my money there. I missed a whole fucking day of work to get a new phone number.

And then I realized that I didn't remember anyone's numbers because I'd always saved them in my phone, which was too beat up to transfer any information over. So I showed up to the softball game Friday night in my pink jersey and a pair of jeans and boots. I was one of the first ones there, but I saw my sister, Fletch, and Maya were there too.

"I tried to call you," Liv said. "You never told the parents whether you wanted grape or apple juice for after the game.

I handed Liv my new phone.

She looked from me to my device. "What's this?"

"My new phone. Can you add the family's numbers? And figure out what the hell my number is and send it to people? But you can leave me out of the team group chat. I don't give a shit what flavor of juice pouches they bring for after the game."

Liv stifled a chuckle. "Sure thing, Coach."

"Fletcher," I said, "help me unload the truck. Maya, you start warming up."

"No one's here yet," she said.

"You and Graham are."

She rolled her eyes and then ran to the field with her dog while Fletcher walked with me to the truck.

"What's with the new phone?" he asked on the way.

"A girl showed up last night while I was at my house with Mags."

We stopped by the bed of my truck, and he looked at me, eyebrows raised. "You got Maggie to go to your house with you?"

"Yeah, and it was going really well until fucking Darlene showed up and asked if Mags wanted a threesome."

Fletcher tried so hard to stifle his chuckle he started fucking choking.

"Don't fucking laugh."

That just made him laugh harder.

I lifted the lid to the toolbox in the bed of my truck and pulled out my baseball mitt, throwing it at him.

He caught it, still recovering, and said, "So what did you tell Maggie after Darlene left?"

"I broke my phone to pieces and said I was getting a new number."

Fletcher sobered. "Damn, you really like Mags."

"I always have," I said, my voice haunted. Those months after she left... I didn't want to remember them. And the years that passed after? It always felt like something was missing.

Fletcher motioned behind me, and I glanced over my shoulder to see Maggie walking toward us. She looked adorable in her pink jersey, denim capris, and flip-flops with pink stuff coming from the straps. Her toes were painted silver to match.

"Hey, Coach," she said to me. "Fletch."

Fletcher nodded, taking the bag of baseballs from me, and walked off, leaving Maggie and me alone.

"I got a new number," I said. "Liv's programming contacts in my phone now."

Maggie smiled guiltily. "You really didn't have to do that."

I scratched my neck. "Yeah, I did."

She laughed. "It didn't hurt." We began walking toward the practice field where Maya and Graham were racing around the bases. "I was meaning to ask you," she said. "What do Cam and I need to bring for the rodeo? It's harder to get things here than it is in Austin."

"If you'd like to wear something lacy, that'd be nice," I popped off.

Her cheeks instantly blushed, making me smile. "I meant supplies for the camper that will be getting a new name."

I bumped her shoulder as we walked, liking the feel of us being on good terms. "Just your beautiful self will do."

She looked down at the ground, smiling, and we stopped by the dugout. "Ready for our first game?"

I nodded. "We're going to crush them. What kind of stupid ass name is 'Fire Stars' anyway? Fucking redundant."

Mags's laugh tinkled, sending a warm feeling through my chest. "Maybe don't say that in front of the girls."

I cringed. "Got it."

More players were showing up as Maggie and I got the dugout set up with drinks for the girls and hooked bats through the chain link fence. Then an older woman in a Fire Star jersey walked our way. The jersey looked just as dumb—a yellow star with a blue flame on it.

She introduced herself as their coach, and we went through plans for warmup. The Fire Stars would practice at the bases first while we took the outfield. When she left to talk to her team, I gathered up mine.

"Unicorns!" I yelled. "Follow me!"

We jogged toward the lush grass of the outfield, and I paired up the girls to start passing back and forth. "Overhand throws first," I said.

"Coach?" a little voice said.

I turned to see Esther, one of the younger girls on the team. She had light brown hair pulled into a high ponytail with a pink bow the size of her head. "Yeah?" I asked.

"I don't have a partner." She looked sad, like she was about to cry.

"That's no big deal. I'll pass with you," I said quickly.

But she instantly burst into tears.

I looked around to find Maggie, but she was helping a couple of the girls with their form. Shit.

Taking a breath, I knelt in front of Ester, getting at eye level with her, and her green eyes filled with moisture. "What is it? Do you need me to get your parents?"

She shook her head, wiping at her eyes. "I'm j-j-just nervous for today," she sniffed.

I tilted my head. "Why would you be nervous? You were doing great at catching those grounders at practice Tuesday, and you even got a hit, remember?"

She wiped at her eyes, dragging snot across her cheek. "B-but I'm new here. And if I'm not good, maybe I won't have any friends when school starts. No one even wanted to pass with me." She slumped into my arms.

Caught off guard, I held her and began patting her back. This poor thing, she wasn't even worried about winning or losing. The social aspect was bigger to her than the game.

"Esther, I need you to take a deep breath," I said.

She pulled back, sniffling, and nodded. I could still feel the damp spot on my shoulder.

"Then I need you to get that booger off your cheek."

She looked mortified, dragging the collar of her jersey over her skin. "Did I get it?"

I smiled. "Yeah, you did."

Her lips wobbled.

I put my hands on her shoulders, making sure she heard me. "Baby girl, it's hard being in a new town and making friends. But worrying about whether people like you or not isn't helping."

Her face scrunched up. "But I am worried."

"About the wrong things. You worry about having fun. You worry about being Esther. And friends? They'll come along, because you're a great person and fun to be around, not because you made a good throw or caught a ball, okay?"

She nodded, wiping the last of the moisture from her eyes.

"Okay?" I repeated.

"Yes, Coach," she said.

A whistle blew from the infield, and I looked over to see the Fire Stars coach waving that it was time to trade.

"Ready?" I asked Esther.

She nodded resolutely.

"Good," I said, standing back up. "Unicorns! To the infield!"

20

MAGNOLIA

THE STADIUM LIGHTS were off and the parking lot was mostly empty while Rhett and I finished packing up all the gear from the game, making sure things were locked down. The scoreboard still read 5-4. The Unicorns' first win. Esther scored the run that broke the tie, and when all the girls picked her up on their shoulders, I thought I was going to cry happy tears.

I walked alongside Rhett to his pickup, and he loaded the bag of balls into the truck bed. But then I realized it was time to go home, and... I really didn't want to leave.

"First game," Rhett said, coming around to my side of the pickup. He leaned up against the white exterior. It was dark out here, with just a lone streetlight illuminating the parking lot. A few moths danced in the light, but nothing like the light that danced in his eyes.

"First win," I said with a smile. "You did great with the girls tonight."

He rubbed his arm. "Esther was worried before the game. I hope I helped."

"Are you kidding?" I asked. "She was grinning ear to ear after that run. What did you say to her?"

He leaned back against the truck bed, arms folded over his chest. "Maybe something about—" But he mumbled the last words, his cheeks turning red.

"What?" I asked. "I didn't catch that."

His cheeks were redder as he said, "I told her to have fun and it didn't matter how she played or if we won or lost."

His shyness made it hard not to smile. "Look at you and that sneaky big ol' heart."

I swore he was blushing as he said, "She was crying. What was I supposed to do?"

"You have a heart, you have a heart," I sang, teasing him.

"Oh shut it," he said. "You're the softie. You said good job to everyone, even after Maya tripped running to home base because she was yelling at her damn dog to make sure he saw her score a point."

I laughed. "Hey, that was objectively adorable."

"Uh huh." He smiled over at me, his eyes meeting mine.

There was something charged between us. Something warm, exciting, familiar, but also terrifying.

"Have you ever heard of twin flames?" he asked.

I raised my eyebrows, surprised by the change of subject. "I think I might have read it on a horoscope website or something."

His lips twitched into half a smile. "Some people believe a twin flame is a soul split into two bodies. These people will be so closely tied they always find each other."

"Like soul mates?" I asked.

He shook his head. "Soul mates are people who agree to meet in this lifetime, if you believe that. But it's thought that twin flames are kind of like mirror souls. They show each other what's good about the other, but also what they have to work on."

My breath caught as I listened to his words, deeper than we'd really gone since I'd moved back home.

"And authors have talked about twin flames in stories. You know, Emily Bronte said, 'He's more myself than I am. Whatever souls are made of, his and mine are the same.'"

I searched his eyes, wondering what that meant about us, a relationship that had hurt me to the core, but I still couldn't manage to stay away.

"Sometimes..." He swallowed. "Sometimes I wonder if that's what we are. If you showed me what I was missing so I could get better. And I hate that mistake I made, but I know I've become a better man because of the lesson it forced me to learn."

My lips parted. I couldn't find the words, only overwhelming feelings that came flooding through me at the memories. At the possibilities.

"I'm more patient with people," he continued. "I don't react so quickly, even if I do get hotheaded from time to time. I've learned to laugh through pain. Patience. God, have I learned patience. And most of all, I learned what it means to love someone and hope the best for them, even if it means you can't live happily ever after with them like you wanted to." He reached out and cupped my cheek.

And this time, I didn't just stand still. I lifted my chin, looking into his eyes. "I'm afraid to fall for you."

"You don't need to be afraid."

My voice felt thick. "Why is that?"

"Because I fell first, and I've been waiting fifteen years, hoping I could catch you."

My heart leapt at his words, and all my resistance crumbled. I fell into his arms, fell into his kiss, fell into his promises and all the hope that this time would be different than the time before.

His hand cupped the back of my neck, tangled in my hair as we kissed under the soft orange streetlight glow. My stomach swooped with a hoard of butterflies, and I held on to his broad shoulders, his firm torso, wanting to savor this feeling but also needing to make up for lost time.

He dragged his lips over my mouth to my cheek, my jaw, and when he whispered in my ear, he said, "You have no idea how badly I've wanted this."

But I did, because my body remembered him, longed for him, in a way my brain couldn't even fight against.

I took his face in my hands, kissing him longer, harder. My back pressed against his truck bed, and his large hands cupped my ass, sending a rush of desire through me.

I could feel his erection through his jeans, pressing against me, matching everything I was feeling.

I wanted him, in every sense of the word.

So I decided to take what I wanted, to stop letting logic and hurt stand in the way of something that could be better than I ever dreamed. I reached for his cock, rubbing my palm against it through his jeans, and he moaned against my lips.

I captured his lips with my own, desperate for more of him, when I heard the crackle of a speaker.

When I looked over, a cop car was driving by. My eyes widened with fear. Could you get in trouble for making out in public? Even if you were fully clothed? I'd always played it safe, never getting carried away like I was right now.

The voice said, "Get a room."

Rhett had a wry grin. "Fucking Knox."

"Knox?" I asked. "Knox *Madigan?*"

"That's the one." Rhett lifted his middle finger, flipping off the cop car. As it got closer, I saw Knox's grin and his middle finger pointed right back.

We watched the taillights disappear down the road, and I shook my head, still breathless. "Didn't he get suspended like every other week in high school?"

Rhett shrugged. "Guess he turned it around." He looked at me, cupping my face with his hand.

Nerves sputtered through my body at his touch, realizing what I'd been about to do, how carried away my heart had gotten. "He won't tell anyone, will he?"

His features fell, and he dropped his hand as well. "He won't tell a soul."

Guilt swirled in my stomach. "I didn't mean to say I regret it or anything."

He gave a quick shake of his head. "We should get you home."

21

RHETT

I COULDN'T STOP THINKING about that kiss with Mags as I drove to the rodeo in Rutlage with Cooper, Fletcher, and my brother Tyler in the truck. Usually Fletcher and Tyler couldn't come along with us with work and family, but today was a special day.

I just wished it felt that way.

Tyler was sitting in the back seat with me, and he nudged my leg with his boot. "What's going on with you? I'm thirty-six with a hickey on my neck and you haven't made a joke once?"

In the front seat, Fletcher said, "If not a joke, then at least a congratulations for keeping things hot with the wife after a few years together." He held up his fist from the front seat, and Tyler bumped it.

Cooper nodded in agreement as he drove down the highway. "You've been pissy all morning, Rhett."

Feeling like I was in a fishbowl, I said, "What the hell? Why are y'all keeping tabs on me?"

Tyler gave me the side-eye. "Quit skirting the question."

I let out a sigh. "I kissed Maggie last night."

The pickup got so loud with their cheers I had to cover my damn ears.

Tyler roughed my shoulder. "Dude, that's awesome! Why aren't we doing shots or something?"

Cooper tilted his blond head toward the steering wheel. "Probably cause we're driving."

"You know what I mean," Tyler said. "You've been pining after her ever since she left."

I slouched down in my seat, covering my face with my ball cap. "I'm probably pissy because Fletcher's cop brother drove by in his cruiser and told us to get a room. And the first thing Maggie said was, 'Do you think he'll tell anyone?'"

Their grunts and moans were enough to tell me they got it.

"I don't want to be her dirty secret," I said. "I want her to like me in public and in private. If you know what I mean."

Tyler smirked. "Annnd he's back."

Fletcher looked over his shoulder at us. "You gotta give her some time. You've been thinking about your relationship for years. She might need awhile to get used to the idea."

I frowned. "I hate it when you make sense."

Cooper said, "It seems like if it's just you and her, things go okay. Other people keep fucking it up."

"True," I said.

Fletcher tilted his head. "Well, that's easy enough, right? Just go somewhere no one will find you."

Tyler chuckled. "That sounds creepy as hell."

I reached over and shoved him. "But Fletch has a point. Maybe I'll take her fishing."

All the guys gave me looks.

"What?" I asked.

Cooper said, "All the chicks I've dated talk too much for fishing."

I waggled my eyebrows. "If I have it my way, we won't be doing much talking."

Tyler's cheeks tinted pink to match the red hickey poking out from his collar.

"Look at that," I said. "Your blush matches your love bite."

Tyler flipped me off, and Fletcher said, "Annnd he's back. The only thing you need to do is prank Knox to get even."

AFTER THE RODEO, the guys and I went out for drinks and dinner instead of going to a bar. Cooper was adamant that he not fuck things up with Camryn, even this early in their relationship, and the other two were married.

Sitting there with them, eating overpriced steak, felt like entering a new era of my life. And to be honest, I was tired.

I was *tired* of bringing different girls home just to have an empty bed the next night. I was *tired* of working day after day and still not being where I wanted.

I was ready for the next step. And I needed to remind

myself to be patient while I hoped Mags would be ready someday too.

I drove on the way back home as Cooper sat in the passenger seat texting Cam while Fletcher, Tyler, and I talked about the Little League team. Tyler had some ideas for drills I could run with them, and Fletcher filled me in on how to talk to little girls without having their parents want to wring my neck after.

The highlights? Quit saying "fuck" so fucking much.

But when everyone was dropped off and I was back at my house, Maggie was still on my mind. I took a shower, trying to wash away the emptiness I felt without her, but lying in my bed, I still felt it.

I let out a sigh and picked up my phone. There were only a few text messages between us about the softball team. On my old flip phone from high school, there were thousands between us. Telling each other how much we loved each other, talking about our days, our dreams, everything.

Now, I didn't even know full well how to say a simple hello. But I did my best.

Rhett: Hey Mags.

It was getting late, so I half expected her to be in bed already. I locked my phone screen, stretching to put my phone on the bedside table, when my text tone sounded.

Maggie: Shouldn't you be in bed?

Rhett: I am.

Maggie: Me too.

A million thoughts ran through my mind that I knew I shouldn't say out loud.

Fletcher's words were at the forefront though. *Give her time.*

Rhett: I was wondering if I could take you fishing tomorrow?

The text bubble appeared, and I found myself holding my breath, hoping the best for her reply.

Maggie: I can't. I'm going to the city to get beauty supplies, then having dinner with Dad.

Rhett: Next weekend?

Maggie: Don't you have a rodeo to go to?

Rhett: On Saturday. I'm free all day Sunday.

Maggie: I have dinner with my dad again on Sunday. We agreed we'd do dinners at 5 every week.

Rhett: You copying me?

Maggie: Gah, more than your family can have dinner together.

Rhett: Just teasing. I'll pick you up at ten? I'll have sunscreen and food and fishing gear. We'll be back in time for you to see your dad.

Maggie: Will you have chairs?

Rhett: Does that mean you're in?

Maggie: Only if I don't have to sit on the ground and hope a snake doesn't bite me.

I smiled, ran my hands over my mouth because I should not be this excited about fishing in the middle of a hot summer day.

Rhett: I'll bring chairs.

Maggie: Then I'll be there.

Maggie: You know that means you're spending every weekend for the rest of the month with me, right? Might get tired of me.

Rhett: I could never get tired of you.

Maggie: Good night, Rhett.

Rhett: Good night, baby girl.

I scanned the texts again, almost in disbelief that they were real. My mind raced, wondering what we could talk about, what we would do. My mind couldn't get over the feeling of Maggie's hand touching my cock, even through my jeans.

Fucking Knox.

Fletcher was right. I needed to prank his brother.

I picked up my phone and called Fletcher. "Get your ass outta bed."

22

KNOX

THE DISPATCHER SCANNED the cameras outside the station. She glanced over at me across the desk where I was doing paperwork. "It looks like there's an animal outside. Can you go scare it off?"

I glanced up, trying to get a read on the screen. "A raccoon or something?"

She looked at the camera again. "I couldn't quite tell. Maybe a big white dog?"

I rolled my eyes toward the ceiling. Even though the city had leash laws, a lot of people acted like we didn't and let their dogs run around. "I'll check it out."

I pushed up from the desk and walked down the hall, toward the front entrance to the station. When I turned the corner with the front double doors in view, I saw them opening.

My eyebrows drew together. Cottonwood Falls was usually quiet at night, and no one came here hardly at all.

But then no one walked in. I heard a snorting sound and the scrabble of hooves on tile. What in the world?

Then I glanced down, seeing a small white pig running down the hallway.

"What the hell?"

I looked back toward the doors, seeing nothing, except for the top half of a phone sticking up in the window.

Holy hell.

Someone was *filming* this?

I walked to the door, ready to have a come to Jesus moment with these teenagers. They had to have something better to do with their time. But when I got there, the phone disappeared, the youths running away.

I pushed the door open, hurrying outside, hearing a crack of a branch from the bushes to the right. Tilting my head, I turned off the sidewalk and pushed the branches aside, expecting to find a couple of young idiots.

Instead, I found some older idiots. "What the hell are you two doing here?"

Rhett and Fletcher glanced at each other, still crouched down behind the bush, and burst out laughing.

Fletcher stood up, extending his hand to Rhett, and said, "We had to get you back for cockblocking the other day."

I raised my eyebrows, then remembered driving by Rhett and Maggie making out. I let out a laugh. "I'm glad I didn't show up a few minutes later and catch some 'public indecency.'"

The tips of Rhett's ears went red, making me laugh.

"So I'm guessing the pig is yours?" I arched a brow.

Rhett nodded.

"Give me your phone."

"What?" Rhett asked.

I put on a straight face, holding back laughter. "Offi-cer's orders."

Rhett reached into his pocket, grumbling, "You know, you used to be fun."

"Oh, I still am." I took his phone, turning on the camera. I pointed it at him and Fletcher, putting on an announcer's voice. "Now, these two bad boys are going into the station to catch a pig on the loose."

Fletcher groaned. "I'm a doctor."

I zoomed the camera in on his face. "How do you feel, Cottonwood Falls, about your local medical practi-tioner now?"

Fletcher pushed the camera away as I laughed.

"Night's not getting any younger, boys."

Rhett shook his head and Fletcher said, "I told you a greased pig was a bad idea."

My mouth fell open. "You *greased* it?"

Fletcher cringed. "Seemed like a good prank at the time."

I nodded toward the door. "Go catch it."

They gave each other a resolute look and went into the station.

Thirty-two minutes later, they had a squealing pig in their arms and grease stains on their shirt. And I had a video sent to my phone that would make me laugh for years to come.

23

MAGGIE

ON SUNDAY AFTERNOON, I wrapped foil around the pan of cheesy potatoes I prepped for dinner with Dad. He offered to cook everything, but it felt good to use my kitchen. Since I'd been so busy with work, I'd mainly been picking up to-go orders from the diner on my way home. I put the potatoes in the fridge for later.

From the living room, Cam said, "I'm heading out!"

I glanced over my shoulder, seeing her in an adorable blue dress. "You look amazing!"

She fluffed out the A-line skirt. "Cooper said blue's his favorite color. Is it pathetic I picked that color for him?"

I shook my head, smiling. "That's adorable. Have fun at the movies."

"Thanks, girl, tell Daddy G and Eileen that I said hi."

"Will do. I'll walk out with you."

We both went outside and saw Cooper's freshly washed truck waiting behind Camryn's in the driveway.

Cam let out a happy little sigh, and I smiled over at her. It was like watching a romance movie slowly unfold.

We gave each other a wave, and then went our separate ways.

Dad's house was about a mile away, so I loaded the pan of potatoes in the passenger seat of my car and made the short drive. When I got there, I could already smell smoke from the grill out back.

My mouth watered. Dad made the best food on the grill.

I skipped going through the house and went through the chain link gate at the side of the house, walking to the backyard. I rounded the corner, seeing Dad grilling on the deck that Rhett helped him build out of reclaimed wood the summer after our junior year.

"Hey, kiddo!" Dad waved his spatula at me and then turned his body so I could see the apron he was wearing. I bought it for him last Christmas, and it was a muscled man in a Speedo.

"You're wearing it!" I said, laughing.

"Easier than working out," he retorted as I walked up the steps to the deck. "Between the apron and the hat, you've bought most of my outfit today." He tipped his Gibson Trucking hat.

I giggled. "I do have great taste." Eileen came jogging up to me, her paws tapping against the wood. "Hold on, girly," I said, setting my pan down on the patio table. Then I bent, scratching her behind her ears just like she liked. "Who's a good girl? It's you!"

Dad said, "Gonna spoil her."

"More than the man who is about to make her a separate plate tonight with cut up bits of steak?"

His cheeks heated slightly as he set the spatula down

and then closed the lid on the grill. "Oh hush. And then tell me you brought cheesy potatoes."

I peeled back the foil to show him what I'd made, and he bent his knees, throwing his head back, and hooting at the sky.

Eileen barked too, and I shook my head at the pair. "Incorrigible."

Dad laughed. "Want a beer?"

"Yes, please."

He went into the house, grabbing one, then came back out on the deck with me, sitting at the table. Eileen lay on the egg chair he got specifically for her.

"How's the electrical stuff going?" I asked him as I sipped on my drink. "Everything working like a charm now?"

Dad frowned. "It cost a little more than I was expecting."

I frowned. "How much more?"

He shook his head. "Not for you to worry about, sweetheart. But we'll be having bean burgers on the grill for a while instead of beef. Now, tell me about the salon. How are things there?"

I gave him a long look. He looked older than he had even a month ago. Had I missed something?

"Tell me about work, Mags," he said.

I wanted to press more, ask him if he needed help financially, but I couldn't really afford much either. All my money was going to the down payment for a salon. The banker said since I didn't have collateral like a house or a newer car, I would have to pay more up front or forget my dream of owning a salon.

Letting out a sigh, I said, "It's been busy, which you

know I like. But I've had less time to really settle back into Cottonwood Falls." I shrugged. "And I'm still trying to come up with a service project because Rhonda wants to make sure I'm giving back to the community."

"You're coaching that softball team with Rhett. Shoot, they should be paying you for putting up with him."

I looked down at my hands, thinking I should paint my nails when I got home. "Rhett hasn't been so bad."

Dad was quiet, and when I looked up, he had an eyebrow raised. "'Not that bad'? He completely wrecked your heart and was sleeping around this town the day after and every day since like you didn't mean a damn thing to him."

Each word put more of an ache to my chest. Dad and I usually stayed away from the topic of Rhett, especially since it had been so many years, but Dad didn't let go of people hurting me.

"It's been a long time, Dad."

He shook his head. "The sooner this softball season is over and you don't have to spend time with him, the better I'll feel."

Never mind the fact that Cam's majorly crushing on his bestie and that I might be crushing on Rhett again too.

But what I didn't tell him wouldn't hurt him, right?

Dad stood up, going to the grill and putting burgers onto a plate. After setting the meat on the table, he went inside and brought back out a plate with lettuce, onions, tomatoes and pickles. He held the ketchup and mustard under his arm.

I began dishing potatoes onto my plate while he dressed his bean burger. For the rest of dinner, we chatted about an audiobook series he was listening to during his drives, and then he casually slipped in, "Your mom called me yesterday."

I nearly choked on what little was left of my burger. "What?"

He nodded. "Apparently she set up a new life insurance policy and wanted to list you as the beneficiary. Needed your social."

I lifted my eyebrows. "Did you tell her to go to hell?"

Now he was the one choking over his beer. "Magnolia," he admonished.

"I'm serious," I replied, setting aside my bean burger. It was not the same.

He folded his arms across his chest. "We had a nice conversation. Maybe it's time you gave her a chance."

I shook my head at him. He was mad at Rhett for something he did at eighteen and could talk to Mom? "The woman ran off with another man without any warning, ignored me during my last two years of high school and my first two years of college, then brought her homewrecker to my hair school graduation, and you want me to *give her a chance*?" My chest heaved with my breath, with the hurt and anger that came with those words. What kind of mother abandoned her daughter? "And now she wants to endow me with something when she dies? Screw that. She's already dead to me."

Dad's lips tugged up at the corners.

"Don't you dare laugh," I muttered.

"Tell me how you really feel," he said.

"How can you be so calm about all this? You're holding a grudge against Rhett and he was a kid. Mom was a full-grown adult who messed up like that. She hurt both of us."

"I was a grown man, and I know I wasn't the perfect husband. Running out on us wasn't okay, but I could have been more romantic, listened when she said she was feeling stuck instead of sweeping it under the rug." He shrugged. "I hate what she did to you, and nothing will ever make up for it."

"But?"

"And," he said. "*And* people aren't all good or all bad."

I hated how right he was. I tended to see things in black and white, but Dad had just shown me yet another shade of gray.

Beneath all that anger at my mom, I was hurting too. I missed her like crazy, but I missed all the parts of having a mom as an older woman my friends got to experience. Cam called her mom when her period was late, when she had a bad hair appointment, when she couldn't figure out her health insurance. I wanted that too.

But forgiving Mom? That was scary too. If she could abandon her sixteen-year-old daughter, how loyal could she be to a grown woman in her thirties? So much time had passed it made me wonder... maybe it was better to let sleeping dogs lie.

24

RHETT

ON TUESDAY, I gathered all the girls in a circle at the middle of the infield. I'd been thinking about Esther and her tears before the game ever since Friday. She was so worried about making friends, but sports had been where I'd cemented some of my best friendships in junior high and high school. Why couldn't that be the case for the girls in Little League too?

I held the large yellow softball in my glove and said, "We had a good game last week, you all played well individually, but I want to see us grow as a team too. So this week, we're doing a little something to build team spirit."

The girls all glanced around, and Maggie gave me a curious look, since I'd changed practice plans last minute. But she said, "Okay, Coach, what do we do?"

"We're going to practice getting grounders. I'll roll the ball to someone, and I have to tell that person one thing they did well at the last game." I dropped the ball from my glove to my right hand and rolled it to Esther. She lowered to the ground, capturing the ball in her glove.

When she stood back up, I said, "Great hit at the end of the game, Esther. We might have to start calling you Powerhouse!"

Maggie clapped, and all the girls followed after while Esther smiled bashfully.

She rolled the ball to Guinevere next and said, "You were so fast chasing after balls in the outfield, Gwennie."

We all cheered again and continued that process until everyone had gotten a compliment. I said, "Good job, team. Next, I want to get to know you all better. When I roll the ball to you, tell me one thing you're looking forward to about the school year."

Over the next fifteen minutes, I learned that Tessa was excited to talk with everyone at lunchtime, Mindy missed the big school library, Shayna couldn't wait to play on the bigger playground, and Maya wanted to do more science experiments. She'd heard that this year, they'd get to dissect frogs. Just like her dad.

After that, we went through and said one thing we were worried about for the next game and then one area we wanted to improve on.

In front of my eyes, these little girls were becoming more than players; they were becoming *my* team, little people with hopes and desires and worries. I hoped they could all see each other that way too.

We didn't have much time left in practice, so I had them spread out around the field and I practiced hitting pop flies to them. I noticed them encouraging each other more when they caught the ball and even when they missed it.

I had a proud smile on my face as they jogged back toward the dugout for their parents to take them home. I gave them high fives on the way, saying, "Atta girl! Great practice! Good job!"

Maggie was the last one back, giving me a smile that said she saw too much. She bumped my arm with hers. "Good practice, Coach."

My cheeks felt hot under her compliment. I was trying to do right by these girls, but I was better at being the fun, playful uncle, not the guy digging deeper and encouraging growth. I hoped I'd do okay.

We worked together to pack up the gear while the girls parted ways with their parents, and when we were done, I looked up to see Liv was still hanging out on the bleachers with Maya.

"You know," I called to her, "for someone who was so desperate to find a coach for the team, you sure are at a lot of practices."

Liv gestured at her pregnant belly. "You want a pregnant woman to coach softball?"

"Seems a pregnant woman would have plenty of experience with balls," I retorted.

Under her breath, Maggie said, "You did *not* just say that."

Liv's mouth fell open, and Maya looked confused. "Are you talking about testicles?" she asked.

Oh god, that backfired.

"Forget it," I said quickly. "Ponies. Rainbows. Unicorns."

Maya made a face, and Liv laughed at me. "We're going to get a late dinner from Woody's. You wanna come?"

"Sure," I said at the same time Maggie said, "That sounds fun."

Suddenly, I realized maybe Liv meant the invite to go to Maggie. Maybe Maggie had wanted to catch up with Liv without the pressure of having me around.

"Um, I can eat at home," I offered.

Maggie looked over at me, the bag of extra gloves hanging over her shoulder. "Why would you do that?"

Liv nodded. "Come along."

With a smile, I said, "I'll meet y'all there?"

Maya bounced up and down. "Can Graham and I ride with you?"

"If it's okay with Livvy," I said.

She glanced toward my sister, who nodded.

Maya and Graham ran ahead to the pickup while I walked behind. "What's that sparkle in your hair?" I asked as we got into the pickup.

She swirled her ponytail over her shoulder and said, "Fairy hair. Livvy put it in for me."

I held it in my fingers, looking at the shiny plastic strands. "Makes me wish I had enough hair to do that with."

She giggled. "You'd look silly." Then she got a thoughtful look. "Maggie would look good with it though. Don't you think she's pretty? I *love* her nails."

I'd noticed too, the pink paint on her nails with silver sparkles to match our jerseys. "Mags is awful pretty," I agreed. "Just like Livvy. Just like you."

She folded her arms across her chest. "This boy at the pool told me I'm too skinny."

"Fucker," I muttered.

She gave me a look.

"Shit."

Her eyes widened.

"Damn."

"Uncle Rhett!"

"I mean... Don't tell your parents?"

She laughed. "They already know you cuss, Uncle Rhett."

"True," I said as I drove down Main Street. "Anyway. Where's this kid? I'll beat up his dad."

"Not him?" she asked.

"Can't hit a kid, but I'll teach his daddy a lesson on how to raise young man. You listen to me, Maya girl, you are perfect the way you are, and anyone who can't see that needs a pair of glasses. Got it?"

She didn't seem too convinced.

"You know how Livvy and Mags have bigger bodies, but Tessa's mom is skinny? Or how your daddy is tall and Mindy's dad is short?"

She nodded.

"They're all different. Not better."

She seemed to catch on as we pulled up to the diner. "Thanks, Uncle Rhett."

I smiled. "Any time, baby girl."

25

MAGNOLIA

SEEING Rhett with the girls on the team and at the diner with his niece had my heart all sorts of confused when I went into the salon the next morning. So much so that I put three creams in my coffee because I was too busy thinking about him to keep count.

I nearly started when Rhonda said, "We have a few minutes till we open. Come sit with me."

I refocused on the present and followed her to the couch in the waiting area. I sat across from her, sipping my coffee. "We have a full schedule today for both of us," I said. "I only have one appointment open. That's exciting."

She smiled. "It's great news. I wanted to check in on you. How does it feel so far?"

I paused, trying to sort my logical thoughts from my feelings about the night before. But the more I thought about what it was like to be here, the less logic played a role.

"It feels like home," I said with a small smile. "I really

hope you'll give me the opportunity to purchase the salon at the end of this trial period. How do you think I'm doing? Anything I can improve on?"

Her Cheshire smile grew. "I've always liked your willingness to grow."

I swirled my stir stick in my coffee. "I try."

She listed off a few ways I could do better with the older clients who liked things just-so and then said, "I love how you interact with the younger clients. I can tell they feel so special when you ask to feature them on your social media."

I grinned. "I love it. Although I think Ms. Fields almost had a heart attack when I asked her."

Rhonda waved her hands through the air. "She thinks they're spying on her through the internets."

I stifled a chuckle at the word "internets." "Who's they?" I asked.

She shrugged. "What I want to know is why she thinks *they'd* want to spy on her? To get her grocery lists?"

I laughed. "They must be pretty good lists."

Rhonda winked. "How are your finances? Are you still looking good for the purchase in a few months?"

I nodded. "Especially if we stay this busy. Rooming with Cam really helps me save too, since we're splitting rent."

"Smart," she said. "I think that's half the reason people get married some days. You can go a lot further together than you can apart."

Our first client came in, and while Rhonda got her settled in a chair, I offered to make her coffee. This time with a regular amount of cream.

Thankfully, the busyness of our day kept me from

having time to think about Rhett, until I got a phone call a couple of hours in.

"Rhonda's Salon, this is Maggie. How can I help you?" I asked.

"Maggie!" said a familiar voice. "I heard you were back in town. It's Deidre, Rhett's mom. I was wondering if you or Rhonda could squeeze me in for a cut and color today?"

I already knew I was the only one with an appointment open, but that would mean spending two hours in conversation with Rhett's mom. Liv had been so friendly with me, but his mom? How would she feel about me?

Trying to keep a smile in my voice, I said, "Hi, Deidre. I actually have an opening an hour from now. Do you think you could make it, or should we look at another day?"

"An hour from now is great. You just saved me from shoveling the chicken coop with Jack, so thank you twice."

I let out a breathy laugh. "See you soon."

I hung up the phone, and after my current client was gone, I took a "bathroom" break, locking myself in the ladies' and calling Rhett. He had to have some information to help me prepare myself for what kind of appointment this would be. Unfortunately, he didn't answer. Shit.

I definitely couldn't hide out in the bathroom forever, and like I said to Rhonda earlier, every penny counts.

So I held my head up high and walked back into the salon, taking my next client and trying to stop this worried feeling swirling in my stomach. Deidre took the appointment with me. She wouldn't do that if she hated me.

But the nerves kicked up when I saw Diedre walking

down the sidewalk to the salon. She had her hair clipped atop her head and wore sunglasses I'm pretty sure she'd worn fifteen years ago.

When she came in, Rhonda and her client greeted her, but then she lowered her glasses and said, "Magnolia Gibson, all grown up!" She smiled wide and walked to me with outstretched arms.

Shellshocked, I stepped into her hug, letting her embrace me.

Her perfume still smelled like the vanilla she used to wear, and her hug was warm as ever. It had been so long since my own mom hugged me that emotion rose in my chest at the feeling of a mother's hug. This woman had been like a second mom when Rhett and I were together, and I realized that when I left this town, I'd left her too. I sniffed back tears.

Deidre pulled back. "Honey, are you crying?"

I wiped at my eyes. "I'm sorry. I just realized how much I missed you all these years."

She smiled, letting out a soft laugh. "I missed you too. But I follow you on the gram. That's what my students call it. You've made quite the life for yourself, Maggie Ray."

Shock dried my tears. "You follow me online?"

She smiled. "Always have. You're like another daughter to me, no matter how far you go."

"You made my whole day, Deidre," I said over the lump in my throat. "Now come sit in my chair. Let's get your hair done."

I set her up, pulling a cape around her, then went to mix the color she liked. When I came back, I said, "Catch me up. What's changed in fifteen years?"

She smiled. "Oh, honey, you'd never guess." She filled me in on her family, giving all the details that Rhett had left out. Like the fact that Tyler got fired from his job for getting oral sex on the clock. (Thank goodness Rhonda was in the restroom and finished with her client when that part came up.) Then married the girl who got him fired and that's who ran the senior apartments in town with him. How Deidre knew all that and could say it without blushing, I had no idea.

Then she talked about Gage and his business, how he was doing more consulting with small business owners now to help them build their companies while Griffen Industries ran under a new CEO, who was apparently crushing it at her job.

Then she said she and Jack were redoing the kids' bedrooms at the house, now that they had grandkids who stayed the night sometimes over the weekends and summers. They loved sharing Maya with Fletcher's dad, Grayson.

"If only we could get Grayson set up with someone," she said. "I know he loved his wife dearly, but a widower all by himself in the middle of the country? Sure sounds lonely to me."

I smiled at Deidre, who wholeheartedly wanted everyone to have their happily ever after.

"And how about you, my dear?" she asked. "Is there someone special in your life?"

My cheeks flushed, because this was Rhett's mom I was talking to. "Um..."

"It's okay if it's not my son. I know he hurt you all those years ago. Even if I wish I could be your mom-in-law. You know if you two had made it work, you'd be married over ten years by now."

My heart constricted, because she was right. "We would have had a completely different life."

She tilted her head, hair all slicked with the dye. "You know, sometimes I think things happen for a reason. If you and Rhett had gotten married, you might not have gone to Austin and gotten all that experience you did. You spread your wings, and you have so much to give to this town now. He's had a chance to grow too, even if he still has that goofy streak."

It was a perspective I hadn't really thought of. All this time, I'd thought I was keeping myself busy, trying to move on from my past. What if I was just preparing for my future here?

I smiled and said, "I think it's time to wash that color out, Deidre."

"Okay." She stood up from the chair. "Now, do I close my eyes while you wash? I always forget."

I giggled. "Keep them closed. It's not my best angle."

When I finished Deidre's cut and color, she was so happy with it and asked if I could take a picture "for the gram."

I smiled, obliging, and then asked for a selfie with her to post as well. We said goodbye, and after she walked out the door, Rhonda sent me a smile over her shoulder that said far too much.

"What?" I asked.

She raised her eyebrows, turning back to her client. "Nothing. Nothing at all."

Feeling a blush on my cheeks, I walked back to the

bathroom, using it and freshening up. I was about to walk back into the salon when my phone rang in my pocket.

Rhett.

He had impeccable timing, letting me worry when, it turned out, his mom still liked me.

I held it up and said, "Hello?"

"Hey, Coach." I could hear the wind through the phone, like he was working outside. "I saw you called?"

"I was going to ask you something, but I figured it out."

"Oh, good," he said. "I was happy you called."

My heart fluttered. "You were?"

"Sure as the sunshine in Texas." He was quiet for a second. "Having a good day?"

I smiled slightly at the question. "Yeah. Busy, but good. You?"

"Better now." I heard the smile in his voice. "I better get going. See you for the game on Friday?"

"See you Friday."

26

RHETT

A WEEK AGO TODAY, Maggie kissed me for the first time since we were eighteen years old. We'd stood underneath the glow of a streetlight, and I'd laid myself bare. Let her know exactly what she was to me.

It had been the best kiss of my life.

Tender.

Warm.

Sexy.

Hopeful.

Everything.

And then she pulled away.

Cooper had been right that every time we were around other people things got messed up, so after today's game, I was determined to keep my distance. We'd play the game, I'd pack up my shit and go home. Easy.

The problem with that?

I gave life a plan, and it decided to have one hell of a laugh.

Everything was going great, until the last couple of

innings of the game. The girls were playing hard, working as a team. The batter sent a hit deep into the field, and Gwennie chased after it. Then she threw the ball in to Mindy at second base, and Mindy threw the ball to Maya at the pitcher's mound. And she sent it zipping to Tessa. (Girl had a heck of an arm.)

Tessa had taken off her catcher's mask to see the play, and when the ball got to her, it tipped her glove and hit her square in the nose.

She let out a cry and started spurting blood all over like a fucking fountain.

Mags instantly sprinted to Tessa while I pulled the little first aid kit out of my gear bag, and when I went running up to her, I could see Mag's pale pink lacy thong rising above her denim shorts.

And yeah, I know I'm a fuckin' loser for getting a semi while a little girl was crying with a bloody nose. But I'm a red-blooded male. When I see underwear like that, peeking out over an ass like that, everything kind of... fades away.

But I shook it off, helping her get Tessa cleaned up and walked off the field so her mom could take care of her.

And even though there was a whole inning after that, the image of Mags's fragile lacy thong sliding between her luscious ass cheeks? It was in the back of my mind.

I couldn't get it out of my head.

Either head.

So as soon as the game was over, I hightailed it, packing up as much as I could and making up some lame excuse about needing to check on something at the ranch.

After years of getting a woman's touch any time the

need came up, I was shit at waiting. Shit at being patient.
Shit at thinking about anything other than how it would
feel to have Mags's lacy thong fall apart under my
fingertips.

I CELEBRATED with her and the rest of the team,
loaded up my truck, and made sure I got the hell out of
Dodge before I could fuck anything up.

On the drive home, I rolled the windows down, letting
the evening air rush over my face and clear my thoughts.
At least, I tried. This hard-on was not going away. I got
into the house and went back to my bedroom, already
taking off my pants when a text sounded on my phone.

I glanced at the screen, seeing Maggie's name, her
picture connected to the account from social media. The
photo was of her in a pair of ripped up denim shorts and
a bright red halter top, sunglasses perched atop her head.

Holy fuck, it wasn't fair.

Maggie: Hey, are you okay? You got out of here really
fast.

She had no fucking idea.

I slipped the rest of the way out of my clothes
standing at the edge of my bed, picturing her lying in
front of me, wearing those same daisy dukes, the same
red top with her cleavage spilling over.

Rhett: I'll be better soon.

I grabbed some lotion, spilling it in my hand and then
gliding it over my rock-hard cock. If she were in my bed,
she'd be licking those juicy red lips, wanting a taste of me.

Maggie: You were great with the girls tonight.

I typed back a message in my phone.

Rhett: I don't want to talk about the girls.

I rolled my head back, picturing her in my bed, head in the pillows, brown hair contrasting my white pillowcases.

Maggie: What do you want to talk about then?

I tossed my phone down, thinking my response instead of texting it.

You. I want to talk about how good you would look on my bed, how I'd taste your pussy, lick, and suck, and blow until you were fucking screaming. I want to talk about how your tits are my wildest desire. How I want to put my face in them and suck your nipples until they're as hard as I am right now. I pumped myself harder. Faster. *I want to talk about how it would feel when I finally plunged into your hot, wet sex, quivering for me. How you'd cry out my name and dig your pretty pink nails into my back as I fucked you like no man ever has or ever will again. I want to talk about how I'd spill my whole fucking load into you, claiming you, once and for all, as mine, only mine. And how you'd shake underneath me, taking every. Fucking. Drop.*

I grunted with satisfaction, thick ropes of cum spilling into my hand, and then I rubbed it over my stomach, still looking at that picture of her.

With my clean hand, I texted back.

Rhett: We could talk about what you want to eat for lunch on Sunday.

27

MAGGIE

"I CANNOT BELIEVE your dad did that," I said to Cam as I swiped mascara through my lashes. "Where did he even find a pool of Jell-O anyway?"

The night of the softball game, Cooper went to her house to meet her parents, and then she worked all day Saturday, so this was the first chance she had to fill me in on all the details it would have taken too long to share over text. Which was worth it because I was in stitches over the impromptu Jell-O wrestling between Cam's dad and Cooper.

"I guess he was at the store when they were going to throw out a bunch of expired boxes. He took them home, and the rest is history." She shook her head with a laugh. "My mom was so unimpressed."

That made me laugh even harder. Her mom was so put together, the thought of Jell-O wrestling anywhere near her house was as strange as snow falling in the middle of July.

Cam leaned back against the wall. "Honestly, I think

Dad's going to like him better than me if they spend too much more time together."

I tossed my head back, laughing. "There's no way Coop could replace daddy's little girl."

"Fair," she agreed. Her older brother lived on the East Coast, so she had seen the most of her parents, even when we lived five hours away in Austin. They were always there for her. Even when she had an ingrown toenail removed, they came to town.

I put down my mascara and started with my lip liner.

"Seems like you're putting in a lot of effort for 'fishing.'" She did finger quotes.

My cheeks warmed. "Just because I'm hanging out with fishes doesn't mean I need to look like one."

"I'm sure it has nothing to do with the guy who's taking you."

Butterflies swirled in my stomach. I knew I shouldn't like him, and I was trying to keep myself safe, but I was having a hard time reminding myself of all the reasons I should stay away. "I know I should leave the past in the past, but I can't stop thinking about him."

She pointed her finger excitedly in the air. "I KNEW IT! That twin flames thing? Genius. How could you hold back after that?"

I glanced at her. "But it sounds so much like a line. Like he's *too* good, you know?" I capped my lip liner and started with lipstick, waiting for her to reply. Waiting for her wisdom, because Lord knew I needed it.

"So I was reading this post online—"

"You mean you saw it on TikTok," I said.

She blushed. "Okay, so I heard this person on TikTok, and they said that if you believe it's too good to be true, it might be because you think you don't deserve something that good."

The air left my lungs for a second. That was way too close to the truth. "Why wouldn't I deserve it?"

She shrugged. "I mean, think about it. You were dating Percy, and he didn't take your job seriously. Then before that it was Jeremy, who was always trying to get you to drink green juice so you could lose weight." She made a gagging face. "And then there was Hansel—"

"His name was Ansel."

"And he was constantly bitching about your social media."

I frowned.

"It's like these guys are great except for one part of them," she said, twirling the ends of her hair and eyeing the split ends. "Maybe there's a reason for that."

"But that's a relationship, right? Nothing's a hundred percent perfect."

"And yet..." she said. "Rhett's gone above and beyond, and you're expecting him to have all the same flaws as he did before. It's almost like you're not getting over the past anymore but worrying what he'll do in the future to hurt you again."

My throat felt tight.

"What if—" She held out her hands. "Just humor me. What if there was someone who could meet your needs? Who wasn't perfect, but who was *good* in all the ways that counted? And *what if* it took him fifteen years to become the version of himself that deserved you? How would you act then?"

Fear gripped my chest, and I swallowed. "I probably wouldn't be as scared as I am now."

She smiled. "You know, fear is just excitement's ugly cousin."

I laughed. "You need to write fortune cookies."

"Who says I don't already?" She winked.

A knock sounded on the door, and she got a smile like the Cheshire cat. "Destiny's knocking."

"And here I thought it was Rhett." I shook my head at her and then kissed her forehead. "He may be my twin flame, but you'll always be my soul mate."

She smiled. "Back atchu, bugaboo."

I gave myself one last glance in the mirror, admiring the way I looked in my favorite distressed denim shorts and a black tank with a bow that drew the eye to the girls. I paired it with a paisley red headband and some casual sneakers, giving myself that effortless look that actually did take effort.

"You look good," Cam said, slapping my butt. "Go get him."

I pretended to be a horse, whinnying and galloping out of the bathroom. I still had a smile on my face as I opened the door to see Rhett Griffen waiting for me.

He looked so good in his faded blue jeans and his cut-off white shirt that showed the sides of his muscled chest. Don't even get me started on his strong, broad shoulders with veins that...

My mind was getting carried away, and judging by the way his gaze dipped over my body, his was too.

He cleared his throat. "You look good, Mags."

"Could say the same for you, Coach."

He smiled, stepping back for me to exit the house. "Today, it's just Rhett."

I smiled and followed him out to his truck, thinking to myself that he was never "just Rhett." Not to me.

As I walked to the passenger side, I noticed a cooler and a couple of fishing poles in the truck bed, along with a tackle box. "Looks like you've got everything we'll need," I said. "But I don't see any chairs."

He held the door open for me, a coy smile on his lips. "Just you wait."

I got in the truck and buckled up as he shut the door. My eyes wandered over him while he walked around the front of the truck. That cut-off shirt was doing him far too many favors.

I glanced down at my lap when he got in so he couldn't see I'd been staring.

"Thanks for coming out with me," he said as we drove off.

I smiled. "How was the rodeo yesterday?"

"I won a nice little purse."

I raised my eyebrows. "They give out purses to men for winning?"

He laughed, the sound warm. "No, a purse is what we call the prize money."

"That makes a lot more sense," I said with a chuckle. "I forgot about that." I was beginning to relax, and it looked like he was too, one arm on the steering wheel, no tension in his broad shoulders. "What do you do with your winnings? Shopping spree?"

He shook his head. "Tuck it away for Grandpa's land. There's a reason I'm not driving a new truck or have any new furniture in my house. I have goals, and sometimes it takes sacrifice to reach them."

My lips parted because I felt what Rhett was saying to my core. I related to him. "I get that. Saving for the salon hasn't been easy. Especially since I can't take as many appointments here. Not enough work for two full-time stylists in town."

He nodded. "I think it's cool that you bet on yourself."

My cheeks warmed. "It's been different, moving back home when all of our classmates have their own houses and families. In Austin, so many people room together because cost of living is high, but here? I can tell some people from our class look down on me because I haven't accomplished more yet."

"Fuck the haters," he said. "No one has to live your life but you. As long as you're good with it, that's all that matters."

I smiled, the action instinctive, natural. "You make it sound so easy."

"It doesn't have to be hard."

I was quiet, thinking as he turned off the blacktop and went down a dirt road. Why did I make it so hard for myself?

"Have I been to this pond before?" I asked.

"Nope. We dug it out a few years ago to help water cattle and let them cool off in the summer, but we've been resting this grass so the pond's all fresh and full of fish now."

"Nice," I said. "Do you remember that time we went 'fishing' before senior year? And you got that leech on your..."

He shuddered. "I'd rather not remember it."

I laughed.

"I'm traumatized, okay?" he said, half laughing with me.

"*You're* traumatized? You made me pull it off! I was seventeen!"

He laughed. "Serves you right for suggesting we skinny-dip."

"I wasn't ruining my first Victoria's Secret." I laughed too. But my throat closed up as we crested the hill and the pond came into view. "Did you..."

He drove into the pasture through the open gate and took us closer to the pond where he'd set the couch from his living room by the water, afghan and all. There were even end tables on both sides of the couch and a red cooler nearby. "You said you required seating."

I let out a laugh. "I meant camping chairs or something. You didn't have to do this."

"Only the best for Maggie Ray."

There was no helping my smile as he parked the truck. "Go pull up a chair," he said. "I'll bring you the fishing pole. I know you're not touching worms with those pretty nails."

28

RHETT

I'D HAUL the contents of my whole damn house into a pasture if it made Maggie smile and laugh this way. Her laugh was so contagious, carefree. The one time my over-thinking girl truly let go.

While she went to sit on my couch, skin dusted with early morning sunshine, I baited up a fishing pole for her. This pond had been stocked with catfish, so we'd catch a plenty. Maybe I could talk her into coming over to my place tomorrow for dinner so I could make her some of what we caught.

Once I had both our poles bated, I grabbed a couple beers for us out of the cooler and brought them over to her. She was standing on the edge of the water, her toes dipping into the dark brown sand.

From here, I could see the way her denim shorts hugged her ass, and it added a whole new element to the images I had in my head two nights ago. The images I knew would cross my mind tonight.

"Damn, you're looking good," I told her.

She turned toward me, her cheeks blushing, and took her beer and then her pole. "Thank you." She took a drink from her beer. "I have to admit I was a little worried about what you'd think of me when I came home. I'm bigger than I was in high school."

My eyebrows drew together. Was she being serious right now? Mags was a bombshell, and the extra flesh of her thighs, her chest, even her stomach? It was a turn-on, because I knew how fucking good it would feel to have her on top of me, pressing me into the bed, surrounding me in every way. "Why would you be worried about that?" I asked.

She set her beer down, then focused on casting for a minute. Her fingers slowly spun the reel, making sure it caught. "You clearly haven't tried online dating as size twenty-four."

I raised my eyebrows. "People say shit?"

With a sigh, she backed up and sat on the couch, careful not to get her damp feet on the upholstery. "Some guys are really into bigger girls. It's like they have a fetish or a bucket list item to check off. *Sleep with a fat chick.*" She rolled her eyes like what she told me wasn't making me see red. "Other guys will date you, fuck you, never introduce you to anyone in their life. Keep you as their dirty little secret, like it's embarrassing to date a bigger girl."

I swore I was getting tunnel vision from all this anger.

"The worst are the guys who say they're okay with your size, but when they see you naked for the first time..." She blinked quickly. "They act like they didn't know you were fat under all your clothes."

My voice scraped out of my throat as I said, "I had no idea. Mags, I'm sorry."

She shrugged, looking down and fiddling with her reel. "I've thought about losing weight, tried some diets, but in the end, I'm a big girl. Even if I lost fifty, a hundred pounds, I would still be a big girl." She lifted her chin. "I figured if a guy wasn't okay with me, a relationship shouldn't move forward, because odds are, if I have a daughter, she'll be my size too. I wouldn't want her to be raised by a dad who wasn't supportive of women at every size."

"Wow," I breathed. I couldn't believe she'd had to worry about that, had to feel like someone might not like her, or her future children, because she had some extra pounds on the scale. "Maggie, I don't want you to think I'm blowing smoke up your ass, but those guys? They're a bunch of fuckin' dumbasses if they think you're anything but drop-dead fucking gorgeous."

The laugh that passed through her lips warmed my heart. "You didn't have to say that."

"But I mean it."

She glanced toward me, a hint of skepticism in her gaze.

We were getting rid of that real fucking fast.

"You know what I did Friday night?" I asked.

She looked at me, eyes wide, curious. "What?"

I held her gaze, knowing there was a chance she'd think I was a fucking creep, but she had to know there was no part of me that didn't like *every* part of her.

"I got away from that game as fast as I could because when you were bent over, helping Tessa, I got a view of that lacy thong you wore under your shorts, and I went fucking feral. I know you want to take things slow, so I got out of there before I could mess anything up. And when I got home, you texted me. Your picture came up, and I stared at it as I fucked myself, thinking of tasting you, being inside you, making you scream my name as you came on my cock."

Her full lips parted, her cheeks full of color.

"You don't have to say anything back, and if you want me to take you home, I get it, but I need you to know, Mags, you're sexy as fuck. Every inch of you."

Her tongue darted out, wetting her lips in the most tantalizing way. "You really did that?" she asked.

I gestured down at my crotch, at the erection growing against my jeans. "I'm like a horny fucking teenager around you, Mags. Holding back is taking all of my willpower."

Her voice was so soft, it almost disappeared in the wind. "Then why are you? Holding back?"

"Is that an invitation?" I asked, my own voice raw.

Her chin lifted. "Don't make me beg."

My lips curled into a smirk, but it didn't last long because I was shoving my fishing pole aside, taking hers out of her hands, and crossing the couch to kiss her like I'd been dying to from the moment I saw her at the salon her first day home.

I tried to hold back all the crushing force I wanted to use on her, but her kiss was frantic as she gripped my shirt in her fists and worked her pillowy soft lips against mine. I wrapped my hand around the back of her neck and gripped her hip with my other hand.

I slid my tongue along the seam of her lips, and she let out a little whimper.

Fuck, I was hard, feeling her body against mine, her skin hot and sweaty under the summer sun. I slid my hand down, cupping her ass and pulling her closer to me so she could feel my length through my jeans.

"Rhett," she moaned against my lips.

I dipped my head down, kissing, biting, licking her throat, her collarbone. I shoved her tank top aside, taking a nipple into my mouth and sucking until she moaned and gathered my hair in her fists.

I pulled down the other side of her top, giving me access to her luscious, salty tits, and she gasped out, "Are you sure you want to do this here?"

"Why the fuck not?" I hummed against her breast.

"What if someone sees?"

"Then they'll know just how much you turn me on, *exactly* as you are."

I continued playing with her taut nipples, loving the taste of her, the way she held on to my hair, my shoulders, how she moaned and shivered under my touch.

I brought her back to the couch, laying her down and then fiddling with the buttons of her shorts, her luscious, glistening tits spilling out of her askew top, nipples hard and pink in the sunlight in contrast to her creamy pale skin.

The button finally came undone, and I grinned down at her.

"What?" she asked.

"I've been wanting to do this..." I lowered my mouth to her stomach, kissing her apron belly and working down to her pubic bone. I took the panties in my teeth and pulled, feeling the fabric come apart.

"Rhett!" she cried.

"You wanted me to show you what I imagined. Now shut the fuck up and let me make you feel good."

Her head rolled back as I pulled her shorts down the rest of the way. Her pretty pussy was full and waxed aside from a patch of short hair in a landing strip pointing to everything I wanted.

I drew my finger along her seam, then slid my fingers between the folds, feeling a rush of moisture. "You're so fucking wet for me. Those panties were ruined before I touched them."

"Mmm," she moaned. "You have no idea what you're doing walking around in a shirt like that. It's not fair."

My chest got all puffed up, knowing my girl was turned on by me too. My fingers still between her folds, I dipped two deeper into her pussy, loving the quiver I felt around me. "Is this fair?"

She let out a whimper.

I turned my fingers inside her, curling them toward me, making her cry out. "This?"

"Rhett," she panted.

My favorite fucking sound.

I lowered myself over her, spreading her folds with my fingers, loving the sunlight hitting the barest part of her. I blew softly over her clit, making her whine.

"This?"

Her head rolled back.

"Look at me," I ordered. Her eyes met mine, heavy, hot, glazed with desire. "I want to see exactly how beautiful you are when I make you come."

Her pretty blue eyes widened, and I smiled at her like a wolf would at Red Riding Hood before lowering my face to her hot sex and working my tongue over her clit.

She reached down, holding my hair tight in her hands.

"That's it, hold on, baby girl," I hummed against her clit.

She moaned, and I looked up to make sure she was watching.

Her eyes were solidly on mine.

"Good girl."

A guttural sound fell from her lips.

She liked to be praised; that would be easy to do.

I dipped two fingers in her, then three as I ate her juicy pussy, working her from every angle, one hand reaching up to tweak her nipples, one inside her and my tongue tasting my sweet Maggie Ray.

"Fuck, Rhett. *Fuck*, Rhett." Her cries became incoherent, closer together. I felt her building around my fingertips and kept going, knowing I was giving my girl exactly what she wanted.

She screamed out in the middle of the countryside, her walls crashing around my fingers, taking me wave after wave.

I kept going until every pulse had subsided and she lay limp on the couch, the sun falling on her glistening skin. She had me so hard, I knew I'd be seeing this in my mind's eye as I made myself come tonight.

I stepped back, wiping my face with my shirt.

She looked up at me, cheeks flushed, hair falling out of her ponytail. "What about you?" she asked.

I shook my head. "Today was about you."

Her lips parted.

"You. Only you. On my shirt. On my face. On my tongue."

29

MAGNOLIA

I WALKED in the front door of my house and yelled, "CAM!"

She turned on the couch, looking up from the crochet project she had in her lap as she watched reality TV. "YOU DON'T HAVE TO YELL. I'M RIGHT HERE."

My eyes were wide as I leaned back against the front door. "Rhett made me come."

"HOLY SHIT!" she yelled.

"I KNOW!" I yelled back.

She set aside her crocheting and beat on the couch cushion next to her. "Tell me *everything*."

I ran over to her, dropping onto the cushion, images of a completely different couch flashing through my mind. "So he took me fishing and brought his couch there so I had something to sit on."

"That's so sweet," she said, "but FAST FORWARD TO THE SEX."

"He ate me out in the middle of the country where anyone could have driven by and seen us."

"Hot," she said, biting her fingernails. "And then?"

I bit my lips together. "I asked if he wanted me to take care of him, and he said," I lowered my voice, "Today was about you. Only you. On my shirt. On my face. On my tongue."

She lifted a throw pillow and covered her face, screaming into it.

"RIGHT?!" I said. "It was so hot I think my ovaries spontaneously combusted."

She lowered the pillow. "When are you seeing him next?"

"I don't know." I bit my lip. "Practice Tuesday?"

"How are you going to keep your clothes on?" She was only half joking.

"We can't hook up like that again," I said, my chest already tightening.

"What the fuck do you mean?" she asked. "You need to have sex like that every day. Twice a day if you can get it!"

I grabbed another pillow and held it in my lap. "I can't think clearly around him! He's like a vagina whisperer."

"Why are you holding back?" she cried. "He's into you. His mom likes you. You clearly like him. Don't even try to say you don't."

I had to bite back a smile, but it quickly turned into a frown. "You should have seen my dad last Sunday when I mentioned I was coaching with Rhett. He about lost it and said the sooner I get away from him the better."

"You know your dad," she said. "He's just worried about you."

I bit my lip. "I don't want him to be disappointed in

me. He did everything for me after Mom left, and then he helped me pick up the pieces after Rhett. He'll be so upset when I tell him about me and Rhett. If there is a me and Rhett."

She tilted her head. "Oh, hon... it's still so new. You don't need to worry about telling your dad until you figure out what it is, right?"

I nodded slowly. "That's true."

She tossed her pillow at me. "Stop looking so worried! Rhett just made you come *in public*. You should still be in your post-orgasm glow."

I laughed. "I definitely am."

Grinning, she said, "That makes two of us."

I raised my eyebrows. "Today?"

"He left half an hour ago." She winked. "I already disinfected the table, if you were wondering."

I shook my head at her. "Look at us, two girls in their thirties having the best sex of their lives. We should have a show. *Sex and the Country*."

She laughed. "I'd watch it."

"Me too." I pushed myself up from the couch. "Now I need to go have dinner with my dad and hope he can't tell what I was doing earlier."

Cam laughed. "Good luck. I'm covering for a night shift tonight, so I won't be here."

I went and hugged her shoulders. "Thanks for being my bestie for the restie."

She smiled up at me. "Thank you for adding to the spank bank."

"Cam!" I cried.

She laughed, pointing at me. "Oh my gosh, you should have seen your face."

My cheeks were still blushing. "Okay, *goodbye.*"

"Wait," she said. "I forgot to tell you. Shelley's bach party. We're both invited, along with forty of her closest friends."

I laughed. Shelley was always a good time, but she had a million friends from her time in the sorority with Cam. But she was the kind of person who knew and remembered and loved everyone too, so I wanted to be there for her. "When is it?"

"Next weekend."

I frowned. "Weren't we supposed to go to the rodeo with Cooper and Rhett?" Now I was actually looking forward to it.

She said, "I already talked to Cooper, and there's another rodeo the weekend after. We're going to that one."

I smiled. "Sounds good. Do we need to book a hotel?"

Shaking her head, Cam said, "Apparently Shelley's dad booked some kind of mega house for us all. Totally paid for."

"Nice," I said. "Okay, now I really do have to go."

I went to change, and I was out the door, getting in my car when Dad called.

"Hey, sorry I'm running behind. Should be there in a few," I said.

"Actually, I was wondering if I could call in a rain check."

"What do you mean?" I asked. "Everything okay?"

"It's great, but wheat harvest just started, and the Fernandezes asked if I'd be willing to help haul grain on the weekends. Apparently their custom cutters had a truck break down and it's slowing them down quite a bit. Plus, I could really use the extra cash."

I frowned. "Dad, is everything okay? I mean, financially."

"I'm working on it," he snapped.

My head jerked back by the force of his words. Dad never talked to me like that.

"I'm sorry, I'm just stressed, sad I'm missing you tonight."

The tightness in my chest eased. "I could come keep you company?"

"We'll be working late, 'til midnight or later probably. Plus, Eileen might be jealous if you take her seat at shotgun."

"You and that dog," I said with a small smile. "Are you sure you want to work that late?"

"Don't you worry about me, hon. Part of being an adult is paying bills, yeah?"

"Okay. Let me know if you change your mind. I can bring you some food."

"No worries," he said.

I turned my car back off and walked inside. When I opened the door, I heard Cam call, "You're early! I'm in here!"

Drawing my eyebrows together, I turned the corner to see her in the kitchen wearing nothing but our oven mitts and holding an empty glass pan.

"Oh my god!" I yelled, covering my eyes. "YOU SAID HE LEFT."

She dropped the pie pan, and it shattered to a million pieces on the tile. "You're supposed to be at your dad's!"

I peeked at her through my fingers, seeing her trying to cover up with the mitts.

"Come on, we cook with those!"

"Well I was going to wash them when Cooper and I were done."

I shook my head, saying, "I'll give you two the house."

I turned to walk out of the kitchen, finding Cooper looking from me to Cam to the glass on the floor. He must have come in when I was leaving.

He got a thoughtful look and shrugged. "I can dig it."

30

RHETT

WHEN I PULLED up to practice Tuesday, my sister and niece were already there, sitting on the tailgate of their truck Liv insisted on calling "Bernice." She named everything, from the bunny that crossed their yard every morning to the freckle on her right shoulder.

I got out and walked over to them. "Why the hell are you two here so early?"

Maya had a big ol' grin on her face. "We wanted to have cupcakes with you before practice!"

My eyebrow quirked at her giggle. "Why do I feel like you poisoned them?"

She laughed. "Don't be silly."

I studied Liv, who was smiling in a slightly less ornery way. "You pee in them? Fletch told me you're using the bathroom all the time lately."

Her jaw dropped open. "He told you that?"

"I think when you were on a bathroom break."

She sent me a glare. "Just have a cupcake with your baby sister and your niece, will you? I had a craving and I can't eat this whole box, but I don't have enough to share with the entire team."

"I mean, twist my arm," I said, reaching for one of the vanilla cupcakes with white frosting and pink and blue sprinkles. I was midway into a bite when I realized they were watching me.

"What?" I asked, giving the cupcake a second look. What the hell had they put into this thing? But all I saw was white cake with a strip of pink down the middle. "Why's it pink?"

Maya and Liv shared a look.

I drew my eyebrows together. "Are you laughing at me for eating a pink cake? Because you know men can like pink too. It's just a color."

Liv laughed.

Maya laughed harder.

I stared at the two of them. "Keep laughing this hard and the baby will fall out before it's due." Then it hit me. *Baby. Pink.*

"Holy shit!" I yelled. "You're having a girl?"

She nodded happily, and Maya jumped up, yelling, "I'M GOING TO HAVE A BABY SISTER!"

I picked up my niece, spinning her around and grinning at the great news. "Congratulations!" I set Maya down and hugged my sister close. Fletcher had confided in me that she'd struggled with endometriosis and they didn't know if they'd be able to have a child at all. Knowing they'd have a little girl made it that much more real.

"Rhett, are you crying?" Liv asked.

"No. I just have something in my eye, like a sprinkle from the damn cupcake."

She and Maya laughed.

"Have you told Fletcher?" I asked.

Liv gave me a look. "You think I'd tell you before my husband? No, Maya and I tried to decide which gender reveal we liked best, so we've done all of them. We did smoke bombs with Mom and Dad, a balloon pop at Grampy Madigan's, a confetti bomb for Fletcher—that's all over the doctor's office now. We did pink rose petals in an umbrella at Tyler and Hen's place. We drove all the way to Dallas and did scratch-off tickets with Gage and Farrah's family. And you get cupcakes."

I finished eating the cake. "I hate to tell you this, but I think I got the best one."

Mags drove up in her cute little car, and Maya said, "Can I bring her a cupcake?"

"Sure, babe," Liv said, and Maya hopped off, running toward Mags.

I rubbed my sister's back and said, "I really am happy for you. And it's sweet that you included Maya in it all."

Liv's smile was a bit tearful. "I don't ever want her to feel like we're replacing her."

I shook my head at her, watching alongside her as Maya pulled the stunt on Maggie too. "That little girl knows she's loved. That's why she's such a shit."

Liv laughed. "You're going to be a great uncle, again."

"It's my honor and my duty," I teased, then I bent down, speaking to the belly. "But you're kidding yourself if you think I'm coaching your softball team. You're shit out of luck."

"Rhett!" She covered her belly. "You know they can hear you in there! She'll come out with a potty mouth!"

"Literally, you know some babies eat their own poop on the way out?"

She shoved my shoulder. "You're the *worst*."

Mags came up and gave Liv a hug. "I'm so happy for you! Congratulations!"

"Thank you!" Liv said. "Now can you please get my brother on the field before I injure him and he ends up with a bruise or something?"

Maggie laughed happily. "That I can do. Let's go, trouble."

We had a great practice. Maggie took half the team to the infield, practicing batting with them, while I took the other half to the outfield, practicing catching hits close to the fence. Not a lot of girls hit it that far in the last couple games, but it was good for them to practice maintaining focus while being aware of their surroundings.

At the end of the practice, I called the girls into a huddle. They all looked up at me, waiting for me to talk.

"I'm proud of you girls," I said. "We've got just a few games left—it's a short season—but you've come so far. Esther, you're a hitting machine!" She blushed, toeing the dirt. "Maya, you're not allowed a softball when we're at home because that arm is a rocket!"

She dropped her mouth. "I already have tons of tennis balls for Graham!"

"Mindy, you're catching flies like a frog out there!"

She stuck out her tongue and said, "Ribbit."

I chuckled and congratulated a few more girls on their skills. "Be good for your parents and come to the game Friday ready to play hard."

I stuck my hand in the middle, but Mags said, "Actually, Coach, I think you should lead the Unicorn Roar."

My cheeks flushed hard as a muscle in my jaw ticked. "What a *great* idea. Fingers up."

All the girls put their fingers up from their foreheads.

I dragged my toe through the dirt at the pitcher's mound and yelled, "UNICORN ROAR."

And when the girls started jogging back to the dugout, I spoke low in Maggie's ear. "You're going to pay for that."

I saw her breath catch in her chest before she whispered, "I'll be looking forward to it."

31

MAGNOLIA

MY HEART WAS STILL RACING, my skin feeling hot as we said goodbye to all the players and parents and loaded up the gear into Rhett's truck. The way Rhett's gaze had shifted after what I said earlier had me ready for whatever he wanted to do to me.

And let's be real; I couldn't get our country tryst out of my mind. Rhett may have admitted pleasuring himself to a photo of me, but I'd been getting off to the memory of him since it happened. I knew what had happened was only the beginning. And I had my hands in the air, ready to scream along to this wild roller coaster ride.

But when we finished putting all the gear in his truck bed, he didn't make a move. Disappointed, I said, "I'll see you next week at practice. I'm sad I won't make the game."

His gaze was heavy as he looked across the truck bed at me. "Get in."

I raised my eyebrows. "In?"

"Get. In. The. Truck." His voice had a hint of danger, another of desire.

My lips parted in stunned silence.

"Don't make me ask again," he growled.

"Why?" I asked, my voice all breathy.

"Because bad girls need to be punished. Now get in the fucking truck, Mags."

My heart sped as I walked to the passenger door, knowing I'd follow whatever direction he gave me if it led to me feeling as good as I had on Sunday.

When I got in and he joined me, he hummed, "Good girl."

Fuck.

At this rate, I'd soak through my panties and my shorts and ruin the upholstery.

"Where are we going?" I asked, already feeling my nipples tightening under my T-shirt.

"Somewhere I can teach you a lesson." He sent me a salacious wink, his hand was tight on the steering wheel as he drove out of the parking lot, sped onto the highway and turned onto a dirt road.

I instantly recognized the directions. We used to drive to this field when we were dating. They always had it baled into big round haybales we could hide behind when we needed a private place to make out or hook up.

Excited jitters sped through my stomach as the past collided with this very handsome, very sexy man in my present. He had a spark of this when we were younger, but I loved seeing the way he'd grown into his dominant side. It turned me on like none other.

I glanced his way, seeing his cock, long and hard

under his jeans. I wanted to free it, taste it, give him a hint of the pleasure he'd given me.

But his voice was dangerously, low and sultry as he said, "I see you looking."

My eyes trailed up, meeting his.

They were all heat, molten fire, ready to consume every part of me. He pulled into the field and parked behind a haybale. The truck turned off, leaving us in complete darkness. "Get that pretty ass out."

My heart stuttered.

"*Now*."

I unbuckled, acutely aware of the heat growing between my legs, the part of me that needed to be filled by him.

Goose bumps rose on my arms as I waited for Rhett. Even the summer night air felt cool compared to the heat of my skin. His truck door opened and he got out, boots crunching over dried grass.

"Hands on the bale," he said,

I moved over the ground, crossing the space as his eyes tracked me, a game of cat and mouse we both would win.

I pressed my hands against the haybale, the baled grass coarse under my palms.

"Good girl."

A shiver went down my spine, and I parted my legs for him.

His chuckle was low, salacious. "You want me, don't you?"

My answer rasped out of me. "Yes."

He walked over to me. "Bad girls have to learn their lesson before they get what they want."

I dropped my head, desperate to move on to the part where he fucked me raw and eased this ache inside of me. "What do I need to do?"

He came behind me, speaking in my ear. "I'm going to pull your shorts down and ream that pretty ass of yours."

I shuddered with desire.

Wordlessly, he reached his fingers into the waistband of my shorts and pulled them down around my ankles, leaving me bare to the night air. It was so dark in the middle of the country, no houses or cars for miles. The only light came from the moon and stars above, casting a glow on my pale skin.

He ran his palm over the swell of my ass. "Such a beautiful body," he whispered, almost to himself. Then his fingertips moved to the crevice between my legs, dipping down to my dripping sex. He let out a moan, sliding his fingers inside once, but then removed them, making me whine. I wanted *more*.

"No pouting. You earned this."

"Punish me," I begged. I didn't want sweet, patient sex with him. I wanted to ache, to burn, to take everything we'd both been holding back for years.

He leaned forward, lips near my ear. "What do you want me to do?"

"Spank me," I uttered, the words slipping out of my mouth before I had a chance to be embarrassed by them.

Who even was I? This woman getting it on in the open air? The woman asking, unapologetically, for what she wanted? I liked the version of me brought out by Rhett, and I especially liked the way he made me feel.

He slid his hand over my ass cheek and then pulled it

away and brought it back down over my flesh, the most delicious mix of pleasure and pain spreading through me.

"Fuck," I whispered.

He brought his hand back again, slamming it down over the crack.

And then a third time. "You're so fucking bad."

In some part of me, I knew I should not like this so much, but my blood was racing, and his touch just brought more attention to the area that wanted him desperately.

He lowered himself to his knees, bringing his lips to my ass, kissing the spots he'd made tender. He slid his tongue over the seam, making me shudder.

"Spread your legs," he said.

I shifted my feet, barely able to feel my legs at all with every nerve ending in my sex begging me to pay attention, begging to be satisfied.

"Good girl," he said. "That's my good girl."

My head dropped down, eyes barely able to focus on the ground I stood on.

He swirled two fingers around my clit, making me cry out in relief, in desire, but before I could process that, he brought his lips to my pussy and gripped my thick thighs with his large hands, consuming every one of my senses.

"Rhett," I gasped.

He hummed against my sex. "That's it."

I moaned, knowing how much he wanted to hear the sound, not worried about anything but this man and the pleasure he brought me.

He continued his pursuit, bringing me closer and closer to the top, to the point where everything disappeared.

"Rhett," I cried out, unable to form any other word but his name. "I'm co-I'm co—"

Waves of pleasure wracked through my body, and he continued until they faded away, leaving me spent and sensitive to even the cool night breeze.

I held on to the haybale as he stood behind me, convinced it was the only thing holding me up. He gently guided my legs, helping me back into my underwear and shorts, and then he took my arms, spinning me into his embrace and kissed my forehead.

"Holy shit," I whispered into his chest.

"I know, baby," he said against my forehead.

I looked up at him, and he took my lips in his, claiming me with his kiss. Soft, patient, and tantalizing all the same.

When we broke apart, my lips as raw as the rest of me, I said, "I want to make you feel good."

He smirked down at me. "I haven't heard you begging yet."

My lips parted, but before I could speak, he said, "Let's get you home."

32

RHETT

I PULLED up to my family's Wednesday night dinner, seeing several cars already in the driveway. We started doing this way back when Gage left for college, and it had been the one thing that kept me grounded throughout the years.

I grabbed the bouquet of sunflowers I picked from the patch in front of my house and walked down the sidewalk to the front door. There was already chaos around as my nieces and nephews played corn hole in the backyard while Dad was at the grill working on a set of burgers and hot dogs. There were way too many people for us to have steak every week like we used to.

The front door was already opened when I reached it, and my mom pulled me into a hug. "Good to see you, hon."

I smiled back at her and held out the flowers. "These are for you."

She looked at them, smiling. "You are such a sweetheart."

"It's what you get for planting them and sneaking over to water," I teased her.

She blushed. "Just because you're grown doesn't mean you're not still my baby."

From behind Mom, Tyler coughed, "Suck-up."

Mom turned, bopping his shoulder. "Oh shush."

My oldest brother, Gage, was farther back in the house, sitting at the dining room table with a bottle of beer. "Don't listen to him. He brought over fresh baked cookies for Mom."

The tips of Tyler's ears went red. "Yeah, well you bought Mom and Dad a damned cruise. Gotta earn my inheritance somehow."

I laughed. "If we're talking inheritance, I better step up my game. Mom, you sure do look lovely. Did you get your hair done?"

Mom shook her head at me, turning to walk in the kitchen to put her flowers in a Mason jar. "In fact, I had a lovely time at Rhonda's Salon. Maggie did a fabulous job on my hair, didn't she?"

Tyler and I followed her back, sitting at the table.

Mom finished filling the jar with water and turned to us. "She's so beautiful, Rhett. It's just too bad you two had a falling out all those years ago. Maybe now that she's back in town..."

There it was, the comments about me being single, me needing to settle down. I'd heard them often throughout the years, but they were getting more and more frequent lately. I glanced over my shoulder, not wanting to say too much to get Mom's hopes up. But out the patio door, I saw... Gray and Agatha talking with my dad.

"What's Agatha doing here?" I asked. It was normal for Fletcher's dad, Gray, to join us for dinners, but Agatha hadn't been over before. We were friendly when she waited on us at the restaurant, but never more than that.

Mom folded her hands under her chin. "Doesn't it look like she's having a good time with Gray?"

Gage spoke up. "Mom's trying her hand at match-making again."

I groaned. "Ma, you can't play Cupid."

"Why on earth not?" she asked. "They're good people. They deserve to be happy."

"First of all, because you can't run around in a diaper. We'd have you locked up."

She rolled her eyes at me, setting the flowers on the table.

"Secondly, they're adults. If they wanted to get together, they would. Plus, Gray's a good ten years... fifteen? Older than she is."

Mom shrugged. "Age doesn't matter so much when you get older. Sometimes people need a little push to see what's right in front of them."

Gage said, "That is true."

"Hey," I said, "don't encourage her."

Gage chuckled, and Tyler said, "Speaking of things right front of people, how's it going with Maggie?"

I glared at him, then jerked my head to Mom. I hadn't said a word to her about the extra time Maggie and I had spent together lately.

She had way too big of a smile on her face. "What's happening with Maggie?"

"We're coaching Maya's team together," I said, but

my grin gave me away because we'd done a hell of a lot more than that last night.

Gage's mouth fell open. "What? You haven't told me anything!"

Mom was clapping her hands excitedly. "You're together?!"

My cheeks and neck were getting hot. I got up from the table and passed Mom, going to the fridge to grab a beer. I'd definitely need a drink for this conversation. "I don't kiss and tell."

Mom's smile got even bigger. "There's been kissing?"

"Kissing?" Gage echoed.

My neck got hotter. "Y'all need to go outside and stop talking about other people's relationships like a bunch of old hens."

I reached the sliding door, and Mom said, "Invite her over for dinner next week! Or maybe I should swing by the salon and ask her."

I turned back to her, my jaw dropping. "You wouldn't dare."

"You don't think Gray invited Agatha, do you?"

I shook my head. "Diabolical."

As I opened the sliding door and stepped outside, she called, "Just want you to be happy!"

"You just want some more grandchildren," I retorted.

I could hear the smile in her voice as she said, "That too."

33

MAGNOLIA

"SHOULD we get snacks now or in Rutlage?" Cam asked as we pulled out of our driveway to leave for Shelley's bach party. Her car had more room for all her suitcases, because she *always* overpacked, so she was driving, even though mine would do a little better on gas.

"Is that a rhetorical question?" I teased. "Now *and* Rutlage."

She laughed. "I knew there was a reason you're my best friend."

I settled back into my seat and got out my phone. "I know this sounds silly, but I'm going to miss the girls tonight."

Cam sent me a knowing look. "The girls or the man who made you scream in the middle of a pasture? Twice?"

My cheeks heated. "The girls. Definitely the girls."

But I pulled up my text messages anyway, clicking through to the thread between Rhett and me. Over the last few days, we'd texted each other on and off, talking about our days, sending some flirty messages. But his last message meant the most.

Rhett: Text me when you get to Austin. I want to make sure you're safe.

My heart melted at the words he sent this morning, but I still hadn't replied. I tapped out a few different responses before settling on one.

Maggie: I will. Take care of the girls tonight, yeah?

While I waited for his reply, Cam and I stopped at the only gas station in town and went inside, loading up with snacks, sweet to savory. We dumped our haul on the counter, and the clerk, Silas, who'd worked there forever, gave us a toothy grin. "Reminds me of when you girls were little. You'd come after a day at the pool and dump all your quarters out of plastic M&M containers."

We laughed, and Cam said, "Not much has changed."

Silas checked out our stuff and gave us the total. I paid for it, and then we told him to have a good day before going back out to the car. I picked up my phone from the passenger seat and looked at it as I buckled in.

Rhett: I'd rather take care of you. ;)

I smiled at the text, biting my bottom lip.

"Oh my god, I just had a flashback to when you two started dating in high school," Cam said. "I swear you're making the same face now."

I laughed. "You have no room to talk. You and Cooper are so freaking gooey together."

She got a lovestruck smile. "He is pretty great."

I shook my head, turning up the music, and glanced down at my phone, trying to figure out what to text back.

Maggie: I'd love to continue this line of conversation, but I'm sitting next to Cam.

I looked at the screen, already seeing the text bubble come up.

Rhett: Then I definitely shouldn't say everything I would like to do to you after the game tonight.

Maggie: Definitely not.

Rhett: I won't tell you that I'd rip your jersey open to see those perfect tits.

I shifted in the seat, glancing at Cam. She was focusing on the road and eating her bag of Muddy Buddies.

Maggie: Don't tell me.

Rhett: I definitely won't tell you that I'd shove your lacy bra down to see your nipples, hard and ready for my mouth.

Maggie: Rhett...

Rhett: I won't tell you that I'd suck on your tits while reaching into those jean shorts you like to tease me with and feel how fucking wet you are...

I shifted again.

Maggie: You're being mean.

I could just imagine the salacious grin he'd have on his face right about now, and it turned me on that much more.

Rhett: I certainly will keep it to myself how I'd lean you up against my truck, hook your leg on my arm and ease my cock inside you like we both know you've been wanting me to.

Holy fuck.

Maggie: I'm so fucking wet, Rhett. I can't do this in the car with my friend!

Rhett: Then I *won't* tell you that I'm stroking my cock while I think about you pressed up against my truck, your head rolling back because I'm filling you like no man fucking could.

I bit my lips together.

Cam said, "Why is your face so red? Are the Cheetos too hot?"

"I'm fine," I said too quickly.

She looked from me to my phone. "Holy shit, he's sexting you isn't he!?"

"NO!" I said too loudly.

She shook her head, picking up her phone. "Hey, Siri, call Rhett Griffen."

"No!" I yelled at her Siri. "*Don't* call him!"

But it had already obliged her request, and she held the phone to her ear. I swore I heard the whisper of his voice through her phone as he answered.

"Can you quit sexting my friend while she's in the car with me? We're close friends, but not *that* close, m'kay?"

I shook my head at her. "I hate you."

Ignoring me, she said, "Good luck at your game tonight... Yes, we will. Bye!"

She hung up, grinning over at me. "He says to text him when you get there."

"I hate you both," I grumped.

A new text came through my phone.

Rhett: You need to work on your poker face.

♡

FIVE HOURS, two playlists, and one gas station stop later, we turned off the highway onto a winding dirt road outside of Austin. I'd never been to this part of Texas, and I could tell why, judging by the mega mansions with beautifully landscaped driveways we passed every so often.

Seeing me stare out the window like a kid in the candy store, Cam said, "Shelley always did have expensive taste."

"This is like golden underwear taste."

"Is that a thing?" she asked.

I shrugged. "Hell if I know."

The GPS on her car started glitching. "Shit," she muttered.

"Do you need my maps?" I asked, pulling up my phone. And then I realized... "I don't have service out here."

"Crap." She frowned, slowing on the winding road.

"How the hell do all these rich people live here without demanding a cell tower?" I asked.

"They probably have butlers sitting in their passenger seats telling them where to go because the GPS voice is grating." She laughed, still driving slowly. "Or better yet, drivers to take them there. Should we turn back to town and see if we can memorize the directions?"

I frowned, looking around. We'd been driving on these windy roads for a good forty-five minutes, and it was already dark. "I guess we don't have another choice..."

She nodded, pulling the car alongside the road. "Just have to wait for these people to pass."

I twisted to see the car passing and caught sight of a bright pink SUV.

"JESSICA!" I yelled. "That has to be her!"

Cam honked the horn, following her, and the SUV slowed. The window rolled down, revealing our pink-obsessed friend Jessica.

"Cam! Mags! It's been a month, and I miss you bitches like crazy!"

Cam and I laughed, and Cam said, "Good thing we have this weekend to hang out. Do you have any clue where we're going?"

Jess nodded. "Follow me?"

"Thank you!" Cam and I yelled through the window. As Cam rolled up the window and pulled onto the road after Jess, she teased, "Guess you did get lucky after all."

My mouth fell open as my cheeks flushed. "I didn't tell him to send me those texts!"

"Yeah, sure, you didn't like it at all." She sent me a knowing smile.

"Okay, the messages were kind of hot."

"When are you going to admit you're crazy about him too?" she asked.

I bit my lip. "I'm just..."

"Afraid," she finished.

I nodded. "I don't know how to get over that."

"Do you remember when my parents booked that vacation to the Bahamas for spring break before senior graduation?" she asked. "I'm pretty sure it was the only vacation we ever went on that required an airplane."

I nodded. "I was so jealous. And I missed you like crazy."

She laughed. "Well, I didn't tell you that I was completely freaking out in the airport. I almost had a panic attack on the plane, and they had to ask if there was a nurse on the flight."

My jaw dropped. "You're kidding."

She shook her head. "So freaking embarrassing."

"What did you do?" I asked.

She twisted her lips to the side. "My mom told me that we could cancel the vacation and go home to where I was comfortable, or I could calm my ass down and stay on the plane so I could see something more beautiful than I ever imagined." She took a breath. "You know what I chose. We had turbulence the whole damn flight and it was scary as hell, but when we got there——" She smiled at the memory. "I was so glad I didn't let fear keep me home."

"You're wise, Cam Childers."

She smiled.

"But imagine if you were getting back on a plane after surviving a crash. You might feel a little differently."

"Maybe if it was the same plane that crashed before," she replied. "I don't think Rhett's the same guy anymore." But I didn't have time to argue because Jess turned down a winding driveway lined with trees lit by twinkle lights. "Looks like we're here."

I stared in stunned silence as we drove up to a mansion with cars filling the driveway. Cam had been right in her estimation—there had to be at least twenty or more cars here, just for her bachelorette party. Part of me was thankful Shelley and her fiancé were eloping to another country because no way could I bring a salad spinner and wear a thrifted dress to a wedding of this caliber.

We stopped behind Jess, and there were valet drivers dressed in tuxedo pants, suspenders, and nothing else waiting to take our cars and our bags. The three of us giggled with each other as we walked up the wide stone steps to the "cabin."

The front area was like a massive great room that had

been decked out like a bachelorette party store exploded on the place. There was pink gauze along the walls, a penis-shaped balloon arch, and even a giant cutout of a naked professional football player holding a helmet over his privates.

"Oh my god," Cam whispered. "We know him."

My eyes widened as I took a closer look. "That's Ford Madigan!"

On the other side of Cam, Jess said, "You *know* him?"

Cam said, "He was in eighth grade when we were seniors."

I swore there were stars in Jess's eyes. "Can you *please* introduce me?"

Cam and I exchanged a glance.

"What?" Jess asked.

"Cottonwood Falls is pretty protective of their own," I explained. "He would have to be okay with it."

Before Jess could reply, a woman yelled, "IF IT AIN'T MY COUNTRY BUMPKINS!"

Cam laughed at the blond walking toward us. She had on a lacy white dress, a pink sash that said BRIDE and a silver tiara atop her head. "Shelley, there's no service here and you're calling US bumpkins?"

"I'm just joking," she said, hugging Cam and then me. "I've missed you two! Are you sure you can't move back to Austin?"

"Not with Cam in love," I teased.

Cam rolled her eyes at me but couldn't hide her smile.

"Oh my god," Shelley said. "We need the story. EVERYONE. SIT DOWN. IT'S STORY TIME." Shelley began dragging Cam toward the pink bean bag chairs spread about the room, and Jess hooked her arm through mine.

"Isn't it good to be back?" she laughed.

"You know it." I smiled. I liked being back in Cotton-wood Falls, but I missed this too. I'd made so many friends in Austin. I needed to do better about staying in touch, even when life got busy. "Tell me about you!" I said to her. "How is your job going?"

As we got settled in, Jess told me about rising through the ranks at her pharmaceutical sales company. It sounded like she was in line for a major promotion.

"That's amazing," I said. "I'm so happy for you."

She grinned. "And how's the salon? I love seeing all your posts online."

My heart warmed just thinking about the salon. "I was really worried after leaving Austin that Cottonwood Falls would feel smaller than it did before, but I think that time away made me appreciate it more." I told her about all the sweet clients who came in and wished me well, and even a little about Rhett.

"He sounds hot," Jess said.

"He is..."

A wave of squeals sounded through the room, and Shelley yelled, "WHO BOOKED ME A SEXY COWBOY STRIPPER?"

I looked to the door, an amused smile on my face until I saw who walked in...

Rhett. Freaking. Griffen.

34

MAGNOLIA

RHETT AND I CONNECTED GLANCES, and he opened his mouth to say something, but Shelley yelled, "Don't be shy, cowboy! You've got a hundred-dollar tip waiting for you. But take the shirt off. Show us those abs!"

I saw the moment the realization hit Rhett: if he danced with this girl, he could make a hundred dollars and probably recoup whatever money he spent driving here for some harebrained reason.

Then I saw him decide against it, giving a slight shake of his head. Shelley clapped her hands together, chanting, "DANCE! DANCE! DANCE!"

I looked to Camryn to see if she was as horrified as I was, only to find that she was chanting along!

My jaw dropped open as Shelley got on her feet and tottered over to him on fuzzy pink heels. Music had already been playing, but someone changed it to "Oh Yeah" by Yello.

I laughed so hard it bordered on a cackle. Shelley had

him completely cornered. So he did what any guy would do.

He began unbuttoning his pink sparkly jersey.

I put my face in my hands, laughing at the ridiculousness of the situation. Once he had the jersey off, he spun it over his head in a few quick loops and then sent it flying through the air to me. I caught it, and Jess and the other girls around me cheered. Grinning, I put it over my shoulders, vaguely wondering if Rhett was a work-for-hire stripper back home. He definitely had the body for it.

The song changed to "Save a Horse, Ride a Cowboy" by Big and Rich, and my stomach hurt from laughing as all hell broke loose. He lowered Shelley on the couch and gave her a lap dance, his back to her as she tucked a hundred-dollar bill into the waistband of his Wranglers.

And from the looks of it, he was *earning* that hundred dollars.

He took her tiara off her head and put it on his, prancing around in front of her while he swayed his hips left to right. Tears were coming out of my eyes I was laughing so hard.

Why wasn't I filming this??

I got out my phone, sliding over to the camera just in time to see him twerking while all the girls screamed and cheered. His brothers would *never* let him live this down.

But then the front door opened, and two guys walked in, wearing police uniforms. The music paused, and everyone looked at them curiously.

Shelley got up, saying, "I'm sorry, officers, we'll turn it down."

The two guys looked at each other, and one asked, "Did you hire a different stripper service?"

Confused, Shelley looked from Rhett to the "officers." Her best friend, Lindsey, said, "I only hired one."

"We're it," the guy said, thumbing toward his chest.

Then everyone swung their gaze from the officers to Rhett. Shelley said, "If you're not a stripper, then who are you?"

Before he could say a word, I piped up, "I'll get him out of here! Carry on with the party!"

Everyone watched as I marched to Rhett, taking his bare muscled arm in mine and walking him to the front door. A Marvin Gaye song was playing before it closed behind us, leaving us alone on the massive covered porch.

I passed Rhett his jersey and he slid it on but didn't worry about closing the buttons. The view of his chest and abs was *highly* distracting.

"How did I do?" Rhett asked with a smirk. "I've never considered stripping before, but they seemed to be into it."

"Rhett!" I half laughed, half cried. "What are you doing here?"

He rubbed the back of his neck. "You said you'd text me, and when you stopped replying... I got worried."

My lips parted. "You drove five hours in the middle of the night because you were *worried* about me?"

"It was better than searching the news for a car accident." His eyes were so full of emotion I couldn't fault him. So I took him in my arms, hugging him.

He held me close, saying, "I'm sorry. I just had to know that you were okay." He pulled back, running his hands over my arms.

"How did you even know where to go?" I asked.

"I called in a favor with Knox to ping your phone

where you last had service since I was so worried. I drove around a little and saw what I thought was Cam's car, but I had to come inside and make sure."

I tilted my head. "You didn't have to do all that. I'm sorry I didn't call you."

He shook his head in return. "Just my overactive imagination. I'd hate it if something happened to you. But I hope you have a good time with all your friends. The bride seems like a *lot* of fun." He held up the hundred dollars, waving it.

I laughed, and he turned to walk away down the front steps.

"You're leaving?" I asked.

He winked. "I already got what I came for. I just wanted to know you're safe, not interfere on your time with your friends." He smiled gently. "Have a good night, Mags."

I smiled after him as he walked past the half-naked valet drivers to his truck parked in the driveway.

He was more than a knight in shining armor.

He was a cowboy in a pink jersey with a heart of gold and an insane amount of rhythm.

So. Much. Better.

35

RHETT

I PULLED up to the practice field early Tuesday and waited for the rest of the team to arrive. Maggie and I had been texting on and off since the party, but I wanted to see her in person. I needed to ask her to dinner with my family tomorrow night, and the thought had me all itchy and nervous.

I'd never brought a girl to meet my family aside from her. Not once in all these years.

Esther got to practice first, running up to me. "Look what my mama got me!" She held up a bright yellow bat. "It's lucky," she said. "This should help me hit the balls at our next game."

I grinned. "That's a cool bat, Esther! We'll practice batting today so you can use it."

She jumped up and down happily, then looked over my shoulder. "Maya! Look at my bat."

I followed her gaze to see my niece approaching while my sister sat on the bottom row of the bleachers holding

Graham's leash. That dog was as much a part of the family as I was.

A few other girls arrived, and I had them go out to the field to start stretching, then I saw her.

Maggie.

She was adorable in her black athletic shorts and a matching crop top that showed a small strip of her bare midriff. Fuck, did that sliver of stomach do something to me. I wanted to pull that top up and see her beautiful chest, pull her shorts aside and fill her the way I've been wanting to do since I heard she was coming back to town.

But I kept my cool, and when she got closer to me, I whispered, "That hangover feeling better?"

She eyed me over the top of her sunglasses. "I'm *never* drinking again."

I laughed. "That's what we all say."

"Keep teasing me and that video I have of you is getting posted on the internet."

My jaw dropped. "You took a video?"

"How could I not?" She smirked. "I've watched it three times already."

"You're devious, Maggie Ray."

She shrugged and then scanned the field of our girls, who had abandoned stretching and started playing tag. She used her fingers to count them off and said, "Gang's all here."

I called out for them, and we started a batting drill, beginning with Esther and her brand-new bat. It was practically glow in the dark with how bright it was.

At the end of practice, we went through the familiar motions of cleaning everything up, and Maggie lingered by my truck. Her standing there reminded me of the last practice, when I'd taken her out to the country and "punished" her. The way she screamed my name still played over and over in my mind.

But I needed to keep my head on straight because I had a question for her, a big one.

"Hey," I said.

She smiled over at me. "Hey."

My stomach turned over with something like butterflies. What was the manly version of that? A beehive? Those killer wasps everyone was talking about a few years ago? Whatever it was, Mags did it to me. But I needed to set aside my distracting thoughts and just ask her already.

"Mags, I was wondering if you'd come to my family's farm for Wednesday night dinner tomorrow. Dad's grilling, as usual, and my brothers and sisters-in-law always bring a side dish, and there's always a bunch of kids running around playing. It's a good time, but I know it would be better with you."

She smiled softly, but there was a reservation behind that smile. I could see it in the tightness of her eyes. "It's so nice of you to invite me."

"But?"

She rubbed her arm. "But would it send your family the wrong message?"

"What do you mean?" I asked, those butterflies/bees/wasps quickly turning to lead.

"I mean, they might think we're a couple."

Forget lead; now her words were like a punch to the gut. "You don't want them to think we're together?"

Her mouth opened and closed, then she spoke carefully. "I only mean that we're still figuring out what we are. We haven't discussed labels or anything."

I raised my eyebrows. "Labels? I'm a grown adult. I don't need to call you my girlfriend to know what you are to me." I shook my head. "Mags, I know what I want." I put my hand to my chest. "I think you're the only one who doesn't know."

She reached for my hand, but I felt stiff under her touch. "Rhett, we're having so much fun together. Isn't that enough?"

I stepped back, pacing the ground in the dim dirt parking lot. "I don't want to 'have fun' with you, Mags. I told you I was done fucking around with girls just for the hell of it, and I meant it."

Her eyes studied me, looking darker than usual under the dusky light. "I don't know if I can give you a relationship, Rhett."

A lump was growing in my throat, all that hope I'd been holding on to, all that progress I thought we'd made... it was disappearing, leaving me just as hollow as I'd felt before she came back home, and I realized, I'd been holding out for this girl for the last fifteen years in one way or another.

Three more years of this, and I will have spent more than half my life hung up over Maggie Ray.

And after what happened last year, I knew; life was short.

I couldn't do this anymore.

"Rhett?" she asked.

I met her gaze, taking her hands in mine and knowing this could very well be the last time we touched. "Maggie, I understand that you don't know what you want, but I can't stick around hoping you'll decide it's me. If you're not ready to move forward, to give *us* a real shot, then I think this is it for us." My voice barely held out to that last word, and I blinked quickly to hold back tears. I didn't want her to try and console me or be with me because she felt bad, but because she truly wanted to see what the future could hold for us as a couple.

I held on for one more second, memorizing the feel of her soft hands under my calloused ones. Remembering the way her blue eyes held mine like no other woman's eyes ever had. But also holding on to that knowing in my chest that said I deserved someone willing to give me their heart.

When she didn't speak, I let go and said, "I'll see you at the game on Friday, Maggie Ray."

She didn't say a word, and when I got in my truck and drove away, I still saw her standing there in my rearview mirror.

36

RHETT

I PICKED up a six pack from the liquor store in town before driving out to my parents' place. Griffen Farms had meant a lot to me over the years. It was the place I learned to walk, to drive a stick shift, how to swim in the creek, and how to rein a cutting horse. It represented a dream, a piece of land to call my own and raise my family, but also, it reminded me that no matter how alone I felt, I still had a place to call home.

I drove under the Griffen Farms sign, my chest just a little lighter than it had been before. At the end of the drive stood that white farmhouse with the flower boxes under the windowsills Mom kept planted and blooming in the summertime. There were cars all over the driveway— Henrietta's pride and joy, her red SUV, Gage's white minivan, Liv's truck, my parents' vehicles, and now my truck too.

I parked behind the old pickup with white doors and a red cab and bed we called Candy Cane, then I grabbed the six pack and walked inside, bracing myself for Mom to ask where Maggie was. I still didn't know how I'd answer, because there wasn't an easy way to say the girl you loved didn't want to be with you.

I made it a few steps down the sidewalk before my nieces and nephews sprinted past, spraying each other with water blasters. Except Maya missed Andrew by a good two feet and completely soaked the front of my shirt with water. I took a deep breath against the cold burst, and Maya and Drew stared at me wide-eyed.

Great. Just fucking great.

Maya said, "Uncle Rhett?"

I kept my eyes closed, cooling down. This was exactly the distraction I needed right now. "You're gonna pay for that," I said, grinning. "Go on, I'll give you a five-second head start."

They didn't move, so I started counting. "Five...four..."

She and Drew screamed and sprinted off, making me smile despite that well of sadness in my chest.

When I got to zero, I ran around the house to the backyard, where they were trying—and failing—to hide behind the doghouse. I hauled Maya over one arm and Drew over the other, carrying them kicking and screaming toward the spigot.

Drew's siblings, Levi and Cora, were cackling and snorting at the pair of them about to get payback.

"Cora," I said, "get me a couple water balloons, will ya?"

She dutifully walked to the bucket full of balloons and carried two to me as Drew and Maya struggled in my arms, half laughing, half arguing.

"Okay, Cora, right on their heads!"

Maya said, "Cora, you're my favorite cousin, don't do thi—"

With an evil grin, Cora smashed the water balloon on Maya's head, sending water right down her face.

I cackled at Maya's stunned expression, but then Cora got Drew with another balloon, making me laugh even more, despite the fact that my clothes were getting wetter by the second.

Still in stitches over Drew's sputtering face and Maya's protestations, I let them go, but that was a mistake.

They both went to the balloon bucket fast as lightning and proceeded to rocket water balloons at me, with Levi and Cora's help, until I was soaking wet and had to yell uncle.

They finally let me go, and I walked around the side of the house where the patio was, water literally dripping off me. Dad, Gray, and Agatha were out there, drinking and talking, but when they saw me, they burst out laughing.

Wiping his eyes, Gray said, "Just like when you all were kids."

I smiled. "Grow up, don't grow old, right?"

Gray nodded. "That's right."

Out of the corner of my eyes, I think I saw Agatha giving him a warm look, but it was gone before I could be sure. She had a reputation for dating the worst men when I was younger, but I couldn't remember seeing anyone for years. Maybe both counts would change soon.

Dad said, "I have some extra clothes you can borrow."

I saluted him and walked past them, taking off my sopping-wet boots at the door. Mom let me go without questioning about Maggie, probably just so I wouldn't mess up her floor, and I went back to the main level primary bedroom, pulling some sweats and a T-shirt out of Dad's drawers. Thankfully, Mom had just bought him a pack of underwear, so I pulled back the plastic, getting out a fresh pair. Something about having my balls in the same place Dad's had been gave me the willies.

Ha. Willies.

I shook my head at myself, finished dressing, and tossed my wet clothes in the hamper. We'd call it a trade.

When I walked out, my hair was still damp, but Mom smiled at me. "All dry?"

I rubbed my hair. "Mostly."

She smiled at me as Fletcher and my brothers sat at the table, drinking their beers. Fletcher said, "The kids came in bragging that they got you."

The tips of my ears warmed. "Yeah, but I got them first."

The guys chuckled, and Mom shook her head at me.

She reached into the fridge for a beer and handed it to me. "Maggie couldn't make it?"

After all the levity earlier, I found myself quickly sinking back to the depths I'd been in before I arrived. "Actually... well, Maggie..."

The front door opened, and we turned to see Maggie coming in, holding a glass pan covered in foil.

She smiled nervously and said, "Sorry I'm late, Deidre. I had to finish making a side for tonight."

I took her in while Mom fussed over her and the pan.

Maggie was here, which meant...

We had a chance.

37

MAGNOLIA

I COULD FEEL Rhett's gaze on me as his mom took my pan of cheesy potatoes. My heart was in my throat, and my stomach was full of butterflies, because we both knew what this meant. I was going all in on what could be the start of happily ever after or a really big disaster.

But I was stronger now than when we first broke up. I knew I could survive heartbreak, forge a life for myself, even date and love other men.

Still, there was a part of me that knew what Rhett said was true. In some unexplainable way, we were linked to each other.

While his mom brought my pan of food to the back patio table, Fletcher leaned back and said, "Well, well, well."

"Shut up," Rhett muttered, coming to me and putting his arm around my waist. He looked down at me, hope and wonder in his eyes, and he kissed me in front of his brothers and his brother-in-law like we were the only two in the room.

His embrace left me breathless, like it always did.

"Want to get out of here?" he asked low.

I laughed. "I just got here."

Tyler, Gage, and Fletcher were already hooting and hollering.

Their noise had the screen door sliding open and Rhett's sister, Liv, coming inside, followed by two other women.

"Oh my gosh!" Liv said. "Mom said you came, but I couldn't believe it."

My cheeks felt hot as Rhett's grip on my waist tightened slightly.

"Yeah," Rhett said, "we were just leaving."

"Oh hell no," Liv said. "She's coming with us."

I raised my eyebrows, wondering who would win in this standoff.

Rhett said, "Like hell she is."

Fletcher cut in. "Come on, Rhett, you get to see her all the time. This is new to the rest of us."

Rhett glared at his friend. "Traitor. Marry my sister and all of a sudden you're on her side."

I laughed at the pair. "It's okay, Rhett. I'm happy to go with Liv."

Liv stuck out her tongue, then came and looped her hand through my arm, marching me away from Rhett.

"Where are you taking her?" Rhett asked.

"Nunya!" Liv teased.

I giggled. "Just like old times."

Liv nodded happily as she walked me to the stairs, the other two women following. When we reached the top of the stairs, it was like déjà vu. I used to sneak up here with Rhett when his parents weren't home to make out. But this time, Liv steered me toward her room, and once the four of us were inside, she shut the door.

And maybe I regretted telling Rhett it was okay.

But I knew, if I was with Rhett, I was with his family too. It had been that way back when we first dated, and I knew that much hadn't changed.

Liv clapped her hands together happily. "I knew you were together! I definitely saw sparks between you two at practice."

My cheeks heated as I glanced toward these other women I didn't know.

"Oh," Liv said, "this is Tyler's wife, Henrietta." She gestured toward a beautiful black woman with natural hair that almost brushed her shoulders.

"You can call me Hen," she said with a smile.

And then Liv gestured at a white woman with dark brown hair and a heart-shaped face. She looked so familiar. Had we gone to school together? "This is Gage's wife, Farrah."

"I knew I recognized you," I said. "I saw that press conference they had when you two first started dating." I cringed. "You handled all the media well. I think I would have melted into the floor."

Farrah batted her hand through the air. "All water under the bridge now. The real news item of the moment is Rhett bringing a woman to dinner!"

Hen nodded. "I've been married to Tyler for three years now, and I've *never* seen Rhett bring a woman over."

Farrah agreed. "Not once."

Liv added, "Not since you left town."

My heart warmed. I was starting to believe Rhett when he said these other women occupying his time were just that—a distraction from what he was really feeling. Maybe I wasn't the only one who had been hurting after we broke up. We just had a different way of coping.

"I think your mom's excited," I said with a laugh.

The three laughed too, and Farrah said, "I like her."

The compliment made my cheeks warm. "Tell me about you two."

Liv said, "Take your time. Rhett will go crazy wondering what we're talking about."

We laughed as Liv settled on the desk chair. Then Farrah, Hen, and I sat on the full-sized bed. It was like a sleepover, but we were all grown. Warm, fuzzy feelings flooded my chest. Is this what it would be like if Rhett and I stayed together? I'd get instant best friends?

Henrietta and Farrah shared a glance, and then Hen said, "I grew up in California, I have three older brothers, and I'm super close with my parents and my grandma. I worked in property management, and the company Tyler worked for was building a new complex for us. One thing led to another and..." She shrugged.

Liv said, "She makes it sound simple. Tyler was fired from his job for—"

Henrietta said, "Ah, ah, ah. She does not need to hear that the first day."

Liv and Farrah laughed, while I gave Hen a bashful look. "Deidre already told me."

A ruckus broke out in the room, Liv laughing so hard she started coughing, and even Farrah was wiping tears from her eyes while Hen shushed them both. "Don't tell me you two've never gotten carried away."

Speaking as someone who'd had two public trysts recently, "I mean, that does sound super hot."

"It was," Hen said, "until he got fired, and I got put on probation, and we had to break up. Anyway, I eventually got my head on straight and realized I couldn't let a man like that go."

Her story warmed my heart. I wanted that, the peace that came with knowing you had your person forever, even after a few wrong turns.

"Your turn," Hen told Farrah.

Farrah laughed. "Okay, I'm in the hot seat." She told me about leaving her ex and moving in with her parents at thirty-four years old with three kids. Gage hired her, and even though they both tried to deny their attraction for each other, they couldn't help but fall.

Liv said, "We thought Gage was going to be single *forever*. But now I get a sister and three nieces and nephews!"

Farrah reached out her hand, holding Liv's for a second. "This is the best family," she said to me. "You picked a good guy to date."

There were still nerves, fear, swirling in my stomach. But I couldn't tell these women all that. They loved Rhett to pieces.

But then Liv explained to her sisters-in-law, "Mags is the one that got away."

Hen and Farrah had a look of understanding, and Farrah said, "That makes so much sense."

My eyebrows drew together. "What do you mean?"

Farrah and Liv exchanged a look, and Liv nodded, like she was giving Farrah permission to go on. Farrah said, "I don't know. It always just seemed like Rhett was looking to fill a hole in his life."

Hen snickered.

"Oh my god!" Liv said, laughing. "You're as bad as the boys."

My cheeks warmed, and I shifted on the bed. I didn't want to be another "hole" to fill.

Noticing my change in mood, Liv said, "Mags, I've known Rhett the longest out of everyone in this room, and I can tell you that he wasn't the same after you left. It was like there was this sadness underneath all the jokes and that smile he always has."

"And now?" I asked.

Liv shrugged with a small smile of her own. "Now, you're back."

38

RHETT

I PACED the floor in the dining room while my brothers and Fletch sat at the table, drinking beer and talking like nothing major was going on.

"What the hell could they be talking about for..." I glanced at the clock on the wall. "Half an hour?"

Gage glanced up at me, totally unbothered. "They've been up there half an hour?"

"Twenty-four minutes, but still."

Tyler laughed. "Dude, it's girl talk. Takes forever. I swear Hen's on the phone hours a week with her friends from back home."

I shook my head. "I barely got Maggie to come here, and I swear if, she leaves after this because they talked her out of it or scared her off..."

Gage got up, patting my back. "It's going to be okay. All those girls up there love you. Including Maggie."

My heart constricted. "I'm not so sure about that last one."

He shook his head. "You think she would have come

to the lion's den and walked up there with those girls if she didn't like you? You're dumber than I already thought you were."

I shoved him, making him laugh.

From the direction of the stairs, Liv asked, "What's so funny?"

I saw Maggie coming down the stairs behind her and breathed a sigh of relief. Just seeing her made me feel better. Still, I studied her, waiting to see if she'd beeline toward the door. Instead, she walked toward me, putting her arm around my waist.

The tension in my shoulders instantly eased.

Gage chuckled.

"Shut up," I muttered.

The sliding door opened, and Mom said, "Dinner's ready."

For the next hour or so, it was chaos as usual. People passed food around the two patio tables shoved together, the kids were up and down up and down, taking bites between playing on the swing set in the backyard. It was hot, but the overhead fan kept the bugs away. And Maggie was sitting next to me, talking with everyone like she'd been joining us all this time.

It felt *right*.

Mags looked over at me, speaking around the bite of hamburger in her mouth. "Why are you staring like that?"

My chest warmed, and I rubbed her back. "Just glad you're here 'sall."

She smiled up at me and then swallowed. The movement of her throat was so fucking distracting I had to look down and take a drink from my beer. Couldn't I keep it in my pants for a couple hours?

She looked worried. "Do I have something on my face?" She wiped at the corners of her lips.

I caught her hand, kissing her palm. "You're perfect."

Her cheeks warmed. "You're a sweet talker, Rhett Griffen."

Suddenly, I felt eyes on me, and I looked over to see almost everyone at the table staring at us.

Quickly, everyone looked away and talking resumed.

Maggie chuckled, and I shook my head. If we made it through this night, it'd be a damn miracle. And hopefully a sign of good things to come.

Luckily, we finished the meal without too much awkwardness. My mom asked about Maggie's dad and said she could invite him next time.

Even though Maggie thanked her for the offer, I could see the tightness in her eyes, the way her lips dipped down for a fraction of a second. So when dinner was over and I walked her to the barn to look at the horses, I asked about it.

She glanced down at her feet, pink toenails showing in her sandals. "My dad holds grudges longer than I do, despite the fact that we were young."

"That's saying something," I teased.

She ribbed me. "You know, I'm his little girl."

I nodded, my throat feeling tight still. "I hope I can prove to him that I've grown and matured a lot, especially in the last year. I want him to see that I'm here for you in a way I wasn't capable of then."

Her fingertips brushed mine, and she squeezed my hand, lifting it to her lips. "He will. It'll just take time."

I nodded and stopped as we reached the corral. I lifted my boot on a rung of the fence panel and hung my arms over the top as we looked at the horses.

"Oh my gosh," Mags said. "You still have Fred?"

I grinned. "He's an old shit. But he's real good for the kids to ride."

She chuckled. "Remember riding horses to the creek and going skinny-dipping?"

Heat flooded my cock at the memory of her naked body before she plunged into the water. "You want me walking around the farm with a hard-on?" I asked, giving her a heated stare.

She swallowed again, and all I could think of was laying a trail of kisses on her thick throat, how it would feel under my hand, the color that would flood her face.

My voice was low as I said, "We should go. I'll follow you to your house?"

Excitement spread through my body as she nodded.

When it came to Maggie, holding back was so fucking hard. Tonight, if she let me, I'd give her everything I had.

We walked together back to the house, said goodbye to my parents, and then I drove behind her car into town, my cock tight in my pants. I took deep breaths to cool myself down, but when we got to her house, I marched to her car and took her in a kiss right there in the driveway.

Her fingers wound up my back and then tugged in my hair, making me moan.

I angled my head, working my lips down to her neck, and then I rumbled against her ear. "Maggie, if you want me to be a gentleman, I need to leave now. I'll walk you to your door, and then I'll turn around and drive home, and fuck myself again until you're ready for me." I pulled back, waiting for her answer.

She looked up at me, baby blues pale and wide, her cheeks full of heat. "I don't want you to go home. But we can't stay here. Cam will be home this evening."

My cock twitched at her words, at the throaty sound of her voice. "Baby, don't tease me."

She arched an eyebrow, lips lifting to a smirk. "Do I have to beg for it?"

"Fuck no." I bent, lifting her over my shoulder, and she squealed on the way up.

"Rhett!" she cried, legs dangling. "You're going to hurt yourself. I'm not light!"

I opened the truck door, putting her inside. "Don't insult me, baby girl. Or I'll show you just how much weight I can take directly on my face."

Her thighs shifted in the seat. "Is that a threat?" she breathed.

My fists clenched the loose fabric of her cotton shirt, pulling her closer to me. "It's a fucking promise." I released her shirt and reached for the seatbelt, crossing it over her waist. Then I shut the door, fire still in my veins, my cock begging not to wait.

I went to my side of the truck and pulled out of the driveway, tempted to take her to a field and fuck her till her screams made birds fly from treetops. But I'd waited this long, and there was no way our first time back together was going to be anything less than perfect.

I sped out of town and onto the blacktop, reaching for her thick thigh and grabbing it in my hand. I kept my eyes on the road as I uttered, "These thighs are going to look so fucking good riding my cock tonight."

She let out a guttural moan.

"Even better when they're shaking as you're coming, over, and over, and over again."

"Rhett," she whimpered.

I clenched her thigh, fingers sinking into soft flesh. "Wrapped around my waist as I pound into you."

My cock ached, tugging against my jeans, and I shifted. "You have no idea how badly I want you, Maggie Ray."

"Let me see," she breathed. She put her seatbelt strap behind her back, reaching for my jeans. I shifted forward in the seat, giving her access to my belt buckle.

She undid it with her pretty pink nails as I flexed my jaw, trying to focus on the road. The zipper cracked as she pulled it back, and I let out a sigh of relief as the pressure against my head eased.

The blacktop ahead was dark and empty, and my short-circuiting brain was only good for staying between the lines, feeling her hands on my cock, and counting down the time until we made it home.

Two minutes left.

I slowed at the sign for Finnigan Farms and turned down the dirt road.

Liv's hands moved my underwear down, exposing my cock to the warm air in the cab. She wrapped her fingers around the shaft, pumping in a maddeningly slow motion. "I want your cock in my mouth," she breathed.

"Now's the time to beg," I said roughly, slowing on the dirt road.

She undid her seatbelt, moving closer. "Give me that cock, Rhett Griffen. I can't wait another second."

"Taste it," I ordered.

She dipped her head, hair falling around her face, and I held it back with one hand as her warm lips surrounded my head.

"That is so fucking good," I told her, my balls already tightening. "Now, suck."

She took my cock deeper in her mouth and sucked like the good fucking girl she was. Then she took my hand and placed it on the back of her head.

My lips formed a salacious grin. She wanted me to guide her.

I pressed against the back of her head and then pulled her hair to bring her up, over and over again on my cock as she moaned, the vibrations so fucking good I let out a string of swears as I pulled up to my house.

Parking in the driveway, I drew her head away from my cock, her lips red and wet, eyes wide. I could look at her like this all night long, but as good as her mouth had felt, I knew her pussy would be even better.

"Get in the house," I ordered. "I want to see your ass as you're walking inside."

Her eyes were wide as she unbuckled and got out of my truck. She pulled her jersey up so I'd have a good view of her ass in the denim capris, and... damn. I bit on the crook of my index finger.

This had to be a fever dream. Something better than reality, because I'd hoped for this day for years, and now that it was here, I realized nothing I imagined had done this moment even an ounce of justice.

She glanced over her shoulder, hair swinging, and sent me a flirty smile.

I shook my head at this woman. Too good to be true.

I got out of my truck and followed her through the

door. She was already walking down the hall, past the bathroom.

"Bedroom's on the right," I said.

She opened the door and turned on the light, looking around. I was glad I made my bed this morning. My room was pretty bare, decorated simply with clean sheets and a thin quilt on the bed. I couldn't wait to see her naked in my sheets. It would be an image I'd never forget.

"Let me get a condom," I said, going to my dresser. "I was tested a month ago, and I'm clean."

I got a rubber from the drawer and turned back to her to see her arms wrapped around her middle.

My eyebrows drew together as I set the condom down and looked her over. "What's wrong?"

She blinked quickly, eyes shining, "I'm sorry, I just..." Her lips trembled, and she covered her face.

My gut sank, and I went to her, putting my arm around her. "Don't apologize, Mags. We don't have to do this if you don't want to or you're not ready. I can take you home right now. We can sit on the couch and eat cookie dough with our clothes on. Whatever you want."

She uncovered her face, looking up, "I'm sorry, it's just... I came in here and I can't stop seeing that girl walking into your house like she'd done it a million times before. And I don't want to be just another girl you've had in your bed."

Suddenly, my past collided with my present. All these years, I'd been fucking girls, looking for a good time and trying to get Maggie out of my system. But now it was reckoning time.

So I did the only thing I could do.

I told her the truth.

"I'm going to be honest with you, Mags." I gestured at my bed. "I've fucked a lot of women over the years. Sometimes when I was feeling lonely, sometimes because I was bored, and sometimes just because it was what I was used to. But I mean it when I say I want to *make love* to you."

"Will you do that?" she asked.

"Do what?"

"Make love to me tonight."

39

MAGNOLIA

I WAITED for Rhett to shy away, but he tilted his head, closed the distance between us, and took my face in his hands. He lowered his lips to mine, kissing me so gently that tears were already forming in my eyes.

I wrapped my arms around his waist, holding on to him as he kissed me slowly, softly, and we got used to the taste and feel of each other all over again. He drew his lips along my cheeks, my jaw, my forehead, his hands never straying farther than the small of my back or my waist.

When I felt comfortable, I reached up, unbuttoning his shirt. The realization of what we were about to do made me smile against his lips.

"What?" he asked.

I looked up at him, speaking what I knew to be true. "You are a good man, Rhett Griffen."

His gaze softened, and he watched me remove his shirt before peeling off his white undershirt. I led him back to the bed, letting him sink into the sheets before straddling him, kissing him, letting my hair become a veil that hid us from the rest of the world.

His hands teased the waistband of my pants before going to my back, and this time I knew he was waiting for me to make the next move. I leaned back, straddling his waist, his cock hard through his jeans, and took off my shirt, revealing the lacy bra I'd worn.

His eyes were hungry on my chest, spilling from the cups. And knowing how much he wanted me gave me the courage to unhook my bra, to show him all of who I was. The large stomach, lined with stretch marks. My breasts, one larger than the other, large areolas puckered with desire and nipples pebbled from only his kisses.

He looked up at me as if I were the most beautiful thing he'd ever seen. "Mags," he whispered.

My lips trembled, because maybe he was right about us being twin flames. It felt like being reunited. It felt like being joined. "I know," I whispered, my voice quivering.

He took me down to him, kissing me slow, one hand holding my ass, the other teasing my nipples between his thumb and finger.

I could feel my panties getting soaked, my sex tightening, begging for him to fill me in the way only he could.

I grinded against his hips, and he let out a moan before rolling me over, getting on top of me and kissing me before quickly removing his jeans. Then he went to my pants, unbuttoning the denim. "Lift your hips," he said.

I did as he asked, and he slid the denim and my panties over my dimpled hips and thighs. My ass wasn't as tight as it was when we were last together, and my body had aged, marked with spider veins and cellulite.

But his eyes were hungry on me, on my soft, naked body bare before his muscled one. "You're so beautiful," he breathed.

My lips pulled into a smile. "Let me see you."

He unbuttoned his pants and bent to lower them, revealing his cock, full, thick, long. The soft skin had felt so good against my tongue. With the jeans off, I could see his strong legs, the heavy way his sack hung under his hard dick.

"Come here," I breathed.

He walked to the dresser, reaching for the condom, but I shook my head, reaching out for his hand. "I'm on birth control. I want to feel you make me yours."

With his jaw flexing, he reached for the condom anyway, sliding it over his length. "You're still mine." He came to me, settling between my legs. His cock brushed my stomach, and I reached for it, pumping the hard length through the condom as he sucked and licked my nipples.

"Rhett," I breathed. I *begged*.

"Baby, I know." He lowered himself over me, his chest against mine, his stomach against mine, and angled his tip at my entrance.

As he pressed himself inside, I cried out. With pleasure, with pain, with hope, and everything in between.

"Magnolia," was all he said, shuddering over me as he carefully controlled his movements.

I wrapped my legs around his hips like he'd said earlier and brought him closer to me, deeper inside me.

He filled me in the best possible way, but even better was the way he held my gaze. He looked at me so lovingly, adoringly.

"You are the most beautiful woman I've ever laid eyes on," he said, increasing the rhythm of his thrusts. "You're irresistible. Funny. Kind. Beautiful. Everything I could dream of having in my life."

All these years, I'd dated men who found my flaws and had trouble seeing past them, but Rhett saw all of me. And loved me anyway. Tears filled my eyes, rolling down the sides of my face and dampening my hair. "Rhett," I choked out.

He lowered his mouth to mine, kissing me, capturing everything I couldn't say with our kiss.

And the intensity, the closeness, it broke something inside me, the last piece that was holding back from everything we could be.

The realization pushed me over the edge, making me come around him and cry out against his kiss.

Feeling me come set off his own orgasm, and he grunted against me, releasing everything he'd been holding back.

When all the waves had passed, he slowly rolled away from me. Once he removed the condom, he pulled me into his arms, holding me close against his bare chest, both of us spent.

He kissed the top of my head, his voice raw as he said, "I know I shouldn't say it this soon, but I love you, Mags. I have since I was sixteen years old."

Tears spilled down my cheeks, and I held on to his arm draped across my chest. "I'm sorry it's taken me this long to say that I forgive you. And that I love you too."

He cupped my face, kissing my forehead.

Warmth spread from the point of contact, and I lay with him. Enjoying his warmth, this closeness, the feeling of his arm around me. I glanced down, noticing the black ink on his bicep.

"That's new," I said, nodding toward it.

He lifted his arm as if to check where I was looking. When he spotted the windmill tattooed in black, he said, "My siblings and I got that a couple years after I graduated. Gage and Dad had a big falling out, and Liv had this idea that we could get a sibling tattoo to remind him that we'd always be there for him."

I ran my fingertips over the ink. "The windmill from your family's ranch?"

"You know how windmills are always spinning in the wind?" he asked.

I nodded.

"No matter how much they move, they're always there. Just like family's always there for each other."

I lifted my lips in a smile. "That's sweet of you."

"I can be sweet sometimes," he said.

I blew out a small laugh.

"What was that?" he asked, mischief in his eyes.

"Nothing," I said quickly.

He tickled my side. "Is that so?"

Giggling, I squirmed to escape him and rolled to his other side. He stopped tickling me, but I got a view of the surgical scars on his back, one on his shoulder, another on his neck, and one farther down his side.

It felt hard to get air. "Rhett, what are these scars from?"

40

RHETT

MY SHOULDERS TENSED.

"What is it?" she asked, moving to sit in front of me. She held the blanket over her chest and looked at me with wide, worried blue eyes.

I hated the fear I saw there, because just moments ago, everything had been the definition of perfection.

I reached out to hold her hand, console her. "You don't need to worry about me."

She tilted her head with a frown. "Tell me."

My jaw clenched. I didn't want to relive the memory, but to have a future with someone, you needed to understand their past too. "A year ago, we found a spot on my back. When Fletcher sent it in for testing, it came back cancerous."

She covered her mouth with her hand. "Cancer?"

Running my thumb over the back of her hand, I said, "We were able to remove it all with surgery, and since then I've had regular appointments to check for more. Some of the scars heal different than others."

Her chest heaved with deep breaths. "That's so scary."

I rubbed her back, loving the soft feel of her skin under my hand. It grounded me enough to continue, because I knew if Darlene hadn't seen the spot when we were last together, I never would have mentioned it to Fletcher. Who knew how differently things might have gone if diagnosis was later?

"If I'm being honest, it was the wake-up call I needed. I knew I had to finally make something of my life, because we're not promised tomorrow."

She reached out, hugging me, and we held each other for moments. It was the healing touch I didn't know I needed.

"Thank you," I breathed.

I felt her smile against my shoulder.

Emotion rose in my throat as I said, "We need to celebrate."

"Celebrate?"

I nodded. "How do cookies sound?"

She smiled at me. "Sounds amazing."

I made us cookies from the dough I kept in the freezer, and we ate cookies and milk in bed before falling asleep. Some younger, dumber version of me might have considered this lame, but I'd never been happier in my life.

I waited until she fell asleep and got my phone from the nightstand, texting Fletcher.

Rhett: It happened.

Fletcher: Who is this?

I grunted at the phone.

Rhett: Who the fuck do you think it is?

Fletcher: You're sounding a little murdery.

Rhett: You're sounding like a bitch.

Fletcher: Rhett.

Fletcher: You got with Mags???

Rhett: Multiple times. For her of course. ;)

Fletcher: TMI TMI TMI

Rhett: Nothing should be TMI for a doctor.

Fletcher: I'm off the clock. And I'm happy for you.

Fletcher: So when are you putting a ring on it?

Rhett: We just slept together!

Fletcher: You asked me the same thing when I got with your sister. At least I'm not asking in front of Maggie.

I could feel his pointed stare, even through the phone.

Rhett: I messed up once before, asking her when she wasn't ready. I can't mess it up again.

Fletcher: You're both older now. And I can guarantee she's wiser.

Rhett: Hahaha. *Middle finger emoji*

Fletcher: Love you too.

WHEN WE GOT up in the morning, I woke up to find Mags already in the kitchen, cooking in her underwear and my oversized T-shirt. Liv got it for me because she said it was "on trend." I hadn't ever worn it because it looked dumb on me, but *damn*.

I leaned against the wall, biting my bottom lip. "Fuck, do you look good."

She glanced over her shoulder at me, smiling. She'd washed off all her makeup and pulled her hair off her neck into a ponytail. It was all natural, the rawest, best version of her. "I haven't even brushed my teeth."

"You could borrow my toothbrush," I offered.

She winced. "Gross."

"Babe. You had my cock in your mouth last night."

She arched a brow. "You're right. Maybe I shouldn't do that again. You know, for sanitary reasons."

"Fuck no." I went to her, pulling her away from the stove and kissing her deeply.

But this time, the doorbell interrupted our kiss.

She looked at me, half exasperated, half threatening. "I swear to God, if that's another girl at your door…"

"I'll just make a no soliciting sign," I teased, grabbing a pen from the junk drawer and writing on the magnetic notepad on the fridge.

NO FUCKING ALLOWED (Unless you're Maggie. Then fucking is encouraged.)

She rolled her eyes at me and continued cooking. "Just get rid of them fast, will you?"

"Sure thing."

I went to my door and pulled it open, ready to tell whoever it was that I already had a woman in my bed and I wasn't letting her go any time soon.

But then, I saw who was standing there.

From behind me, Maggie said, "*Dad?*"

41

MAGNOLIA

WITH MY DAD standing in Rhett's doorway, I was suddenly very aware that I was only dressed in Rhett's shirt. I tugged at the hem and asked him, "What are you doing here?"

Rhett cleared his throat. "You're welcome to come in, Mr. Gibson."

My dad's face was pale as he stood frozen in the doorway. "Magnolia, can you get dressed, please?"

I nodded, quickly going to Rhett's bedroom and pulling on my capris. I went ahead and changed back into my top from the night before and found Rhett and my dad standing awkwardly on the front porch.

Rhett's skin was paler than normal, and my dad's jaw was tight.

"What's going on?" I asked.

They both looked down.

Shit. What had they said to each other?

Dad cleared his throat. "My mechanic can't get my truck in until next Thursday, and I can't afford to sit out that long. I knew Rhett was trained in diesel mechanics and wanted to see if he'd do me a favor by fixing my rig."

I looked from Dad to Rhett. "Can you do that, Rhett?" I asked.

He nodded. "Course I can. But he doesn't want me to do it anymore."

I tilted my head at my father. "Dad, of course you can have Rhett work on your truck."

"I was having trouble asking him before I knew you were in the sack together." Dad folded his arms over his chest, bringing his chin down and then back up. He scrubbed his hand over his scruff and shook his head. "Shit, Mags, I thought you were smarter than this."

My stomach sank. "Dad..."

He shook his head. "You might not remember, but I do. You were a little girl, eighteen years, old, lying on my couch for an entire summer, crying your heart out, broken, because of him." He jabbed his finger toward Rhett.

Rhett's jaw muscles ticked, but he didn't say a word.

Shame and anger swirled in my gut. I knew I'd have to talk to my dad about this eventually, but I hadn't prepared for it to happen today. And now I wasn't just defending Rhett to him; I was defending myself.

I gritted my teeth, squared my shoulders. "Kid," I said.

"What?" Dad asked.

"You said I was a little girl, a kid, back then. Well, Rhett was too."

Rhett glanced over at me, and the gratitude in his hazel eyes nearly made me melt.

Dad just seemed more frustrated. "You may have

been out of Cottonwood Falls for over a decade, Maggie, but I haven't. I've heard everything about this *kid*, and yes I say *kid*, because a man doesn't toy around with women the way he has."

"The women agreed to what they were doing, Dad." My voice shook, half from shame, half from worry. I didn't want to choose between my dad and the man Rhett wanted to prove he could be.

"I don't want you to be just another notch on his bedpost, because that's what you are to him," Dad said. "A means to an end. One he already got by the looks of it."

My heart split at his words. "That's over the line, Dad."

Dad shook his head, turning to walk away. "Forget it about the truck." But then he turned back. "Come over on Sunday, okay, Maggie? We'll talk this out then."

I froze, shaking my head. "I'm busy this weekend."

Dad looked between Rhett and me. "Mags, I expected more from you."

He started walking off, but I was so angry I had to follow him the few steps to his pickup. "Dad, wait," I called.

He stopped and looked at me, a questioning look on his face.

"So it's okay for you to call on Rhett when you need a favor, but it's not okay for me to get to know him again?"

"It's different."

"Why?" I asked.

"Because you're not desperate." He got in his truck and drove away, but I stayed where I was, feeling torn between these two men as tears brimmed in my eyes.

Rhett came to me, putting his arms around my shoulders, but I felt stiff under his touch. "I'm sorry," I said, wiping at my eyes.

"It's a lot to get used to," Rhett said gently.

"What did he say to you before I came out?"

Rhett cringed.

"Tell me."

He took a breath. "He said you deserve better than a..."

"Rhett, tell me."

He cringed again as he said, "...a piece of shit womanizer who only cares about getting his dick wet."

My lips parted, feeling a punch in the gut just from hearing the repeated words. "He said that? In those words?"

Rhett nodded curtly.

I couldn't imagine how hard it was for Rhett to hear firsthand. "What did you say back?"

Rhett tilted his head. "I told him that I was trying hard to be what you deserved."

"And he didn't believe you," I finished.

His lips quirked at the side. "Looks like you're not the only Gibson with a hard head."

Smiling despite myself, I leaned into his hug, but my features quickly fell. "I can't choose you over him, Rhett."

He kissed the top of my head. "It's too soon to worry about that. Why don't I take you back to your house so you can get ready for work?"

I turned in his hug, looking up at him. This really was a different Rhett. The one I knew was hotheaded and said what was on his mind. He was a lot like my dad that way. This confrontation could have been disastrous.

Instead, he was kind, understanding to my dad, to me. "So this is what it feels like to fall all over again?"

He brushed back my hair. "This is what it feels like to have me catch you on the way down."

42

RHETT

MAGGIE and I texted each other, talked on the phone Thursday night, and had a hell of a game Friday night that the girls barely won in an extra inning. But when I asked her to stay over at my place Friday, she said she had to pack and get ready for our rodeo trip the next day.

I tried not to read too much into it, but I could still feel myself stressing as I put fresh sheets in the camper Saturday morning. I was so lost in my thoughts I almost didn't notice Cooper walking over with his duffel bag. I nodded his way as he opened the storage space underneath and shoved it in.

"Why do you look like you stepped in shit?" he asked.

I continued into the camper. "I slept with Maggie Wednesday night."

"WHAT?" he yelled, hauling himself inside. "Why aren't you over the fucking moon?"

I began spreading the sheet over the queen bed up front. "Probably because her dad came over the next morning." I'd been planning to tell Cooper at work, but after all the drama, I wasn't feeling quite as chipper.

"Shit. Why?" Coop asked.

"He wanted me to do some mechanical work on his semi, but he wasn't so happy about seeing Mags in my shirt and her underwear so early in the morning."

Cooper said. "Think he'd be better with it after a little breakfast and some coffee?"

I shot him a glare and then straightened, bringing the sheets back to the bunks at the back of the trailer. "Seems he holds a grudge the same way Maggie does." I handed him one, and he climbed to the top bunk.

"What happened after?" he asked from above me. "She still coming today?"

I nodded, crawling into the bottom bunk to get the back corners of the mattress. "But she said she couldn't choose me over her dad."

"Shit," Cooper muttered. "Isn't that what marriage is though? You leave your parents and cleave to each other?"

"Don't start quoting Bible shit at me," I said, working the sheet over the back of the mattress. "It's too early to be talking marriage."

"In the day or in the relationship?" he asked.

I climbed out of the bunk and looked up at him, still struggling with the sheet. "Both." I took the extra corner, helping him out. "You got marriage on the mind?"

His smile got all dopey.

"Well I'll be damned," I said, shaking my head. "Come help me with the food."

We went into my house, each taking a couple grocery

bags sitting on my table. When we got back to the camper, Coop said, "I'll put the fridge stuff away."

I nodded, taking the produce. "I get to open the slutty oranges."

He gave me a look. "What the fuck are you talking about?"

I smirked, holding up the bag. "Gotta rip that fish net apart to get to the goods." I winked.

He threw a small bag of shredded cheese at me. "Weirdo."

I held up the oranges, ripping the netting, and made a lewd sound.

A bag of lettuce sailed my way, but I dodged this time, laughing.

We finished unloading the groceries, and then I said, "Are you ready for this?"

He wrung his hands. "It's my first long trip with Cam. I don't want to ruin it."

I patted his shoulder. "If your toilet didn't do it, I don't think anything can."

We got out of the camper, and he chased after me. He shoved me, and I used the momentum to jog to my side of the truck. When we got to the girls' house, I smiled at the metal art wind chime hanging on the front porch. I hoped it was a good omen, that last night was just what Maggie said it was—time for her to pack and not time for her to decide against being with me.

"You've got it bad," Cooper muttered.

"Okay, pot." I got out of the truck and walked up the front steps, Cooper just a few feet behind me. When I knocked on the front door, Mags pulled it back, a single duffel bag over her shoulder visible through the screen door.

"You pack light," I commented, holding the door open for her.

From behind Maggie, Cam said, "That's because she gets all her extra shit from me." She came into view with two large rolling suitcases, each strapped with a smaller bag.

"Holy hell, woman," Cooper muttered behind me. "You know we're just leaving for a weekend, right? And it's already Saturday!"

Cam glared at him. "I come with a lot of baggage, okay?"

Maggie only had an echo of a smile as she stepped down the front stairs. "Good thing we have some strong men to carry them for us."

Cam walked behind Mags, carrying her phone. She slid a pair of big dark sunglasses over her eyes. "Chop, chop, boys."

Cooper and I exchanged a glance. He was still grinning like a puppy in love.

We carried the bags back to the trailer and put them inside before joining Cam and Mags in the truck. Maggie sat up in the front passenger seat, leaving Cooper room to sit in the back with Cam. The instant he got in, he pulled Cam into a long, heated kiss.

I stared across the cab at Mags. "You know that was a mistake, right?"

She held up her off-brand AirPod case. "I thought ahead."

"What the hell am I supposed to do?" I asked.

She held up another pair still in the store wrapping.

"Have I mentioned you're amazing?" I asked.

She grinned, leaning across the cab to give me a quick kiss. Then she set up the headphones for me, connecting them to my phone and playing a station for me from my music streaming account.

We drove the next few hours in mostly silence, sharing a few smiles when her arm snuck across the cab to hold my hand.

She was mine, at least for the moment.

TRAFFIC GOT THICKER the closer we got to Dallas, and I had to let go of her hand to keep both of mine on the wheel. She took out her headphones too, using her phone to navigate for us since my truck wasn't new enough to have a Bluetooth screen.

Eventually, we reached the campground, and I found a place with hookups to park for the night. Coop and I set up the camper with water and electricity while the girls checked out the trailer and got their things situated. When we were all done, we stood outside the trailer, and Mags said, "What happens now? Do we go to the rodeo grounds to check in?"

"Actually," I glanced at my phone where I'd gotten a text. "Gage, Farrah, and my nieces and nephews are coming to the rodeo. They weren't going to be able to, but Levi's ballgame got cancelled. Do you mind sitting with them?"

Her eyebrows rose. "You want me to spend time with your family twice in one week? Without your supervision? I saw how you were sweating on Wednesday."

"I promise they love you a hell of a lot more than your dad loves me."

She laughed, and Cam hugged Cooper a little closer.

Grinning, Maggie said, "You know, it's not every day you get to sit at a rodeo with a celebrity. Gage will probably have paparazzi all over."

I rolled my eyes. "He'll try to be incognito with his damn Ropers hat, like no one can tell it's him."

"It's sweet he wants to support you," she said, walking with us toward the pickup. I held her door open for her while Cooper and Cam got in on the other side.

"The windmill on my arm means something," I said.

She looked up from at me from where she sat. "I wish my mom..." She blinked quickly, shaking her head.

From the back seat, Cam said, "Are you okay?"

We both remembered how hard it had been for Maggie when her mom left town. Maggie blocked her mom's number she was so angry and hurt. As far as I knew, they never got back in touch.

I cupped Maggie's face and kissed her forehead. "I'm here for you."

"Me too," Cam said from the back seat.

She smiled, looking ahead. "Let's go see Gage and Farrah. I have years of information for them to fill me in on that we didn't get to cover at your family dinner."

"I'm going to regret this," I muttered, shutting her door and walking around to my side of the truck.

43

MAGNOLIA

WE PULLED up to the rodeo grounds and parked near the registration building. When we got out, we waited by the building for his family. I thought I would find Rhett's billionaire brother stepping out of a Lamborghini or something equally flashy and expensive. Instead, when Rhett pointed them out, we saw them climbing out of a plain white minivan. So that was their vehicle at the farm Wednesday night.

The youngest girl, Cora, screamed, "UNCLE RHETT!" and came sprinting up to him.

Rhett didn't wait for her to reach him, instead jogging toward them, picking her up, and spinning her in a circle. "Princess Cora." He knelt in front of her. "So good to see your majesty."

She giggled, pushing his shoulder. "I'm just Cora now."

I glanced up, seeing Gage and Farrah grinning at me and then back at their children interacting with Rhett.

Andrew, their middle child, followed behind Cora,

and Rhett said, "Drew, you're getting so fuckin' big. I swear you grew since a few days ago! Is it the green beans?"

"LANGUAGE," Cora said.

Drew rolled his eyes, smiling. "Uh huh. I *definitely* don't feed them to our dog."

Farrah laughed, shoving him slightly.

Standing beside Gage and his wife was their oldest, who chuckled.

Rhett grinned at him, sticking out his hand for Levi to shake. Then Rhett turned to me and lowered his voice to a whisper. "So everyone's on board, we're calling Gage, Shmage Shmiffen, in public."

Gage took off his sunglasses and rolled his eyes at his brother. Then he said to me, "It's good to see you again. We didn't get to talk much with my family grilling you and Rhett hogging you."

I chuckled. Gage and I had never been close since he was already out of the house when Rhett and I started dating, but I always felt like he was my big brother too all those years ago. "I never got to tell you that you have a beautiful family, Gage."

The way he grinned at the kids and his wife, I could feel how much he loved them. "I'm lucky," he said.

Farrah reached out to hug me too. Then she said, "Are these your friends?"

Rhett and I had almost forgotten Cam and Cooper were still there. Gage said, "This is Camryn Childers. She's from Cottonwood Falls too, and I think you met Rhett's friend Cooper last time we came to a rodeo."

"Right!" Farrah said. "Gosh, I'm bad with faces."

Cooper chuckled. "I probably was covered in dirt the last time you saw me. No worries."

Rhett said, "We better go check in. We'll catch up with y'all when it's over?"

We agreed and started walking toward the stands. This rodeo was a lot bigger than the one in Cottonwood Falls. On the way, Farrah and the kids decided to get snacks, and Gage caught up with Cam and me. She told him all about nursing at the retirement home, and he told us what his life had been like since he'd stepped down as CEO at his business. It sounded like he had more of an advising roll now instead of being quite so hands on.

"What about you, Maggie?" Gage asked as we found a good chunk of open seats a few rows back from the arena.

I told him about my trial period at Rhonda's and wanting to buy the salon.

"That's amazing," he said, his smile genuine. "If you ever want some business consulting, please reach out. I've been doing more to help small women- or minority-owned businesses lately."

My eyebrows rose. "Seriously?" It wasn't every day a literal billionaire offered to advise you. "I'm not sure I can afford your consulting fee, Gage."

He tossed his head back, laughing. "Dealing with my brother is payment enough. He seems happier than I've seen him in a long time."

My heart warmed. Even after the rough morning we had Thursday, it made me glad to know I was somehow making Rhett's life better. He'd certainly shaken mine up since I'd moved home.

Farrah and the kids reached us then, carrying arms

full of nachos and popcorn, and passed them around for everyone. Cam leaned in my ear and whispered, "Sounds like it's more than Rhett that's happy you're home."

I hugged her side, then let out a heavy sigh. "Why can't everything be good at once?" I said so only she could hear. It was like the pieces were starting to come together with Rhett, yet my dad was disappointed in me. It put a storm cloud over every good thing happening now.

Farrah slid into the bleachers on the other side of Gage, and we started chatting about interior design. She was so friendly; I swore we talked all the way through the barrel racing and the steer roping before the bronc riding started. She gave me her number too so we could start texting back and forth.

I was both happy and scared to be entwined in Rhett's world. Because I knew how good it was to be with him and how heartbreaking it was when it was all over.

The announcer came over the speakers, saying, "Up next to ride broncs is Cooper Lawson of Cottonwood Falls. You have to love these small-town rodeo guys. They've got the heart and the skill."

I glanced over at Cam to see tears falling down her cheeks.

"Are you *crying*?" I asked.

She had a napkin wadded up in her hands, holding it tight at her chest. "I'm just nervous! I don't want him to get hurt!"

I tried not to laugh. "Is your period starting soon?" She always got weepy when it was her time of month.

Her eyes glanced toward the ceiling like she was doing

mental math. "Maybe that's it. I don't know why I'm so damn surprised every time."

I could see Levi's cheeks getting red on her other side, and Farrah giggled. "You are definitely not alone. Gage got an app to track mine."

"Aw." I laughed. "That's kind of cute."

"I need to know when to have chocolate and flowers ready," Gage teased, bumping her shoulder.

The buzzer sounded and the gates flew open, and we watched as Cooper clung to the back of a bucking bronc.

"Breathe," I urged Cam.

She only bit her lip.

Before we knew what was happening, Cooper lost his grip and went flying through the air. He tucked and rolled at the landing and popped up, taking a few limping steps before catching his stride and jogging to the edge of the arena while a couple people on horses caught his bucking bronc.

The announcer said, "Not quite eight seconds, but a good ride from Lawson!"

Our little section of fans cheered loudly, and Levi, put his fingers in his mouth, whistling loudly.

"That is so cool!" I said, turning to where he sat in the row behind us. "Can you teach me?"

For the next several moments, he showed me how to do it, and I got a lot of slobber on my fingers while making absolutely no progress toward a whistle. Everyone was in stitches as I wiped my hands on my jeans.

Then they called Rhett's name over the speakers. I pulled my fingers to my mouth, trying again to whistle, and a sharp sound peeled through the audience.

I'm pretty sure Rhett's family was cheering as much

for my successful whistle as they were for him. I was
smiling as the gates flew open and my man flew out on
the back of that bull.

I held my breath, just like Cam had, saying a quick
prayer that he'd be okay and come out of it with a good
ride. The seconds slowly ticked by as Rhett was jerked
along the back of the bull with long, sharp horns.

And then the buzzer went off, and Rhett let go, falling
off the bull. A rodeo clown distracted the animal while
Rhett jogged to the edge of the arena, pointing right at
me, and then shaping his fingers into a heart.

"Aw," Cora said, "he loves us!"

Farrah rubbed her daughter's arm. "He sure does."

Gage and Farrah stayed for a few more rides, but
when Cora started yawning, they told us goodbye so they
could get her in bed.

As they walked away, I asked Cam, "Wanna come to
the bathroom with me?"

She nodded, and we went to the crowded bathroom
on the other side of the arena. We each took a stall, and I
sat down on the toilet. The door opened and closed, and
one woman said, "Did you see Rhett? He looks so fucking
good riding a bull."

Another woman said, "You should have seen how
good he looked riding *me* last year." She cackled deviously,
and the other girl joined in.

"Are you meeting up again tonight?" the first woman's
friend asked.

"I tried to text him, and it didn't go through. I'm
going to find him after. He's always worth the wait."

In the stall next to me, Cam cleared her throat.
"Rhett's taken."

The women were quiet for a moment. Finally, the first one said, "What?"

"He's dating my friend," Cam said through the stall.

The second woman laughed. "Sure he is."

Cam piped up. "He is."

"Did he make it official?" the first woman asked.

"Of course he did," Cam said, "Tell them, Maggie."

My mouth went dry. Now was *not* the time to be having this conversation. But I finished my business and left the stall, trying to put on my big-girl pants. I was not the kind of person to be arguing with another woman in a bathroom.

But when I came out of the stall, there they were. Two women a few years younger than me. Thin. Wearing jeans and cute shiny belt buckles and tight shirts that showed off their assets. They were conventionally beautiful, not like me. And I had to remind myself that Rhett chose me.

"We're together," I said.

The first woman, white with blond hair and dark brown eyes, looked me over. "Sure you are."

Her obvious disbelief rubbed me the wrong way. "He said he loves me," I told them. "So I don't think he'll be hooking up with either of you tonight."

Cam came out of the bathroom just as the blond and her red-headed friend started laughing.

My cheeks heated, and I couldn't find words, but Cam said, "What the hell are you laughing about?"

The girls exchanged a look, and the one with red hair tilted her head at me. "I'm sorry, honey, he says that to everyone he sleeps with."

They exchanged a glance with each other and left

Cam and me in the bathroom, people walking in and out around us, and I wished the floor would swallow me whole. I was so freaking humiliated.

"Mags..." Cam said gently.

I shook my head, going to the sink to wash my hands. "Who was I kidding? He has all these women to choose from. He might like me now, but maybe my dad was right. I'm just another notch in his bedpost."

I finished washing my hands and turned off the water. Cam walked behind me toward the paper towels saying, "They're a couple jealous twats. You can't believe everything they say."

I turned and looked at Cam. "Why are you Team Rhett? Is it just because you're happy with Coop and you want me to be happy too?"

She smiled, rubbing my arms. "Babe. Of course I want you to be happy. I think you're so afraid of history repeating that you're not really giving him a chance to be different. He's a good guy, Mags. I *know* he is."

"But last time..." My jaw trembled. "I was a mess."

"You don't give yourself enough credit for all the ways you've grown. Even if he hasn't changed, you have. You're not one to lie around and wallow about a man. Not anymore."

I loved her faith in me, but I didn't have the heart to tell her. Rhett wasn't just any man. For better, for worse, he was the man who could bring me to higher highs and lower lows than I'd ever known.

44

MAGNOLIA

CAM and I left the bathroom, and she called Cooper to see where he and Rhett were. We agreed to meet at the pickup, and when we got there, Rhett held up a thick envelope.

"What's that?" I asked.

"My purse!"

Cam held up the cross-body bag I'd paired with her outfit. "This is a purse. That's an envelope."

Cooper and Rhett tossed their heads back laughing, and I held back a smile. I'd had the same question not long ago.

Cam folded her arms over her chest. "What on earth is so damn funny?"

Cooper wiped at his eyes. "Sorry, babe." He put his arm around Cam's shoulders. "A purse is what you make when you win."

"You won, Rhett?" I asked. "First place?"

He had a bashful grin. "A thousand bucks should pay for gas and food with a little extra to spare, right?"

"Hell yeah." Cam held her arm up to high-five him, and then I hugged him, saying, "Congratulations, babe."

He looked down at me, holding me close. His hat cut off the glow of the parking lot lights, and he looked like a haloed cowboy with eyes for only me. "I like the sound of that."

"Congratulations?" I teased.

He put his arms around my shoulders, bending me over and tickling my sides until I hit him, yelling to stop. He let me up, both of us laughing. The tension from those girls' comments earlier lessened off my shoulders.

"Let's go to Bandwagon," Rhett suggested.

Cooper whooped while Cam and I exchanged a shrug.

I said, "Sometimes, I swear Rhett and Cooper are the ones in a relationship."

"A true bromance," Cam added. "But can we stop at the store on the way? I forgot to pack something."

All of us stared at her, but Cooper was the one to talk. "In all those bags, you forgot something? What was it? The kitchen sink?"

She narrowed her gaze at him.

He held up his hands. "To the store, right, Rhett?"

Rhett smiled as he walked beside me, his arm around my shoulders. "To the store."

We got in the truck and drove to a supermarket. I asked Cam if she wanted me to go in with her, but she said she'd go on her own. So the two guys and I sat in the truck, talking about the rodeo while she walked through the parking lot.

About twenty minutes later, she came back out, looking pale.

"Are you okay?" Cooper asked her as she slid in next to him.

She nodded. "I think the nachos didn't sit right. I got some antacids."

After she buckled in, Rhett got back on the road, weaving through traffic toward Bandwagon, a dance hall on the outskirts of Fort Worth. When we reached the parking lot, I saw it was full of trucks, probably most of the people who'd been at the rodeo earlier.

When we got inside, Rhett offered to get us drinks while Cam and I used the bathroom.

"Just a soda water for me," she said. "I don't think my stomach can take any alcohol or sugar."

He nodded, and Cam and I made our way to the bathrooms. They were crowded, but she pulled me into an open stall, barely enough room for the two of us.

"What's going on?" I asked her, worried. "Do you need me to hold your hair or something?"

She locked the stall door, the bolt clicking loudly against the metal. "Mags, I'm pregnant."

My brain short-circuited. "What?" I couldn't have heard her right.

She put her hands on my face. "I took a pregnancy test in the store, and it came back positive."

My mouth opened and closed. This couldn't be real. "How did you pay for it after you took it?"

"Mags!" she cried. "I'm pregnant!"

And it hit me. All of it hit me. "Holy shit, you're having a baby?"

She nodded, her blue eyes wide, blond hair moving.

"Is it Cooper's?" I had to ask.

She nodded again. "He's the only guy I've been with since we moved home."

"How?" I shook my head. "I mean, I know *how*, but I thought you were on the shot?"

"I was a little late taking it," she admitted. "But I didn't think a week would make a difference, and things with Cooper were so intense I didn't think to ask him to wear a condom or take something the next day." She covered her face, giving herself tunnel vision and breathing deeply.

The backs of my legs butted up to the stall door as I rubbed her shoulders. "It happens. Birth control's never a hundred percent."

"I'm thirty-two years old. I've been so careful." Tears began sliding down her cheeks. "I mean, I've had scares, but never actually been... pregnant..."

I hugged her tight, rubbing her back. "What do you want to do? I can call a cab to drive us home. I don't care how much it costs."

She held on to me and spoke into my shoulder. "I'm so scared. And I know this sounds crazy but I'm... also kind of... happy about it too."

"You are?" I pulled back, taking her in.

She nodded, wiping her eyes. "I've always wanted to be a mom, and you know how it is when you get to be in your thirties. You feel your clock ticking. Now I don't have to wait anymore."

I definitely understood that part. "But Cooper? Are you sure about raising a child with him?"

She smiled slightly. "You know how they say when you know, you know? I felt it. With him."

My lips parted. "You did?"

She nodded. "Dirty toilet and all. He's my person. Who knows? My grandparents only knew each other a week before getting married, and they were together over fifty years. Maybe insta-love is in my blood."

I wiped at her tears with my thumbs. "If you're happy, I'm happy." Even if I was also nervous for her too. A child was a life-changing responsibility.

She grinned, nodding. "I'm happy."

My heart soaring for her, I yelled in the bathroom, "I'm going to be an aunt!"

Women in the stalls around us cheered, and Cam laughed happily. "Now I just need to tell Cooper."

I nodded. "Do you need me to do it with you?"

She shook her head. "It's him and me now."

She opened the stall, smiling bashfully at the people around us, and walked out of the bathroom. As I stepped behind her, I couldn't help but feel like she was moving forward. And I tried to remember that didn't mean I was getting left behind.

45

CAMRYN

I WALKED into the crowded bar, looking around for my person. He was over six feet tall, so it usually wasn't hard to spot him and his sandy-blond hair in a crowd. Except now I was extra aware of what I carried with me.

I knew I wouldn't be able to feel the baby for weeks to come, but I sensed its presence as I looked for Cooper. I found him near Rhett, still waiting in line at the bar. When I found him, I slipped my hand through his and said, "Come with me?"

Coop nodded, then turned back to Rhett. "You're good to get the drinks?"

He patted his pocket, where he kept his "purse," and nodded.

It was different, seeing Rhett through Cooper's eyes and Maggie's eyes. Cooper thought Rhett was the best friend in the world, always there for him when his back was against the wall. Maggie knew him as the guy who promised her forever and then broke her heart. And I was getting to know him too, as a good man and a good friend.

But I couldn't think about it now, with Cooper's large, calloused hand enveloping mine. I led him past the dance floor and out to the back patio. There were still people out here, but not as many as inside. We found a private corner, and he smiled down at me.

"If you wanted to get me to yourself, we could just go out to the truck," he hummed, leaning down and grazing his lips, his teeth over my neck.

My body shivered with desire, and a part of me wanted to take him up on the offer. Make love until the responsibilities of our future faded away, but I couldn't hold on to this secret any longer.

"Cooper," I said as he continued dropping kisses along my neck, my jaw.

"Yeah?" he asked against my cheek.

I reached up, tangling my fingers in his hair and then palming his cheeks so he could see me. I searched his pale green eyes, hoping like hell he was the man I thought he was.

"I need to tell you something," I said. "And I'm not sure how you're going to react."

He tensed under my hands and studied my face. "What is it?"

I rolled my lips between my teeth, knowing the words were simple but the aftermath was anything but.

"I'm pregnant," I breathed.

His eyes widened, much like Maggie's had.

I continued, unable to stop the spill of words because I didn't want him to be disappointed; I didn't want him to leave me. "I know it's a lot, but I want to keep this baby. I want to raise it with you and have a crazy, passionate, fast, fun life full of sex and laughter and happiness and everything in between. And if you don't want that I understand, I'll raise this baby on my own, but I really—"

He covered my mouth with one hand, holding the nape of my neck with the other as he studied me, a small smile playing along his lips. "Will you shut up for a sec?"

I let out a small laugh through my nose.

Slowly, he removed his hand from my lips and held my face so carefully in his hands, you'd think I was made of gold. "Camryn Childers, I loved you the second I laid eyes on you. Some people will think that's crazy, impossible, or just plain dumb. But you know what I say?"

I looked up at him.

His lips quirked. "I say that's none of their goddamned business."

I smiled up at him. "You love me?"

He nodded. "And I love the hell out of *our* baby. You just try to raise it without me. You'll get so fucking annoyed by me sitting on your porch and offering to change diapers and mix bottles and shit."

Despite the tears falling down my cheeks, I was grinning like a fool.

He kissed me hard and then pulled back, taking me in, his eyes shining with joy. "I'm going to marry the shit out of you."

I let out a tearful laugh. "Are you proposing?"

"Shit. Right." He got down on one knee in front of me and looked up, a crooked grin on his lips. "Camryn, can I *please* marry the shit out of you?"

I laughed, happier than I knew I could feel. "Yes, Cooper Lawson, you can marry the shit out of me."

46

MAGNOLIA

I FOUND Rhett still waiting in line at the bar, Cooper and Cam nowhere to be seen. But he wasn't alone.

That girl from the bathroom earlier, with her long red hair and thick eyelash extensions, was with him, her hand touching his arm.

He didn't shy away, instead, standing his ground. He held up his hand, showing... a ring on his finger.

My eyebrows drew together. What the hell was going on?

The girl seemed to pout, but Rhett only shrugged. Then he caught sight of me and waved me over. As I got closer, he said to the girl, "That's my wife."

With a sneer, she looked me over, saying, "I don't see no ring on her finger."

Rhett shrugged. "We're getting it resized. But the point is, I'm very happily taken."

She let out a huff and turned to walk away while I stared at Rhett. I reached for his hand, holding it up to see the wire ring, so similar to the one he made me all those years ago.

"What is this?" I demanded.

"A wedding ring."

"No shit. Why are you wearing it?" I asked.

He hugged me, hooking his hands behind my waist. "I wanted everyone to know I'm yours."

Butterflies swirled in my stomach. "But we're not married yet."

His grin got even bigger.

"What?" I asked.

"You said 'yet.'"

My cheeks flushed. "You know what I meant."

He pulled me closer, bringing his lips to my ear. "I want everyone to know how committed I am to you. I am not available to anyone other than Magnolia Ray Gibson, married or not."

I looked up at him, overwhelmed by everything—the news Cam gave me earlier. The lengths he would go for me to feel safe in our relationship. And all I wanted to do was cry. Because how could I be with Rhett when the man who had always been there for me wouldn't support us? If I had doubts swirling through my mind despite all his reassurances?

Rhett said, "How thirsty are you? 'Cause I'm about ready to give up on this line."

I let out a shaky laugh. "Not really."

"Good. Let's dance." He took my hand, pulling me away from the line and leading me toward the crowded wooden dance floor. Finding a gap in the ring of spinning bodies, he pulled me into the fray, leading me effortlessly in a two-step.

Shuffling with him, I looked up at him, breathless. "How are you so good at this?"

"A little too much practice," he said, guiding us along. "Where'd the other two go?"

I nearly stumbled, realizing he didn't know the news Cam had dropped, but Rhett kept us going despite my stutter step. "Everything okay?" he asked.

The song came to an end, changing to a slow one. He pulled me in a little closer, changing our pace as he waited for me to answer.

"I think it will be, for Cam and Cooper," I added.

He studied my expression. "And for us?"

That hard rock in my stomach grew even heavier as I blinked quickly. "Sometimes it feels so easy with you, and others..."

"It's like swimming upstream," he said.

Knowing he felt it too just made me want to cry.

"Mags, I promise, I'll spend every damn day proving to your dad that I'm the man you deserve."

"And me?" I asked, my voice shaking. "Because I saw that girl at the rodeo, in the bathrooms, and she said you tell everyone you sleep with that you love them."

His jaw ticked, and he stepped back from me, both of us standing still in the middle of the dance floor.

"What are you doing?" I demanded.

"Damn it, Maggie, I don't know what I'm supposed to do." He beat his chest. "I got a new number so chicks couldn't call me. I told you about my cancer diagnosis. I didn't even tell my mom about it until I knew everything would be okay. I wore a fucking wedding ring just so no one would get any ideas. How else can I prove to you that

I'm in this? That I'm not giving up or running away this time?"

I stared at him, my jaw tight. "Maybe do it for longer than a couple months! You say you've made all these changes, but I'm still getting to know you, Rhett!"

He held his chest. "I know me, Maggie. And if this doesn't work out, it's going to be because you're scared, not because I fucked it up."

His words hit me, one after another, and I knew we were making a scene, I knew everyone was staring, but I couldn't find it in me to disagree with him or care what anyone else thought of us.

"You're right. I'm scared. And I don't know how to get that feeling to go away," I said. "Tell me how to make it go away."

A commotion was growing on the other end of the bar, and we both looked that way to find people carrying Cam and Cooper on their shoulders.

"THEY'RE GETTING MARRIED, THEY'RE GETTING MARRIED!"

Soon the entire bar was shouting, and Cam and Cooper were getting closer to us. Rhett and I had no choice but to smile and cheer along as they headed our way.

Regardless of what was going on with us, they needed our support. Now more than ever.

WHEN WE GOT BACK to the camper, Camryn and Cooper took the queen bed, and Rhett and I opted for the bunks. But instead of climbing to the top one, Rhett crawled in next to me, spooning me from behind.

He brushed my hair over my shoulders and placed a kiss softly on the back of my neck. And I cried, because after all these years, I had a chance to live the kind of life I wanted with Rhett without all that heartbreak, and he was right about what he said tonight.

I was more afraid than I'd ever been.

As Cam's breathing slowed and Cooper's soft snores filled the trailer, I turned in Rhett's arms to face him. In the dim light coming through the blinds, I could see his deep hazel eyes open.

For a moment, we watched each other, and I reached up, cupping his jaw, running my thumb over his bottom lip. "You were right, earlier."

He drew his lips to the side. "It's not always fun being right."

"Beg to differ."

He smiled slightly.

I leaned in and kissed him. "Give me time to get used to the idea of us?"

He rested his forehead against mine. "Guess it's not fair of me to think you've been dreaming of me for fifteen years too."

I looked up at him. "Some things are too good to risk dreaming about."

"Why's that?"

"Because when you find out reality doesn't match, it just breaks your heart that much more."

47

RHETT

THE GIRLS LAY in the back seat, both of them slouched against the doors and sleeping as we drove back to Cottonwood Falls Sunday afternoon. The night before had worn out all of us, even Cooper, judging by the way he was slumped in the passenger seat, dark sunglasses over his eyes.

"I'm going to be a dad," he muttered, half to himself.

"Scared?" I asked.

"Shitless."

"I'd be worried about you if you weren't," I replied.

He smiled slightly. "Guess I haven't asked you yet. Will you be my best man?"

"Sure. When are you getting married?"

Cooper shrugged. "Hell if I know."

I chuckled. "So Cam's deciding."

"She gets whatever she wants."

"Happy wife, happy life," I said.

He smiled to himself. "Hell of a happy life."

I glanced over at him, a warm feeling spreading

through my chest. I knew a lot of people in our small town would have opinions, but Cooper had been with a lot of women in the few years I'd known him. I could tell there was something different between him and Camryn from the first night they met. "I'm happy for you, Coop."

He glanced toward our girls, sleeping in the back seat. "I'm happy for you too."

I couldn't find it in myself to smile all the way. My throat felt tight, and I swallowed down the lump of emotion. "Thanks, man."

"I think I'm gonna try and sleep off the rest of this hangover," Cooper said.

"Go for it."

He put in his ear buds and tipped his hat down to cover his face, leaving me the only one awake in the truck. As I drove the rest of the way home, I listened to music and tried to think how I could be patient with Mags, no matter how hard it felt. When you knew who you wanted to spend the rest of your life with, it was hard waiting for them to decide they wanted the same. Harder yet knowing they might not come to that conclusion.

We pulled up to the girls' house, and I said, "Up and at 'em, everyone."

They began shifting awake as I put the truck in park alongside the curb. I got out and held the back door open for Mags. She smiled sleepily up at me and yawned.

"Stoppp," I said.

"What?" she asked, rubbing her eyes.

"You're like a damn kitten. Way too cute."

She purred at me.

Cam laughed. "You two are so cute I want to throw up."

"I think that's the morning sickness," Mags tossed back.

"Shh," Cam and Cooper said loudly at the same time.

Maggie and I looked at them in confusion, and Cooper explained, "We haven't said shit to our parents yet. You know, the walls have eyes here."

"True," I said with a shrug.

We got all of Maggie and Cam's things from the truck, and while Cooper helped Cam carry her multiple bags back to her bedroom, Maggie and I stood in the living room across from each other.

"See you at practice on Tuesday?" she said.

I smiled. "Yeah. And dinner at my family's house on Wednesday?"

Her lips parted. "Are you sure?"

I nodded. "They'll be excited to see you again." I took her in a hug, linking my hands behind her round backside.

She tilted her chin back, giving me a chance to kiss her plush lips.

"You know," I said against her lips, "you could just come home with me."

Laughing, she said, "I have work tomorrow."

"Then I'll see you next Tuesday," I replied.

She gave me a confused look. "And this Tuesday, right?"

"Yeah, but 'see you this Tuesday' doesn't spell CUNT when you write it out."

She rolled her eyes at me, shoving my shoulder. "Get out of here."

I chuckled, leaning in to give her one long, heated

kiss. Because I never knew which one would be my last, so I was going to savor every single one.

When we broke apart, her cheeks were flushed and my breaths came hard. I wanted to take her right now, because one night with her would never be enough. But I knew we both had things to think about.

"Coop," I called. "You ready?"

"No," he yelled back from Cam's room.

"I'm leaving."

Cam yelled, "I'll give him a ride!"

Mags and I shared a smile. "Things are changing, aren't they?" she asked.

"They always do."

⌇

I MEANT to go back to my place. I did. But I found myself parked in front of Maggie's childhood home instead. I knew the way there like the back of my hand, having spent most of junior and senior year there when we were dating, watching movies with her and her dad, helping her dad with projects out in the backyard, doing life together.

Now I was nothing but an unwelcome stranger on his doorstep, but I knew Maggie meant it when she said she couldn't choose between us. I would make sure it didn't come to that.

I got out of my truck and walked up the sidewalk to the faded yellow front door. I pressed the bell and held my hat in my hands, hoping like hell he wouldn't slam the door in my face.

When the door drew back and he saw me, he rocked

back on his heels like he'd seen something repulsive. His smooth-shaven lip curled. "Shit, what are you doing here?"

I frowned. "Gabe, can't we talk man-to-man?"

He lifted his Gibson Trucking hat and ran his hand through thinning salt-and-pepper hair. "Like we did when you promised me you'd never break my daughter's heart?"

I held out my hands. "I know I fucked up, but I'm not giving up on your daughter. And I don't want her to have to choose between you and me. She'll choose you, but she'll hate you for it."

Gabe grimaced, his blue eyes so much like Mags's, seeming heavy. "Fine. We'll go out back and talk."

I nodded, my chest feeling heavy, like I'd won some kind of easy victory at the first line of battle, but knowing the hardest part was yet to come. I walked into his house, and seeing it all took me back to the time when Mags and I dated.

The same couch in the living room where we spent hours watching movies, sneaking kisses when her dad wasn't in the room.

Her bedroom, where we had sex the first time. Her dad was at work and we both called in to school, pretending to be our parents and saying we were sick. We'd spent the entire day in her bed, exploring each other's bodies, trying to make each other feel good with no clue what we were doing.

Gabe opened the back door, and we stepped onto the deck I'd helped him build during my senior year of school. "Looks like the deck's still holding up," I said.

He grunted.

I took him in, his round face, his assessing gaze, and realized something. Losing Maggie hadn't just been losing her. This man in front of me had been like a second father to me, someone I looked up to and tried to please. Now he was a stranger who hated some version of me that no longer existed.

He sat down on one of the chairs at an etched glass table, and I sat across from him.

"You wanted to talk," he said. "So talk."

I glanced across the table at him, noticing the similarities between him and his daughter—the blue eyes, the round face, angular nose. But there were differences too —the ruddiness in his cheeks from years in the sun, the rounded shape of his stomach, his gray eyebrows.

I knew Maggie always wanted an explanation, but with him, it was best to cut straight to the point.

"Gabe, I want to say I'm sorry for what happened back then. I know I apologized to Maggie, but I should have apologized to you too. I let you down when I broke my word to you."

Gabe's expression softened. "You were like the son I never had. And we've lived in this town the last fifteen years together, nary a word shared between us."

"Honestly, I thought you'd never want to talk to me again," I admitted. "Better to put my tail between my legs and run off than admit I fucked up the best thing to ever happen to me."

His lips twisted into a wry smile. "I had some words I wanted to say to you when we finally got face to face."

"Say them," I said. "Get it out. Because if I'm laying my cards on the table, Mags is it for me. I knew it when I was eighteen years old, and I know it now. I hope you and I have to be around each other for years to come."

He shook his head slowly, like he knew so much more than me. "She's been back in town how long?"

I grit my teeth, holding back the retort I had.

"It's easy to show up for someone a few months out of the year; it's harder to be there for them through thick and thin. Through opening a business, and getting sick, and being broke, and everything else life throws at you."

I nodded. "I know that."

"My wife and I did it for eighteen years before something new and shiny came along for her."

My features fell, because I remembered how hard that separation had been on him and Maggie. "I'd never do that to someone I committed to. My word means something now, Gabe."

He lifted his chin, studying me. "It took a lot of guts to come over here."

"We both know I have to make up for what I lack in the brains department."

That earned me a small chuckle. Then he sobered, taking me in for a minute. "I don't trust you. That's earned over time, but I won't stand between you and Maggie. I need to apologize to her too for the way I've acted. I lost my cool the other day when I saw you two together."

"It's understandable," I said. "But not unforgivable."

He chuckled. "I need to get better at that forgiving part. Mags and I both do. She's still holding on to so much anger toward her mom."

My eyebrows drew together. "I thought her mom left her high and dry? How would Maggie reach out?"

"She did." Gabe folded his arms across his chest, straightened his legs a little. "But she's been wanting to connect with Maggie again, and Mags won't have it."

"Wow," I breathed.

"Of course, Mags is angry and hurt. And I think we both know it's hard to let someone back in when they hurt you to the core."

I took a deep breath, leaning forward and resting my elbows on my knees. "Gabe... growing up is hard."

He tossed his head back, laughing. "You're telling me."

With a smile still on my face, I said, "You know, I will help you with your truck, if you'll have me."

He cringed. "I already paid a rush fee and had it towed to a shop in Rutlage. Didn't think there was a chance of you helping me after the tantrum I threw."

The back door of the house opened, and Mags came through, staring at us, her eyes wide. "Dad? Rhett?"

48

MAGNOLIA

I STARED between my dad and Rhett, all the air gone from my lungs.

They were both sitting on my dad's back deck, Eileen lying at my dad's side, and no one looked like they were going to fight each other.

"What's going on?" I asked.

They both stood up at the same time and glanced at each other.

Rhett nodded for Dad to go ahead.

Since when did Rhett and my dad have silent conversations?

Dad wrung his hands. "Mags, I'm awful sorry about what I said the other day at Rhett's place. I lost my temper and didn't give you credit for the woman you are. I told Rhett that I don't trust him yet, but I trust you to make the choices that are best for you. I support you. And him, if that's what you want."

My eyes stung as he spoke each word. "You mean it?"

He nodded, coming and putting his arms around me. I held on to him, relief making my eyes sting.

I didn't need to choose between Rhett and my dad, because they were both here for me. I looked up to see Rhett smiling at us, and he tilted his head. *Thank you,* I mouthed to him.

He nodded.

Dad and I broke apart, and Dad patted my shoulder. "Wanna stay for supper? I can make some extra for you both."

I glanced at Rhett, and he nodded.

"That would be great, Dad," I said, my voice raw.

He turned toward Rhett. "You're staying too, yeah?"

Rhett grinned. "If you'll have me."

Dad nodded. "Have you met Eileen yet?" He gestured at his dog.

Rhett stared from my dad to the salt-and-pepper dog standing next to him. "You got a three-legged dog and named her Eileen."

Dad's cheeks flushed.

Rhett laughed. "Damn, Gabe, I've missed you."

WE STAYED at Dad's house for the next couple hours, and when it was time to go, Rhett and I walked down the cement path to the street.

He said, "This is a change. Usually I was walking you *to* the door wishing the sidewalk would be longer. Guess I'm still wishing it was longer, 'cause I really don't wanna go home without you."

I twined my fingers through his. "Who says you have to?"

He gave me a hopeful smile. "Really?"

We stopped at the end of the sidewalk, and I glanced down before facing him again. "I should have just told you I couldn't go home with you because I wanted to make things right with my dad."

"We must be on the same wavelength, because after I left your place, I found myself driving here." He reached up, brushing my hair back and holding my face in his hands.

My throat felt tight with emotion. "You have no idea how much it meant to me to see you two together at dinner, laughing, joking. It felt like a fresh start for all of us."

He pulled me in, hugging me close. "That's all I've wanted."

I looked up at him and rested my chin on his chest. "Let's go to your place?"

He smiled. "I think that's a hell of a plan."

♀

WHEN I GOT to the salon the next morning, Rhonda had a cup of coffee waiting for me, which was good because I got barely any sleep the night before. She smiled at me and said, "How was your weekend?"

"It was..." I let out an unintentional happy sigh. "Really good."

Rhonda laughed. "It's been a whirlwind of a summer, hasn't it, dear?"

I nodded in agreement. "I can't believe the Unicorns

last game is Friday," I said as I took a spot on the mustard-yellow couch.

Rhonda sat across from me, smiling. "This is the first year that the Unicorns even stand a chance at winning the Little League championship."

"No way. Really?"

"You and Rhett make quite the team." She gave me a coy smile that had me blushing. "But I don't want you to get distracted from what brought you home. It's important to me that I see you giving this salon your full attention."

I nodded quickly. "Absolutely, Rhonda. I don't want to let you down."

"So then you have a plan for your service project?"

"Yes!" I took a sip of my coffee. "Actually, my friend Cam came up with the idea. She thought it would be good to have a monthly spa day for the residents in the retirement home. I could dedicate a whole weekend once a month to do nails, toes, maybe hair if we have the time for it."

Rhonda twisted her lips to the side, nodding along as she listened. By the time I finished, she had a full-fledged grin. "That's an amazing idea. And that way, you'll be doing my hair forever." She winked.

I let out a laugh. "You'll be fabulous always. We'll both make sure of that."

"How about you take a month off after Little League and then solidify your schedule at the retirement home? We can announce the program in the paper. I think that will mean a lot to the people of this community." She paused, taking me in. "I'm proud of you, Magnolia."

My heart melted. "You mean it?"

She nodded and extended her arms for me. I set my coffee cup down, holding her close, wishing I could have a relationship like this with my mom, but so much time had passed I doubted it was even possible.

Our first client came a few minutes later, and Rhonda and I got back into the flow of welcoming people to the salon, cutting and coloring hair, and cleaning up between appointments. When I had someone cancel last minute, I took my phone outside to call Camryn.

It was still hot in the way only early August could be. But I walked slowly, just enjoying the cute Main Street with its flags on the light poles and big flowerpots kept up by the master gardeners.

After a few rings, she answered. "Hey, girl, hey. Can't talk too long."

"No worries, I just wanted to tell you that Rhonda loved the idea of a salon day at the retirement community!"

"No way!" She sounded genuinely excited for me. "That's awesome!"

"Thank you so much for your idea. It really helped a lot. Do you think you could do me another favor and put me in touch with the director there so we can handle logistics?"

"Absolutely," she said. "While I have you, can you come over to my parents' house tonight? We want to talk plans for the wedding, and you're my maid of honor, of course."

I grinned. "Do you know how long I've been waiting for this moment?!"

She laughed. "You won't have to wait much longer."

49

MAGNOLIA

I FINISHED CLOSING up the salon and then drove to the Childers' house on the outskirts of town. Camryn's parents were well-off, her dad working in a cush government position. Her mom stayed home and took homemaking to the next level. The outside of their massive white house had stunning flower beds, cute little ceramic decorations, and even the numbers by their door were fancy—modern and lit at night.

Cam and I had spent so many hours together here that it almost felt like a second home to me, and I hoped I could make my own place look just as gorgeous someday. Her mom was the one who encouraged me to start thrifting, because she always said home is more than the place where you lay your head at night. It's the place that sets the tone for your life.

Back then, I was longing for something that felt like the happiness I used to have with Rhett. I'd found so many beautiful wire art pieces at the thrift store near mine and Cam's Austin apartment, along with junky items we could upcycle and use.

I opened my car door, hearing a truck rumbling down the driveway. Turning to see who it was, I caught sight of Rhett grinning at me through the windshield.

He stopped a few feet behind my car and parked. "Hey, beautiful," he said as he got out of the truck and coming to give me a kiss.

I grinned up at him. "What are you doing here?"

"Guess the whole wedding party had to be here to plan for the big day."

He wrapped his arm around my waist, walking beside me to the house. "Been a while since I've been here."

I nodded, trying to think back to the last time I was here with him. "A week before you proposed. We had a going-away barbecue with our friends."

He twisted his lips to the side as we walked up the front steps. "We played that stupid game... Over Under?"

I laughed, remembering the bet that had Rhett licking a tree stump. "How did you get those splinters out of your tongue?"

He shook his head at me as he reached for the doorbell. "Now I know why I forgot."

The door swung open, and the older version of Camryn smiled at us, wearing a stunning outfit, a full face of makeup, and her blond hair piled atop her head and held there with a clip. "Great to see you two! Come on in."

As we stepped inside, Rhett said, "Your home is as beautiful as I remembered, Mrs. Childers."

"Oh, honey, call me Dina."

"Short for Dinasaur?" he teased.

She laughed. "I haven't heard that one in a while. Can y'all take your shoes off?"

I was already slipping out of my sneakers, but Rhett had to pause to take off his boots. Something about seeing him with his white socks, slightly loose around his toes, was so stinking cute.

"What?" he whispered to me as we followed Dina to the kitchen.

I shook my head. "Nothing."

He was about to ask more, but we both were taken aback by the amount of people and things spread around the table. There were notebooks, piles of cardstock, pens, and a buffet of snack food.

Camryn and Cooper stood up when they saw us, but her dad and two older people I assumed were Cooper's parents stayed sitting at the table.

"Surprise!" Cam said. "We're getting married in two weeks."

My eyes nearly bugged out of my head as Rhett said, "Two *weeks*?"

Cooper nodded, and Cam said, "We talked about waiting, but I've always wanted to have a backyard summer wedding, and Cooper's parents really want us to be married before the baby comes, so this is what we landed on."

Cooper put his arm around Cam's waist. "I woulda married her yesterday, so I'm fine with this, but we need y'all to help us address the invitations tonight, and the girls gotta decide on colors and dresses and shit—" At the pinched look on his mom's face, he said "—uh, I mean, dresses and stuff."

She nodded her approval.

I held back a laugh. "Let's get going, then."

Dina was a sight to see as she leapt into action, giving each of the men a printed list of addresses and then the cardstock wedding invitations and envelopes to start writing on. She must have used an hour-printing service at one of the box stores to have them done so quickly.

I didn't have too much time to think logistics as Cam began talking about the wedding.

"I've always seen myself having a wedding with mint green and robin's egg blue. We can do blue dresses and then more green in the bouquets. We've already got Bora on board for the floral arrangements. Coop's uncle is catering. He does barbecue competitions all over the state. Mags, are you okay with doing my hair?"

"Of course," I said, my voice coming out softly. "I can't believe how much you all got done already." I ran my fingers over an invitation on the table and read the words.

We cordially invite you to the wedding of Cooper Lawson and Camryn Childers.... gifts may be mailed to...

I looked back up at Cam. "Are you sure you don't want the gifts to be mailed to our place? It'll be easier for you to go through them there."

"Oh, honey," Dina chuckled. "Cooper's place is Camryn's place after the wedding."

I raised my eyebrows, and Cam looked down at the table. Cooper's mom glanced between us with a worried look, but Dina said, "Mags, you know Camryn is moving in with Cooper, right?"

"Mom," Camryn whispered, shifting in her seat.

I felt like I'd taken a gut punch. "Of course," I said

quickly, knowing that made logical sense. "It's just been a long day at work."

Camryn's shoulders seemed to relax, but I couldn't help the tightness in my chest. Cam was moving out in two weeks? I hadn't thought it would be this soon.

I felt guilty for wondering if she'd still help with rent. I mean, she had a whole human to take care of, growing inside her, but I hadn't budgeted for living on my own this soon. Maybe I could pick up waitressing shifts at the diner if they needed someone extra. Or find a way to sell something to clients at the salon? But that felt bad too—I wasn't the owner yet.

Dina was looking at her phone, saying, "Magnolia, I'm texting you a link to dresses in the pretty blue color Cam wants. Can you pick one and order it?"

My stomach sank further. A dress, a gift, a bachelorette party... I was happy for Cam to find the love of her life and start a family, but... I wasn't sure I could afford for my best friend to get married.

50

RHETT

AFTER WEDDING PLANNING, Mags offered for me to stay over at her place for what would be the first time since the rodeo when I slept on the couch. But this time, when we got back to the empty house, we walked back to her bedroom.

She sat on the bed, rolling her head in slow circles.

"Long day?" I asked her as I slipped out of my boots.

With a long sigh, she said, "Lots to think about."

"What do you mean?" I asked, sitting behind her, massaging her shoulders.

"I'm going to sound like a bitch if I say it out loud."

I laughed. "That means you *have* to say it out loud."

She glanced over her shoulder at me, then looked ahead, fiddling with the edge of the quilt on her bed. "I wasn't ready for Cam to move out, financially I mean. We have another few months on our lease, and I wasn't planning to cover an extra five hundred dollars a month."

My stomach sank for her. Luckily, accommodations

were included with my job, so I didn't have that stressor on my plate. I could see how much it was weighing on Mags. "You don't think Cam will pay her half?"

"How can I ask her to pay if she's not living here and she has a baby on the way? It doesn't feel right." She let out a sigh. "Maybe I can find another roommate, just for a little while."

Good thing she couldn't see me, because I cringed. Cottonwood Falls wasn't really a big town. "Why don't I help you with rent?"

She turned toward me, making my hands slide down her arms. "I can't let you do that, Rhett. You're saving for your land."

I cupped her face in my hand. "Baby girl, when will you learn that I want to take care of you?"

She leaned into my hand, and my chest warmed like she had a direct connection to my heart. "I love you for that. But I think this is one I need to figure out on my own. I need to talk things out with Cam."

"Okay..." I said, not quite sure how that would go.

"Okay?" She smiled at me.

I laughed. "Okay. But you know what might help you relax?"

She tilted her head in question.

"A warm bath. Come on." I got up, taking her hand, and led her to the bathroom. I sat on the edge of the tub, turning on the water and letting it run over my fingers until it was hot. I plugged the bottom so it would begin filling. "You know what's crazy? Chick bathrooms have so much shit." There had to be at least eight bottles of stuff in the shower.

Mags laughed. "Well, there are two of us here, and we don't use the same products."

"Why the hell not?" I asked.

She came and sat on the opposite end of the tub, her back resting against the cream-colored tile. "Well, first of all, Cam's hair is wavy and bleached. She needs a moisture-intensive product to help it stay healthy, and then she needs a different mousse to add volume. My hair is colored, thin, and tends to get oily, so I need a heavy wash and a lighter conditioner to cut back on the oil."

I reached out and held an end of her brunette hair between my fingertips. "This is your natural color."

"Nope." She shook her head. "It was, until I started going gray."

"No way. You're not old," I said.

She laughed. "I'm also not a man, but that didn't stop me from losing hair at seventeen."

I took her hand between mine. A glance at the tub showed we had plenty of time for it to fill. And when I looked back, I realized she was remembering that time too when her mom left and she got stress-induced alopecia. Her hair fell out in chunks; I remembered finding some caught between my fingers when we were making out and how she burst into tears after.

I told her the words I'd said all those years ago. "You were beautiful then, as you are now."

Her lips lifted. "You know how much I missed you, right?"

My heart twitched at the hope those words caused. "You did?"

She nodded. "Other than Cam, you were my best

friend. When we broke up, it felt like half of me was missing." Her voice broke, and she blinked quickly.

I had to swallow down the lump growing in my own throat. "You have no idea how good it feels to have you back."

Her smile trembled, and she nodded, wiping at her eyes.

I noticed the tub getting full, so I turned it off and pulled a can of bath salts off the ledge.

"Those are Cam's," Maggie said.

I twisted the lid and dumped them in the tub. "I'll pay her back."

I stood up, and she did too. Hot steam filled the room, making sweat glisten softly on her skin under the incandescent lighting. "Put your arms up," I said gently.

She looked up at me, slowly raising her arms. I pulled her shirt over her head, showing more of her beautiful body.

"Turn," I said.

She did.

My fingers made quick work of her bra, freeing her breasts.

She turned back toward me, but instead of taking off her pants, she put her arms around me and hugged me close. I ran my calloused hands over her bare back, higher until my fingers brushed her long hair and lower until I grazed the denim at her waist.

She looked up, resting her chin on my chest, so beautiful with her shoulders bare, and glanced at my lips.

Knowing what she wanted, I bent to kiss her. The brush of my lips over hers was as natural as it was exciting, healing as it was rending. It was a reminder of all I had and all I had to lose.

When our kiss ended, I brushed the tip of my nose over hers. "Enjoy your bath, Mags."

I turned to leave the restroom, but she caught my hand. "Stay and talk to me?"

I smiled, kissing her again. "I'd love nothing more."

51

MAGNOLIA

I WOKE up in the morning, feeling Rhett's strong arms around my waist. His nose was against my back and his knees curled in around me like he didn't want to miss a part of me, even in his sleep.

The warmth that flooded my chest was something I never wanted to live without, and I realized... I loved him.

I loved him with all that I had.

But instead of fear, there was something else there.

Excitement.

Contentedness.

Wonder, at this feeling of knowing all the parts of someone, good and bad, of being incredibly hurt but also wonderfully loved by the same person, knowing they had that power to cherish or destroy and giving it to them anyway.

I rolled over in his arms, wanting to see him.

He smiled slightly, his full lips curving up, but his eyes were still closed as he said, "Good morning, beautiful."

I smiled at him, that feeling of love welling over me and making me want to cry.

When I didn't reply right away, he opened his eyes, taking me in. "What's wrong?"

My voice broke. "I love you."

His brow creased. "And you're crying?"

"It's not wrong. I was just lying here, realizing how good it felt to wake up next to you. And it hit me. I love you. Not the boy you were, not the man I hoped you could be, just you." Tears slid down my cheeks. "I'm sorry for how I've treated you."

"Baby girl." He wiped my tears away and brushed my hair back. "I didn't think you'd be crying when you told me you loved me."

I let out a laugh, which just had me crying a little more.

He smiled with me, eyes crinkling at the corners. "I know it was hard for you to see the new me, but I'm so glad you did."

And I did, see him. This man with beautiful hazel eyes that always had a smile behind them, even when his lips were even. This man with a heart that loved everyone and was brave enough to show everyone, unapologetically, his raw, unpolished self. This man who was a great friend to anyone he met, an incredible brother to his siblings, an uncle who always gave his nieces and nephews a chance to have fun and be themselves too. A man who saw past my anger to the woman I was and the woman I could be.

"You're amazing," I breathed.

He smiled, then nuzzled closer, bringing his lips to mine.

I ran my fingertips over the back of his head, feeling

the hair that was still slightly uneven, and a smile touched my lips.

"What?" he asked.

I opened my eyes, a guilty smile on my face. "I think it's time I fixed your hair."

He laughed, the sound so full and contagious I laughed along with him, my belly aching and my lungs fighting for air.

Across the house, Cam called, "What's so funny?"

Rhett and I looked at each other, only laughing harder.

Rhett called out, "She loves me!" He squeezed me to his side and added, "And I love her too."

RHONDA STOOD off to the side as I fixed Rhett's hair. I cut it short to match the path I'd swathed with the clippers. "I'm *so* glad she's fixing that for you," Rhonda said.

Rhett grinned. "Me too. Just remind me not to let her near with a straight razor."

"Ha ha," I said, turning off the buzzer. "Very funny." I picked up my scissors, trimming up a few stray hairs.

Rhonda and Rhett laughed like old pals, and Rhonda said, "You know, I remember you walking up and down the sidewalk like a lost puppy, waiting for Miss Maggie to be done with her shift back when you were young."

Rhett laughed. "I didn't know I was allowed in if I wasn't paying for a haircut."

Rhonda chortled, and I smiled at the memory.

"I didn't want all the blue-haired ladies trying to steal my boyfriend," I teased.

"Between him and your dad, they'd be covered," Rhonda laughed out.

The tips of Rhett's ears went red, and I had to set down my scissors I was laughing so hard.

Rhonda laughed along with me, and Rhett shook his head. "Y'all have been around these chemicals too long."

With a wink, Rhonda said, "Maybe just long enough." The bell over the door rang, and Rhonda went to greet her client while I finished up with Rhett's hair. I gave him the mirror and spun his chair.

He fussed with his hair, saying, "Would you look at that. The girls aren't gonna be able to make fun of my hair anymore."

I laughed. "I'm sure they'll find something."

He stood up and set the mirror on the counter, then reached into his pocket for his wallet. Have I mentioned the man can fill out a pair of Wranglers? "How much do I owe you?" he asked.

I winked at him. "I think you paid me last night."

He tossed his head back laughing, then whispered, "Baby, that was just a tip."

I laughed too, feeling more carefree than ever.

"When do I see you next?" He looped his hands around my waist. "Will you come to family dinner this week?"

I nodded. "And then we can hang out after the game Friday?"

"That works," he said. "We'll have to celebrate crushing the 'Princess Warriors' in the championship."

"You're pretty snobby about team names for someone who coaches The Unicorns," I teased.

He shook his head. "Unicorns are magical creatures with sharp, deadly horns. I totally get it."

I laughed and kissed his lips. "See you later."

"Love you," he said back.

"I love you too."

Rhonda eyed me as he walked out the door, and her client, Mrs. Briggs, said, "I'd steal him from you."

I laughed. "I'm not letting him get away this time."

My next client came down the sidewalk, and I walked to the door to let her in. For the rest of the day, it seemed like it was nonstop. I didn't even have time to check my phone until I heard it ringing in my pocket.

I excused myself from my client, who was waiting on the bleach to process in her hair, and took the call. "Hi! This is Maggie."

"Hey, Maggie, this is Bernice Williams, the director at the retirement home. Cam gave me your number."

"That's great!" I told her a little about my project, and she asked if I could come in after work to talk and make some plans. Since I had a little time before practice tonight, I said I would.

Rhonda was so happy I was making progress that she offered to close up shop, and I even had time to grab some food to-go at the diner before heading to the retirement home. But when I walked down the sidewalk, I heard someone whistle behind me.

I turned, ready to snap at whoever it was for wolf-whistling at me, but instead saw Rhett getting out of his truck. "What are you doing here?" I asked. "Are you following me?"

"Nope." He walked down the sidewalk carrying a

plastic bag of takeout and then kept pace beside me as we walked to the door.

I stared at him. "What, then?"

He punched in the code at the front door like he'd been here a million times before. "My grandpa lives here. I see him every Tuesday night. We eat dinner together before practice."

52

MAGNOLIA

I STARED at Rhett in shock, almost not moving until I realized he was holding the door open for me. "You see him every Tuesday?"

Cam came walking down the tiled hallway in her cute pink scrubs. "Rhett! I was starting to worry you weren't coming." And then she saw me, looking confused. "Mags? What are you doing here?"

"Me?" I asked. "I'm here for a meeting with the director. Were you waiting on Rhett?"

Cam and Rhett exchanged a glance.

"What is going on?" I asked, an uneasy feeling settling in my stomach.

Bernice came out of the front office and smiled at the three of us. "Maggie, it's great to see you. Why don't we chat in my office?"

I looked between her, my friend, and my boyfriend. Realizing she was waiting on me, I pasted a smile on my lips. "That sounds great."

I could feel Rhett and Cam watching me as I followed Bernice into her office and she shut the door behind her.

While we chatted about potential days and times and logistics, I had the same questions running in the back of my mind. Why had Cam seen Rhett every Tuesday without telling me?

Bernice and I made plans to have the salon set up in the community room the first weekend of every month, and she said she had a volunteer who could help me bring equipment back and forth so I wasn't carrying everything from the salon on my own. We decided to have the first salon day a month from this weekend.

When we were done, she asked if I wanted her to walk me to the door, and I glanced at my watch. We still had an hour until practice started, so I asked, "Can you show me where Rhett and Grandpa Griffen are visiting?"

"Of course," she said with a smile.

I walked after her down a hallway until we reached a big room with lots of tables and benches and even a little theater area. At one of the tables, I saw Rhett, Cam, and Grandpa Griffen all sitting and eating together, laughing and talking like old friends.

My stomach sank, and those old jealous feelings came up. I knew I shouldn't be so upset, especially before I knew all the facts, but I also knew if I approached them right now, I wouldn't behave the way I should.

I made a show of glancing at my watch and said, "Actually, Bernice, I need to get something from the store before it closes. I'll be in touch closer to the day!"

She smiled. "Sounds good. But you better hurry. You've got about ten minutes."

"I will," I replied, booking it out of the building.

When I got to my car, the tightness in my chest wouldn't go away.

All I could remember was going to Rhett's place, knocking on the door and him answering half-naked with Lola behind him, wrapped in a sheet.

This wasn't the same, I told myself.

He and Cam were in public, with his grandpa.

Cam would never do that to me.

Rhett was different now.

But it felt like a betrayal all the same.

Not knowing where else to go, I went to the baseball field and sat in my car, trying to eat my food and not stress out until vehicles started to approach.

I saw Rhett's truck first, and he got out, coming to my car. He opened the door for me. "Hey," he said with a big smile on his face.

I steeled myself, tried to ease that hot, hard feeling in my chest. "Hey." I got out of the car. "Can we talk about earlier?"

He seemed confused. "What about earlier?"

"I mean, you clearly have a standing date with your grandpa and my best friend that no one told me about. Why?"

"I can't just let my grandpa sit by himself in a nursing home," he said. "It's important for family to visit."

I narrowed my gaze.

He rubbed his arm. "I don't know. It didn't feel like something to brag about."

Now my brows furrowed. "What do you mean?"

"I didn't want brownie points from you for visiting my grandpa."

I tilted my head and opened my mouth to argue.

"Don't even try and say I'm wrong," he said. "You loved my grandpa. If you knew I was doing what I should be doing, not even going above and beyond, you would have melted like an ice cream cone in July. I didn't want to win you back that way. I wanted to earn your love, for how I treat you."

My heart *was* melting like that ice cream cone though. "You could have told me."

"I was going to tell you next week. He's been on my ass to bring you in for a visit."

I laughed, feeling relieved. But I still didn't understand, "Why didn't Cam tell me? We tell each other everything."

"I asked her not to," he said simply.

But it wasn't that simple. Since when did Cam keep secrets for Rhett? Since when did she keep secrets from me?

Suddenly that tight ball in my chest was back and getting bigger. She was already getting married; now she was keeping things from me. I felt like I was losing my best friend, the one person who had been there for me no matter what, even when my dad was reeling from the divorce, even when I'd been devastated from losing Rhett. Through all the years.

Liv's truck pulled into the parking lot, and Maya waved at me through the windshield. I placed a smile on my lips and waved back. I never considered myself much of a kid person, never having younger siblings or working around lots of little kids, but hanging out with Maya and the rest of the team had been a highlight of the summer.

The engine quieted and the doors opened, Maya's

dog jumping down first, and then Maya followed. Liv got out, holding up her phone, and the shutter sounded.

Rhett said, "You're taking pictures?"

Liv sniffed. "Last practice with the Unicorns."

"Holy shit," Rhett muttered.

"UNCLE RHETT!" Maya yelled.

He shrugged. "Last practice. Whatcha gonna do? Fire me from a volunteer position?"

I chuckled, shaking my head, and said, "Maya, wanna help me set up the field for practice?"

The two of us went to the field, setting out the bases while Rhett got the rest of the gear. As the summer sun warmed my back and the soft breeze blew around us, I knew this was one of those moments I should cherish.

So I did.

I focused on practice, playing with the girls, making the most of the dwindling moments of our time together. And after practice, when Rhett asked if I wanted to go home with him, I shook my head.

"I need to talk with Cam tonight."

53

MAGNOLIA

TAKING DEEP BREATHS, I pulled out of the gravel lot, preparing myself for an honest conversation with Cam. Neither of us did great with conflict or confrontation, but I knew it needed to happen for the sake of our friendship, for my peace of mind moving forward.

But just a few minutes from my house, my phone started ringing, a call from our landlord. I swiped the phone, figuring he was changing the mowing schedule or something. "Hey, Peter, what's up?" I asked. I could hear the TV going in the background before he replied.

"Hey, Mags, I heard the news about Camryn and Cooper's baby on the way! Can you tell her congratulations for me?"

"Of course, but I can give you her number if you'd rather call her? I know she'd love to hear from you." I pulled to a stop in the driveway, parking next to Cam's car.

"I have her number. I actually wanted to call you because you're the main leaseholder."

I raised my eyebrows. "Oh?"

"My son is moving back to town, and with Camryn moving out, we figured you would need to find something smaller, and we want to give the house to our son and his wife to live in. Technically, in your lease, it says either one of us needs to give a month notice to terminate the agreement, so I suppose this is that month."

Each word was like a punch to the gut. "Oh. Wow."

"Things are changing all around," he said. "We'll sure miss renting to you two. You both made the place look so great from the outside, and you're always paying rent on time. If you need a reference on another place, let me know, okay?"

"Sure thing," I replied, barely keeping my voice from breaking. "I gotta get inside."

"Of course, have a good night, Maggie," he said, and the line went silent.

I slowly lowered the phone in a complete daze.

My best friend was moving out.

And a month from now, I wouldn't have a place to live.

How would I have time to find a new place while working a job and getting ready for a wedding? How would I afford a deposit, first and last month's rent, while waiting for the deposit to come back on this place and being the maid of honor Camryn deserved?

My face contorted with emotion. This fucking sucked.

Tears slid down my cheeks, and I wiped at them, but more just kept coming until my shoulders were shaking with the force of it. I was thirty-two years old, single, with nowhere to live, so far from being the independent woman I should be by now.

I watched the front door of the house open, and Cam come outside in her nightgown, looking at me through my windshield.

I hurriedly wiped my face, trying to hide just how devastated I was, but she came to the driver's side of the car and opened the door. "Are you okay, hon?"

"I'm fine," I said, but my voice cracked.

She looked down at me. "Let me get in. We'll talk." After closing my door, she walked around to the passenger side and got in. "What's going on, Mags?"

I held up my phone. "Peter just called and said he's terminating our lease a month from today."

She seemed confused. "That's a good thing, right? Then you can find a one bedroom instead of having to get another roommate."

My chest ached even more, sadness fighting with frustration. "I didn't realize I'd have to find another roommate quite so soon, or another place to live altogether."

"Mags..." She held her hand over her stomach, even though she wasn't showing yet.

"I know you're having a baby, and I know you're getting married, but it would have been nice to hear from *you* that you were moving out on your wedding day or that your wedding day was only *two weeks away*. I had no time to prepare myself or ask you any questions without having everyone staring at us!"

"I'm sorry I'm not perfect!" she cried out. "I'm pregnant, and my hormones are crazy, and I have my mom telling me not to get married and Cooper's mom saying we'll disgrace the family if we don't. I shouldn't have to worry about where *you're* going to live on top of everything else! You're a grown adult, and I'm not your mother."

My jaw dropped, my heart stinging from her words. "Seriously? I'm not asking for you to mother me! I'm asking for some basic communication, Cam! Like were you wanting out of the lease? Were you going to pay your half of the rent even when you were living with Cooper? Or did you really just plan to leave me high and dry?"

She let out a frustrated groan that just made me angrier. "Didn't you hear me? I have a baby on the way. I'm making appointments for sonograms, finding an OB, planning a freaking wedding, and all you can think about is *rent*?"

"I'm happy for you, Cam, I am, but I didn't think you'd drop me the second you decided to get married! But then again, I also didn't think you'd be hanging out with Rhett for *months* on end behind my back! Why didn't you tell me?"

"Because he asked me not to!" she yelled, gesticulating wildly. "I don't know why you've been so freaking hard on him. He's a good guy, Maggie!"

Her words continued to slice through me. "So you've just been silently judging me this whole time?"

"Of course I have! I can't say anything to you about him, or you lose your ever-loving mind!"

"Because he hurt me!"

"Fifteen years ago, Maggie. Grow up."

My mouth fell open. "You're telling *me* to grow up?"

She flattened her hand over her chest. "I'm trying to move on with my life. I'm sorry I can't be your live-in bestie forever. I want to get married and have kids and live my own life without messing around with you all the time or hearing you complain about a man who's been nothing but good to you since you moved back home!"

Hot tears welled in my eyes, sliding down my cheeks. That's what she thought we'd been doing all these years of friendship? *Messing around*? "Get out of my car."

"Maggie," she said, but I cut her off.

"Get out of my car!"

She let out an angry groan and left, slamming the door behind her. Her pink nightgown swished behind her as she walked away.

I was still crying as I whipped out of the driveway, refusing to stay in the house with her tonight.

I drove half the speed limit, but I made it to Rhett's place, my skin raw and stinging from all the saltwater tears.

I had to look like a mess as I walked up to his door, where the paper he'd made was still taped up.

No fucking around. (Unless you're Maggie. Then fucking is encouraged.)

For some strange reason, I started crying more as I knocked on his door.

A few moments later, he opened it, shirtless and wearing sweats slung low on his waist. As he took me in, confusion registered on his face. "What's going on?"

I fell into his arms, saying, "I need you."

54

RHETT

COOPER and I rode four-wheelers through the pasture, checking on the cattle. We hit a level path and slowed down. With the engines quieter, Cooper yelled over, "Did you hear what happened with Maggie and Camryn?"

I glanced over at him. I'd heard the entire thing last night, holding Maggie as she cried from it all. "Sounds like it was pretty bad."

"Really bad," he echoed.

I nodded.

"What should we do?" he asked.

I gave him a look. "Stay the hell out of it, right?"

He cringed. "But Camryn's already texting me shit from Pinterest. The kind of shit she should be sending a girlfriend. Like Maggie."

I laughed. "Looks like you'll have to see the pins until they figure it out."

"How did you know they're called pins?"

"I have a sister," I replied.

We had to gun it a little bit to get up the hill. But even after, Cooper was quiet for a minute.

"What?" I asked him.

"How do you know I'm thinking something?"

"Cause the only time you're quiet is when you're thinking something bad. Otherwise it all comes out your mouth."

He had a wary smile. "I don't know if I should say it."

"Say it." I took a breath, knowing it would probably be something I didn't like.

"Well, seems like Mags can hold a grudge."

I chuckled. "That's true. But it's all because she wants to protect herself from being hurt. Her mama wasn't there to protect her like she should have those teen years, and I think she learned she has to do that for herself."

Cooper ducked his head in a nod. "I get it, I do, but knowing what I know about Maggie and with what Cam told me she said to Mags, this might not be something Maggie lets go of—before the wedding or after."

The thought hurt me, because those two had been such good friends since we were all in high school. "They'll work it out," I said, more of a prayer than a promise.

"I hope so, but what happens the next time you two have a fight?" Cooper asked. "You're a hothead, and Mags likes to run. Aren't you worried she'll ice you out again?"

I gritted my teeth as his words hit my ears and transformed into an uneasy feeling that churned in the pit of my gut. That fucker was right. If Mags and I were going to move forward, she needed to learn how to forgive.

"I see one up there," I said, nodding toward a cow

separated from the rest of the herd. Without waiting for Cooper to reply, I sped up and went to check it out.

*

MAGGIE STAYED at my place every night that week, and Thursday night, I said, "Hey, what do you say you and I go on a trip after the championship this weekend? We can stay at Gage's fancy hotel and drink champagne and spend some time together?"

She slipped under the covers and said, "I like the sound of that."

I smiled over at her. Sometimes I couldn't believe I had my Maggie back, that this beautiful woman was sharing a bed with me and so much more.

But that niggling feeling had stayed in my gut since Cooper and I had that brief conversation. I knew I wanted to talk to her about it, but I wanted to make sure we talked at just the right time.

She curled into my arm, resting her head on my shoulder. She wore a pink, floral silk cap—she said it kept her natural waves from getting frizzy, but I mostly thought she looked adorable. "I love your little bonnet," I said.

She adjusted the pink headband. "It's not a bonnet."

"Whatever you"—I touched the tip of her nose with my finger—"say."

She batted my hand away and curled into my arms, looking up at me.

"What?" I asked.

Her smile softened. "Lying in bed with you, it makes everything feel better."

I held her closer, kissing her lips. "Everything's better with you, Maggie Ray."

She smiled against my mouth. "Everything?"

I nodded.

Her hand danced around the waist of my pants. "What about this?"

"Definitely."

Her hand slid into my underwear, nails scraping my happy trail, until her fingers gently circled my cock.

"Fuck, Maggie, I have to feed the cows tomorrow at four a.m."

She made a fist around my shaft, growing harder by the second.

I reached back, tugging on her hair through her bonnet so she had to look back up at me. "You're pushing it."

She gave me a bratty grin, pumping my cock. "If you don't like it, you should punish me."

With her neck exposed, I couldn't hold back. I pushed her over on the bed, laying her down and putting my hand over her throat—not enough to choke her, just enough to show her who was boss.

"I'm in charge," I said, my voice low.

Her eyes lit with desire, and her throat moved under my hand with her swallow.

Fuck, it was hot.

"You're in charge," she gasped, desire in her eyes.

I released my grip, leaning back over her. "Now get on your knees and hang on to the headboard. Wouldn't want that pretty head to get a bump."

I moved back, watching her thick body roll under the

blankets, and when she pushed up, her nightgown was already riding up. Holy fuck.

I took off my sweats, prowling beside the bed to get a condom.

"I'm on the pill," she breathed.

We'd only done it with protection to this point, and the thought of fucking her raw nearly had me coming in my pants, but I shook my head, gritting my teeth. I ripped the condom open, rolling it on my cock, and got on the bed behind her. She had both hands on the top of the headboard, back beautifully arched as she waited for me.

I fisted her gray nightgown, pulling it aside to see that beautiful ass of hers, lacy thong disappearing between luscious cheeks. With one hand still on her nightgown, I pulled the thong aside, running my fingers along her sex and finding it soaking wet.

"You're ready for me."

"I'm *begging* for you," she breathed.

My cock jumped at that, begging right along with her. I pumped it in my hand and angled myself at her entrance. I pressed inside, slowly feeling her stretch around me. She let out a moan, and the sound nearly had me coming undone.

I moved my other hand to her juicy hip and took a handful of flesh, pumping in and out of her, then slid my hand down, making quick circles around her clit.

"Rhett," she gasped.

"Now be a good girl," I said, pulling back and slamming into her. "And come when I tell you to, not a moment sooner."

She clenched around me.

"Got it?" I said, my voice low, punishing as I removed my hand from her clit.

She whimpered.

"Say it," I ordered.

"Yes."

"Yes what?" I squeezed her ass harder.

She let out a cry. "Yes, sir."

"Good girl."

She clenched even harder.

Fuck.

"When I count down from ten, you're going to come so fucking hard you'll go to sleep like we should have earlier."

She moaned.

"Ten."

I ran my hand across her ass and spanked it, leaving her skin bright red under my touch.

Her hands tightened on the headboard.

"Nine."

I slowed myself, doing deliberate circles inside her as I tweaked her taut nipples. Her head fell back, the cap sliding from her waves.

"Eight."

I wrapped one hand around her hair, fucking her, riding her, her ass rippling from each slap of my thighs against her.

"Rhett," she begged.

"Patience, babe."

"Yes, sir," she breathed.

"Seven."

I pounded into her, over and over again, slowly making my way down to three.

"Turn over," I ordered.

"Now?"

"Now. I want to see your face when I make you come."

She turned, spreading her legs for me. I bracketed her face with my hands and adjusted my hips, guiding my cock to her hole. The second she engulfed me, I let out a hoarse moan. "Holy fuck, Maggie, you get me hotter than I ever knew I could be."

Her eyes were wide on me as she held on to my forearms, dug her nails into my skin.

"Three," I said. "You're so fucking hot, your tits bouncing in that nightgown, your mouth open, like you want me to fill every fucking part of you."

Her lips parted farther.

"Two... Your thick legs, wrapped around my waist, pulling me in to you," I uttered. "Your hot, wet pussy, fucking quivering, begging for me to spill everything I have into you. And your voice, ready to cry out my name when I say..."

She bit down on her bottom lip.

"One."

She shuddered around me, her eyes crinkling in pain, in pleasure, her luscious lips echoing out a cry that matched my hot grunts as I came harder than I ever had, her pussy clenching and milking me for seconds that turned into minutes.

As the last of the waves faded, her head rolled back into the pillow. I slowly slid out of her and rolled to the side, removing my condom.

Once I cleaned myself up, I went to the bathroom and got her a warm washcloth and another dry one. I brought them both back to her, and she smiled up at me. "I'm never going to get over how sweet it is that you do that."

I grinned, adjusting the sheets and blankets to lie down. "All for you, Maggie Ray."

She tossed the rags to the hamper, along with her underwear, and then curled in next to me. I was such a fucking horndog for how hyperaware I was of her lack of panties. But my cock was beyond dead. Give me twenty minutes and that could be a different story.

Mags curled in my arms and aimed her blue eyes up at me. "Can I ask you something?"

I nodded.

"Why do you always wear a condom? Most men are so eager to take it off."

The thought of other men inside her almost had me going fucking feral. But I took a few deep breaths to cool down. "I'm not most men."

She lifted a corner of her lips. "I know that." But then she waited, quiet.

I knew she deserved this explanation too. "To me, having kids, bringing a life into the world, is a really big deal. It's not something I'm ever going to risk, even if the pill's ninety-nine percent accurate. I'm going to put the condom on and wear it every time until I know that person is the one I'm ready to have a family with."

Her eyes fluttered down and back up at me. "I know it's too soon." She nestled deeper into my arms, her eyes closing sleepily. "But I think this feels perfect."

I kissed her forehead and told her goodnight, because I couldn't completely agree.

55

MAGNOLIA

"GO, ESTHER!" I yelled from the dugout. It was our last inning, and all the bases were loaded. We were down by three, with two outs, and if she could hit a triple, we had a chance at tying or even winning the game.

Her little shoulders moved with her breaths as she stepped up to the plate with her bright yellow bat.

Beside me, Rhett said, "I'm so damn proud of that girl."

I looked up at him for just a second. "Tell me about it."

The pitch went over the plate, and the umpire yelled, "Strike one."

Rhett swore under his breath. "You can do this, Esther!"

I watched her square up to the plate again as I waited for his answer.

"At the beginning of the season, that little girl was in tears before the game even started. Now, she's up to bat, all these girls on the bench are cheering for her, depending on her for the win or loss of the game. And that fucking tiger is taking deep breaths and staring down that pitcher, making her her bitch."

I let out a laugh. "That is pretty amazing."

Another pitch sailed toward Esther, and she swung with all her might, barely tipping it.

"Strike two," the umpire called.

I pressed my hand to my chest. "Gosh, I can't take the suspense. GO, ESTHER!"

Behind me, the girls joined me in cheering, "GO, ESTHER! GO, ESTHER! GO, ESTHER!" The entire crowd joined us, her name echoing around the field.

The ball sailed toward the plate, and Esther swung... and missed.

The girls on the other team instantly started screaming and cheering while my heart broke for Esther. She looked around at her teammates, her bottom lip quivering. But instead of waiting for her to come to the dugout, all her teammates were running out to her. Hugging her, telling her good job, asking us coaches about what snacks were coming next.

I felt tears rolling down my cheeks for these girls, because they'd gotten so much more than a summer playing softball—they'd made friendships that would last years to come. It made me realize how much I missed Cam, especially those simpler times with her when our biggest worries were running out of lip gloss or who to sit by at lunch.

Next to me, Rhett said, "Look at you, softie."

"Shut up," I sniffed, wiping at my eyes. "I'm proud of her too."

He grinned. "Let's call the team in for one last Unicorn Roar."

"Willingly?" I laughed.

"Team! Huddle up!" he said. The girls came running over. A few leftover tears ran down Esther's cheeks, but she wasn't crying anymore. When all the girls had circled us, Rhett looked at me and said, "Coach, anything you want to say?"

I smiled, nodded. "I am so proud of you girls, not for the way you played, but for the way you supported each other. This is a small town, Cottonwood Falls, and these girls are likely going to be the ones you walk through life with. Middle school. High school. Sports. Dances. Maybe even college. I hope you always lift each other up like you did tonight."

"Amen," Rhett said. "I'm so fucking proud of you girls."

Their mouths fell open, and some of the girls giggled while others whispered amongst themselves.

"Oh hell, it's the last game. I can let a cuss word loose," he said. "But don't let fancy words make you miss the main point. I'm proud of you, of how you played, of how you improved, and of how much fun you had. Now don't drink too many juice boxes tonight, you hear?"

They giggled and echoed out a chorus of, "Yes, Coach."

"One last Unicorn Roar?" he said.

They all nodded.

"Three, two, one...."

Everyone stuck a finger to their forehead, pawed the ground, and yelled, "UNICORN ROAR," but no one was louder or smiling bigger than Rhett Griffen.

I'D GONE BACK to the house before the game, while Cam was at work, to pack my bags for our weekend getaway. So after the game, we hung out at the field with the girls to have snacks and drinks, then got in my car and drove toward Dallas.

We didn't have much on the itinerary aside from a dinner at Farrah and Gage's house, but I was excited, nonetheless.

After looking up the hotel where we were staying, The Retreat, I realized it was a five-star resort with a pool, a hot tub, sauna, state-of-the-art gym, and beautifully designed rooms. Rhett later told me Farrah had been the one to design them.

We held hands in the car as he drove and just reflected on the season. Some of the moms had posted photos online that included us, and my favorite was one where Rhett and I were doing the Unicorn Roar with the girls before the last game. I knew we'd both remember this time for years to come, even if we were both reluctant to coach the team at first.

The drive seemed to fly by, and before I knew it, we were pulling up to the cutest hotel. Check in was super easy, and then we were up in the penthouse suite, which looked even more amazing than it did on the website.

"Oh my gosh. Oh my gosh. Rhett, have you seen this bathtub?" I cried from around the corner of the bathroom. It was like it had been hand carved out of marble.

He stepped behind me and got a cheeky grin. "We'll have to try it out later."

My cheeks heated as I wrapped my arms around his

neck. "I thought we could try the hot tub tonight. Relieve some of that tension from the drive?"

He had his shirt off in two seconds flat.

"You really missed your calling as a stripper," I teased.

His cheeks turned bright red, but he quickly recovered. "If you hurry up and get into your swimsuit, I'll give you a lap dance later."

"Can't turn down a lap dance." I smiled and went to my bag, getting out my swimsuit. It was my favorite—a bright red bikini with bottoms that covered my stomach but showed a little bit of cheeks and a wrap-style top that gave the girls an extra boost. As I tied the straps and cinched it up, Rhett took me in.

"Yeah, there's no way we're making it down there," he said, coming to kiss my neck.

BUT I PULLED BACK. "Speak for yourself."

He made to chase me, but I ran to the hallway, pulling the room key off the desk on my way out.

When we made it to the hallway, he lowered his voice, speaking in my ear. "You are so paying for that later."

I couldn't fucking wait.

We rode the elevator to the level with the pool and walked outside. There were twinkle lights hanging around the pool area, a bar, and even light blue lights in the water. "It's so pretty," I said.

"You are."

My cheeks warmed. "Oldest line in the book."

"What book?" he asked. "If it's about us, I'd love to read it."

I smiled. "How would it end?" I asked.

"Probably with me fucking you senseless in a hot tub."

"Let's get in then," I said, smiling. We walked over to the hot tub, and I held on to the railing to step in while Rhett easily lowered himself from the side.

He looked so damn good in his green swim trunks. "How do you not have a farmer's tan?" I asked him.

"I work shirtless. The ladies like it." He winked.

I rolled my eyes at him. "I'm sure Coop does too."

He laughed, skimming his fingers along the top of the water. He didn't have his normal smile like he had moments ago. Something felt... off.

"Everything okay?" I asked.

He shook his head, looking up at me. "I haven't been honest with you."

56

RHETT

I SAW HER FEATURES FALL, the way her breath hitched. "What do you mean?"

I rubbed the back of my neck, water sliding down my forearms. "There's something I've been wanting to talk to you about for the last week, and I've been to chickenshit to do it."

"Tell me," she said quickly. Forcefully.

I knew she had to be imagining a million different things, each new one worse than the last, so I hurried to get it out. "I got in touch with your mom."

Her face went blank. "What? How?"

"I had a little help from your dad." At the hurt, confused look in her eyes, I wrung my hands under the water. "I think I've been clear with my intentions, Mags. I'm in this for the long haul. That means dating. It means marriage when we're both ready. And if you're up for it, I'd love some babies running around that look just like you."

Her eyes studied mine, guarded.

"But when I think about our life, there's one thing that has me worried," I admitted, the words harder and harder to say out loud.

"What do you mean?" she asked.

"I mean, Maggie, a relationship takes a lot of forgiveness. I'm not perfect, I'm gonna mess up, and from what I've seen, you throw these walls up around you the second someone hurts your feelings."

She opened her mouth to speak, but I hurried to get out what I needed to say.

"I'm not saying you need to sing "Kumbaya" with your mom around a campfire or even send her a card on her birthday, but this hurt, this pain, this anger you've been holding for her... it makes me nervous, especially when your dad told me she's trying to reach out to you. And what happened with Camryn? You've been at my house all week, not a call or a text sent to her."

Mags eyes welled with tears, and it hurt like hell to see her crying. "What Camryn said to me—"

"Was awful," I said. "I agree. You need to tell her you won't accept that nonsense anymore."

"But?"

"She's your best friend. She's been your best friend for *years*. She's scared shitless with a baby on the way, and she's worried she'll mess it all up. Sometimes stress makes people say stupid, hurtful things."

Maggie raised her eyebrows. "Cam told you that?"

"She didn't have to," I said. "That's how I'd feel with a baby on the way. And I think it would show a lot of maturity on your part if you were there for her, even when she wasn't lovable. Sometimes, the most unlovable people are the ones who need us the most."

Maggie wiped at a stray tear, but the water from her hands just dampened her face. "It's been *years* without talking to my mom. I don't even know who she is anymore."

"Then now might be a good time to give her a chance to show you who she's become," I said.

"And what if Cam really does hate me?" Maggie continued. "She's been thinking all those things about me behind my back."

I tilted my head "Come on. Tell me you haven't thought a time or two that she and Coop are batshit crazy for doing what they're doing."

Her cheeks warmed.

"Exactly. But you didn't tell her that because you're a good friend. Just like she's a good friend to you by keeping it to herself until now."

Maggie nodded, looking down at the water. When she looked up, she asked, "What did you talk to my mom about?"

I lifted a corner of my lips. "I asked if she'd like to meet us for lunch while we're in Dallas—at a place that doesn't have steak knives or hair trimmers."

Maggie let out a hoarse laugh. "That was probably a good call."

"So you'll go?" I asked her.

The blue water reflected up to her face, catching the circles under her eyes as she nodded. Then I realized this distance between her and her mom was probably weighing on her even more than it had been on me. Maybe we both needed this to move forward.

"Come here," I said, opening my arms.

She crossed the hot tub, sitting in my lap and letting

me hold her close. I brushed back her hair and spoke into her ear. "This means so much to me, that we can grow, together."

She nodded, sniffed, and looked up at me. "You'll be there the whole time, right?"

"I'm never leaving your side."

57

MAGNOLIA

I LOOKED through the windshield of the car to see the building in front of us. It was an unassuming place called Barry's Coffee, and we'd gotten here fifteen minutes early despite me changing my mind a hundred times about whether or not I wanted to come.

Rhett squeezed my hand and said, "I'm here for you, no matter how this goes."

The tension in my chest eased, if only slightly. "I want to show you that I'm willing to work on being more forgiving," I said. "Isn't that the point of twin flames? We show each other opportunities for growth?"

He smiled, kissed my forehead. "That's the point of *us*, twin flames or not."

I leaned into his kiss and took a few deep breaths. "Let's go order and sit down."

As we walked inside, my legs felt shaky, and part of me worried that she'd no-show while another hoped she would. What if she was the same woman who left me all those years ago? Could my heart take another disappointment?

A sweet girl named Jenni took our orders, and then we found a table at the corner of the coffee shop. "I like this place," I said. It had a really nice vibe, with people of all ages hanging out, chatting, doing homework, enjoying their drinks. I wished I could appreciate it more.

Rhett took a sip of his iced tea. "Farrah's dad owns it."

My eyes widened. "Seriously? That's amazing."

He nodded. "I feel like this is the kind of business you'll have when you own the salon. Everyone will feel right at home."

My heart warmed at those words, at his belief in me. "You mean it?"

He nodded. "Absolutely."

The bell over the door chimed, and I looked over, seeing my mom.

She was visibly older, with extra lines on her face and streaks of gray through her brown hair, but it was her. And this time, she was alone.

"Breathe," Rhett reminded me.

I sucked in a gasp, but it didn't seem to do anything. My eyes were already on the verge of watering, and my throat felt tight.

Mom scanned the coffee shop, and I felt it the second our eyes connected. Rhett rose, and I stood by him as we watched her walk our way. She wore a summery yellow dress with flowy sleeves, and her lips lifted into a tentative smile.

When she reached us, she held one arm in her hand,

half crossing her chest. "Maggie, Rhett. I'm so glad you agreed to meet me here."

I always imagined what I would say to my mom if I saw her again, what it would feel like, how she would act, but I never expected how *awkward* it would feel. I could tell how nervous she was, and I was nervous too, lost even. What did you say to a stranger who birthed you?

Rhett spoke first. "Would you like me to get you something to drink, Hazel?"

"I'm alright," she said and gestured at a chair. "Mind if I sit?"

"Of course," Rhett said.

I watched as she carefully pulled out the chair and sat down. Her nails were painted a soft pink, almost the same color as mine. I wondered if it was a sign.

"How have you been, Maggie?" she asked.

I sat back down and glanced at Rhett, not quite sure what to say, but started talking anyway. "I've been pretty good. I'm trying to buy Rhonda's Salon in Cottonwood Falls, so I'm busy with that. Cam is getting married here in a couple of weeks. Rhett and I are back together."

Mom smiled between the two of us. "I always thought you two had something special."

Rich of her to say, since we'd only been dating a few months when she ran out of town.

Rhett cleared his throat. "How are you, Hazel?"

She fiddled with her fingers. "I'm... okay. I was diagnosed with NASH, and that has me rethinking a lot of things."

"NASH?" I asked.

She nodded. "Nonalcoholic steatohepatitis. It's basically fatty liver disease, but not because of drinking. I'm trying to turn my diet around, or it could lead to liver failure."

The news had my stomach sinking, our years apart flashing before my eyes. "Are you doing better?" I asked, hope bare in my voice.

She shrugged. "I won't really know until my next blood draw in a few months."

I couldn't think of what to say, but after a moment, she kept talking.

"I know this is strange, seeing me, and I know we have a lot of baggage in our past, Maggie, but I really do love you. I've watched you online and I'm so amazed by you, the way you help people, how good you are at what you do. I know I left you when you really needed me, but I want to be here now if you'll let me."

My throat was tight, and a mix of anger and hurt swirled in my gut. "*Now* you want to be here? I was *sixteen years old* when you left. You were there one day and gone the next, didn't even look back for your daughter or even make a call. I had to go to my senior prom without you. All the other girls had their moms there, helping them get ready, taking pictures, and you were nowhere to be found. Not because I lost you but because you *chose* to leave me. What kind of mother does that to her daughter?" I demanded, letting all the words pour out of me. Rhett squeezed my knee, giving me the support I needed to keep going. "Why? Why, Mom? I know things weren't perfect with Dad but what about me? You made me think I wasn't worth sticking around for."

She looked down at her lap.

"*Why* damnit?" I repeated.

"No reason would be good enough." She met my

gaze again. "But I want you to know I didn't leave because of you. I hit forty and realized that I was living in the same town where I was born. I married the first man I ever really dated. I failed at having more than one child. I didn't have a degree or any professional skills. I was over-weight, broke, and had nothing to show for all the life that I lived. I felt dead inside. I honestly thought you'd be better off without having a mom around whose only accomplishment was keeping you alive."

My heartstrings ached with each word she said, because so many of those words echoed the fears I had for myself.

"I got online just to talk to people my age," she continued, "to see if I could find someone who under-stood what I was going through, and I met this man..."

I gritted my teeth.

"He was kind, told me I was pretty, said I could be more than what I was. He promised me a life with him that was everything I was missing in Cottonwood Falls. I think it was my last-ditch effort to hang on to life when it felt like it was slipping through my fingers. But he was so jealous and possessive he didn't want me calling back to the house to check on you."

My eyebrows drew together. "What?" I'd never heard this before.

She nodded. "I tried, a couple times. When he found out, he made me change my number, and when that didn't work he took my phone. He got..." She took a shuddering breath. "He got abusive with me. The only way I could go to your hair school graduation was for him to come with me. When I showed up with him, I felt even more worthless than I did before because I had such a good thing with you and your dad and I just didn't appreciate it like I should have."

"Hazel..." Rhett reached out, holding my mom's hand. This lifeline between us both.

"I left him right after your college graduation with the help of an organization here in town, and I decided if you could make something of yourself, I could too. I went to cosmetology school and followed in your footsteps, because you, Magnolia Ray Gibson, are the *only* thing I've ever gotten right."

I covered my mouth with my hand. "You did?"

She nodded, pulling out her phone. "I don't have a big social media following like you, but I've been documenting the journey." She swiped to an Instagram account and showed me row after row of hair and nails she'd done for women and men alike.

Tears fell down my cheeks as Rhett said, "That's amazing."

I nodded in agreement, trying to stem the flow of tears. "I'm proud of you."

Mom's smile wavered, and she sucked in a deep breath. She opened her mouth to speak but was overcome by emotion. "That's all I ever wanted to hear."

My chest ached with guilt, with happiness. Because my mom had been just as lonely, just as lost as I was, and just like she wasn't there for me, I hadn't been there for her either.

I made a commitment to myself, to Rhett, to work on forgiveness while still holding boundaries to keep myself safe. And I made another promise out loud. "Mom, is it... is it okay if we get to know each other again?"

Tears rolled down her face as she nodded. "I'd love that."

We got up from our chairs, hugging each other long and hard.

It felt like we were both finally home.

58

RHETT

WE SPENT hours at the coffee shop, talking and laughing and catching up.

We all said goodbye in the parking lot and made plans to visit again soon. Hazel hugged me goodbye, whispering in my ear, "Thank you. Thank you. Thank you."

I smiled, hugging her a little extra tight. This had been good for all of us. I hadn't been sure how this meeting would go, but Mags had gone above and beyond any expectation. She'd shown me that she was ready to grow and learn to forgive. In the process, she'd rekindled a relationship I could tell she missed like crazy.

We waved goodbye, and when we got in the car, I looked over at Maggie. She seemed a little shell-shocked. "How are you holding up?" I asked.

She sniffed, wiped at her eyes. "I'm happy, but I have *so* many regrets."

I lifted a corner of my lips. "None of us are perfect. We all have to fuck up before we find the right way. The trick is to use those mistakes as lessons instead of reasons to beat ourselves up."

Her hand twined with mine, and she held the back of my hand to her lips. "I don't know what I'd do without you, Rhett Griffen."

"Probably have a lot less sex," I quipped.

She giggled. "Maybe. I'd smile a lot less too."

That warmed my heart. "I'm here, Maggie Ray, and I'm not going anywhere."

She squeezed my hand a little tighter. "Do you mind if we have a little rest and I clean up before we go to Gage and Farrah's place?"

"Of course." I backed her car out of the parking spot, and we drove back downtown to The Retreat.

She napped while I checked out the weight room. Then we showered and changed before driving to Gage and Farrah's place in Denton. Mags looked beautiful in the passenger seat, wearing a flowy olive shirt with ripped black jeans that did her ass so many favors they should be on the payroll.

"What?" she asked as she caught me looking.

I smirked. "Just thinking about how fine you look."

She reached out, running her hand over my thigh. "It's not fair when you just wake up looking like that."

I chuckled. "Growing up, sharing a bathroom with Liv, I have to say I'm happy to be a guy."

We slowed as I pulled into the driveway behind Gage's Tesla.

"There's the expensive car," Maggie said, almost to herself.

"What?"

She unbuckled. "The other day I saw them pull up in

a minivan, and I thought, no way. Gage has to be driving a fancy car."

I laughed. "He loves that thing."

"It's pretty," she agreed.

"I think he keeps the minivan just to prove to Farrah that he's down to earth."

She laughed, and we got out of the car. I held her hand as we walked up the driveway to the light brick house. It wasn't huge, but big enough for all of them—way less assuming than the fancy downtown condo Gage used to call home.

"I love this yellow door," Mags commented as I rang the doorbell.

"We can paint my door yellow if you want."

She turned to me, smiling as the door swung open and Cora grinned up at us. "You're here!"

"Hi, Cora Bug!" I said.

She scrunched her nose. "Bug?"

"Well, you said you're not a princess," I retorted.

Putting her hands on her hips, she said, "Well I ain't a bug either."

Farrah came behind her daughter, laughing. "Let them in, Cora. You're letting out all the cool air."

Cora got out of the way and Maggie chuckled, stepping in ahead of me. When we were inside, I noticed the boys lying out on the living room floor playing video games. "Where's Gage?"

"Grilling out back," Farrah said. "Just like your daddy, always on that grill."

I laughed. "He had to wait until we grew up and moved out to have a turn at the grill. Dad would never let us touch his."

Mags smiled. "Farrah, your house is gorgeous."

"Thank you!" Farrah replied. "Want a tour? We just had some of Drew's newer art framed for decoration."

Maggie nodded, and I excused myself to go out back and talk to Gage. When I stepped on the back porch, he glanced over at me. "Hey, Rhett."

I stared at him in shock. "You call this a grill? Looks more like a rocket ship."

Gage smirked. "I am still a billionaire, you know."

"So what does this thing do?" I asked, going to a cooler in the corner of the patio and pulling out a beer. "For what I'm assuming it cost, tell me it blows you."

Gage chuckled as he closed the lid. "It grills, smokes, and there's a griddle inside if I wanted to cook that way. Best meat you've ever tasted—and you can tell Dad I said so."

"Yeah, you know the whole 'kill the messenger' thing?" I teased.

He took a swig from his beer. "True. Hey, there's something I've been meaning to talk to you about."

"Shoot."

He went to the patio table and sat, gesturing I should do the same.

"Shit."

"It's good news," he replied, looking up at me.

I sat down, waiting.

He folded his hands atop the table. "I checked the investments I made for your brokerage account, and one of the businesses you invested in blew up."

My lips parted. "Blew up how? Like with a bomb?"

His smile was growing by the second. "I mean you have enough money for a down payment on that plot of land, maybe even a little extra to start putting in the water and electric infrastructure."

My jaw was hanging on the floor at this point. "You're shitting me."

Gage shook his head.

"But that wasn't supposed to happen for another eight years!"

"Caught a lucky break," he said with a shrug.

My throat felt tight. "You know you work toward something so long you start to wonder if it's ever going to happen."

Gage said, "I never had a doubt."

"I had doubts. A lot of doubts. Especially last year when I found out..." My throat closed up, and I absently rubbed the place on the back of my neck where the last spot had been removed.

Gage held his hand out for me to shake. "Congratulations, Rhett. You did it."

I gripped his hand, giving him a hug. "Thank you, brother."

After we hugged, he shook his head at me. "You fucker, I told you I would have bought it for you five years ago. I had the money. Still do."

"Yeah, but then it wouldn't have felt like mine." I glanced through the screen door where I saw Mags, Cora, and Farrah chatting at the kitchen table. "And now it can be ours."

59

MAGNOLIA

I FELL asleep on the way home Sunday, feeling more at peace than I had in a really long time. I remembered living in Austin, going to work, taking courses, and still feeling like I'd never get any closer to my dream of owning my own salon, much less having a family of my own.

Now, all within a few months, my life was falling together in a way I'd never even hoped or dreamed, but there was still something missing: my best friend.

When the car slowed at the city limits, I woke from dozing, seeing the streetlights that lined Main Street. "We're home," I said.

"Just ten more minutes 'til we get to my place," he said.

But I shook my head as I sat up straight. "Can you take me to my house?"

He looked over at me, studying me with dark hazel eyes. "Are you sure?"

I nodded.

"I'm so fucking proud of you."

I grinned. "You make me better, Rhett Griffen."

He smiled back at me, turning off Main Street to go toward my place. Cooper's truck was there, but it was still too early for them to have gone to bed. "Can you wait for me, just in case?" I asked.

He nodded. "I'll be here."

I took a deep breath, getting out of the car and smoothing my cotton dress over my legs. The closer I got to the front door, the more nervous I got. Cam and I had never gone a week without talking, but she'd also never said anything as hurtful as she had last week.

I hoped we could move forward as friends, even if that relationship was changing.

When I got to the door, I realized it didn't feel like my home, even with all my decorations on the walls and most of my stuff inside. My sense of home, my life, was changing too.

I lifted my hand, knocking on the door, and when it opened, I saw Cooper standing there. He looked from me to the driveway and said, "I'm gonna wait with Rhett."

I let out a small laugh as he beelined past me to my car.

But when I looked back to the house, I saw Cam standing in the living room in her light blue pajamas and gray slippers, her arms folded across her chest. "You didn't have to knock. It's your house too."

The hurt in her voice, the anger, almost made me want to turn around and hide. I hated this fighting, hated worrying about what she'd say next to hurt me, but I needed to be brave too. "We need to talk."

She nodded, stepping aside, and went to sit on our

couch in the living room. We'd found it by a dumpster five years ago and bought curtains at the thrift store to reupholster it. It actually looked really cool, even for a dumpster couch.

We'd done so much life together, built a home together. But now this was the space I knew would take us forward or backward.

Cam looked at me. "You wanted to talk?"

I nodded, swirling my ring around my thumb. "It's been a hard week after what happened."

"You ran away," Cam said. "I haven't heard from you, haven't seen you in a week. The only reason I knew you were okay was because Rhett told Cooper you were staying with him."

I ran my hand over the back of my neck. "I've learned I have a problem with running away from the people who hurt me, and I'm trying to work on it. But I need you to know, Cam, you did hurt me. A lot."

Her expression softened. "Don't you know how awful I feel about it too? We were supposed to live in this house for six months while I dated around, fell in love. It wasn't supposed to be like this." Tears rolled down her cheeks, and she wiped them away. "I feel like shit for letting you down. I know you don't have money to handle the rent alone or wait on the deposit. So I talked to my parents, and they said they would cover it on your new place until we got the deposit back."

Relief swept over me as I realized how much stress that financial burden had placed on me. "I think I heard about needing to buy the stuff for the wedding and needing to pay the lease and something snapped. I've been working toward this dream of owning a salon for so long that I'm afraid of it slipping away from me at the last moment."

"That would never happen. If anyone's going to put in the work and find a way to make it happen, it's you."

I studied her expression, because sometimes I didn't have that much faith in myself. "You mean it?"

She nodded. "Look at you and all you've done! Maybe part of me feels left behind because you still have all these opportunities ahead of you, and my life is changing so much. I'm going to be a mom and a wife. I have two whole people to consider now."

"Cam..." I shook my head. "I've been feeling left behind because you're getting the man and the family like you always dreamed. I don't ever want to lose you." The dam broke at those words, at the hurt and worry I'd been feeling. "You're not just my friend. You're my family."

She crossed the couch, hugging me and crying too. "I don't want to lose you either." We held on to each other, crying. "I'm sorry about what I said about Rhett. I don't know what I'd do in your position, but I'm so happy you're giving him a chance. He loves you so much."

My heart warmed as she pulled back. "I love him too. He got me to talk to my mom this weekend."

Cam's jaw dropped. "WHAT? Tell me everything."

As we sat on the couch, I told her all about seeing my mom and catching up with her.

"That's amazing," Cam said. "Maybe she could work at your salon one day. Lord knows we need a good nail person around here."

The wheels in my head were turning, but soon got interrupted by a knock on the door. Rhett and Cooper were looking at us through the screen door like a couple of lost puppies.

Cooper yelled, "We wanted to make sure you two didn't kill each other!"

Rhett held up a plastic bag and a drink tray. "And we brought food!"

Cam giggled. "Looks like it's not just us two in the family anymore."

I smiled, hugging her close. "No, but it's even better."

60

RHETT

COOPER and I were getting dressed in the guest bedroom of Camryn's parents' house, and he kept fiddling with his tie.

"Let me get it," I said, going to adjust it.

"Thanks." He took a breath and straightened his suit jacket. "I haven't worn a tie since high school, and I'm pretty sure it had a zipper."

I chuckled. "There's a first and last for everything, right?"

Coop nodded. "Better be my first and last wedding."

From the bedroom door, Camryn's dad said, "Agree."

We both looked over our shoulders at him, leaning against the frame. "It's about that time," he said. "Ready to go?"

Cooper nodded, adjusted his cowboy hat. "Yes, sir. Been ready since I first laid eyes on your daughter."

Cam's dad chuckled. "Right answer. Let's get you two married."

I followed the two of them out to the back door. Coop

had to go out first and walk his mom and dad to their chairs, then Mags and Cam came out from Cam's old bedroom. Mags had on this pretty blue sleeveless dress that brushed the floor and showed just the right amount of cleavage. "Beautiful," I breathed. Then I remembered Cam was there too.

She looked gorgeous in a two-piece white dress, the top all lacy and the bottom flowing around her legs and gold sandals. "You're a beautiful bride, Camryn," I said and went to give her a hug.

She hugged me back. "Thank you, Rhett."

I stepped back and looked around. "Is it our time to go?"

Dina said, "It sure is. Let me get out there first." Dina gave Camryn a long hug and then patted my shoulder before going out the back door. As it opened, I could hear soft guitar strings playing.

Maggie turned, facing her friend. "The last time we're both single girls."

Cam's face softened. "We haven't been single girls since that first rodeo. We just didn't know it then."

Maggie smiled and hugged her friend tight. "I'm so happy for you."

Cam squeezed her back, her eyes closed in the embrace. My heart warmed at the sight of the two of them. There were so many kinds of love in this world, and friendship had to be one of the best ways to experience love.

They let go of each other, and I extended my arm for Maggie. She easily slipped her hand through the crook of my elbow, holding a white and blue bouquet in the other hand.

We stepped outside together, going down the short aisle where a small group of family and friends had gathered for the wedding. Guitar strings played as we walked together, and when we reached the end, Mags and I parted ways, me going to stand next to Cooper, her on the opposite side.

Cooper had his hands linked in front of him, and I patted his shoulder. "This is it."

His smile wobbled. "It sure is."

The back door opened, and Cam and her dad stepped out. Everyone turned to watch her walk the aisle, but my eyes were on my best friend. His jaw shook, and his eyes filled with moisture.

I don't think any of us imagined it going this way for him or Camryn, but seeing the way he looked at her right now, the way she smiled back at him, tears falling down her cheeks—I knew it couldn't have happened any other way.

Just like it had to happen this way with Maggie and me.

We had to go through all those hardships, all this growth, to be ready for each other, to start a life together on solid ground we leveled and fertilized throughout the years. I glanced over at her, seeing how beautiful she was watching our friends with tears in her eyes.

If there was a more perfect moment, I didn't know it could exist. That is, until I watched Cam and Cooper say "I do."

WE WENT to the township hall for a reception with more guests than were invited to the ceremony. Music played over the speakers, and Mags came with me to the dance floor so I could spin her around.

So much had changed since our first dance after the rodeo, but I had yet to tell her about the biggest change— that I was finally buying the land I already saw as ours.

"What are you thinking about?" she asked, looking up at me.

I held our intertwined hands to my chest. "I'm thinking about our life together, and there's news I've been wanting to tell you once I had some details in place. Now feels like the perfect time."

She gave me a curious look. "What is it?"

I couldn't help the grin sliding across my lips. "I'm buying my grandpa's land. The sale will be final a month from Monday."

Her mouth fell open. "What?! I thought you needed longer to save!"

"One of my investments did well enough to move up the timeline." I held her closer to me, just bursting with happiness. "I talked with the banker, and we can start moving forward with infrastructure too. A few years from now, we'll have enough saved to build a home. Picture it —a three-bedroom house, wraparound porch, a picture window overlooking our magnolia tree. A yellow door, just like you like."

Her eyes filled with moisture as I spoke each word. "*Our* magnolia tree?"

I nodded. "It was always for you, Mags. A piece of me always knew it had to be you."

She leaned her head into my chest, holding me tighter while we swayed. "It sounds like a dream."

"Open your eyes, baby. It's all real."

She grinned up at me. "I love you, Rhett Griffen. And I can't wait to see our home come to life."

I kissed her lips until the song closed. As we broke apart, I saw her dad on the dance floor a few feet from us. "Mind if I cut in?" he asked.

I nodded. "Of course," and he swirled Maggie away.

I stood to the side, watching them for a moment, but Maggie wasn't smiling like before.

In fact, it looked like something was really, really wrong.

61

MAGGIE

DAD SMILED DOWN AT ME. "That was a beautiful ceremony."

I nodded in agreement. "I liked the smaller group. Made it feel even more special."

He agreed. "Tell me you'll give me more than two weeks warning for your wedding."

I laughed. "I promise. It's moving that direction, but I think it's still too soon for us to move in together."

His eyebrows drew together. "Why would you move in when you have the rental?"

It struck me that so much had passed that I still hadn't told him about losing the rental house. Cam's wedding and reuniting with my mom seemed like such bigger topics. But I might as well ask now. "Our landlord is ending our lease early. Think I can stay in my old bedroom until I find a place?"

Now his lips pulled down. "I don't think that's a good idea."

"Seriously?" I asked, confused. "I can chip in for groceries and stuff."

"It's not that."

"You got the electric fixed, didn't you?" I asked.

His frown grew deeper.

"Dad, what is it? You always said I was welcome at home."

He glanced down. "It's Cam's night. Let's just enjoy the music."

"Dad, I can't just enjoy the music now. I can tell something's wrong. What's going on?"

He shook his head, letting out a long breath. "It's embarrassing to say."

"Tell me," I urged him, forgetting about the music altogether.

"The house is going into foreclosure."

I covered my mouth, stepping back from him. "*Foreclosure?* How?"

He looked around, whispering, "Can we go outside to talk?"

"*Please*," I said, needing an explanation and needing it now. I followed him outside to the front steps and around the side of the building, feeling everyone watching us on the way. But this couldn't wait until tomorrow. "Dad," I said when we had a semblance of privacy. "Tell me what's going on."

He shook his head, and I could feel the tightness in his voice as he spoke. "I lost one of my biggest contracts a couple months before you came home. I had to use up what little savings I had to keep the lights on while I looked for other options. And then the electrical issue came up, and I had to file a home insurance claim on it. I have a high deductible plan, so I had to miss a couple mortgage payments to cover it. And then the truck broke down, and I've had to pay that because insurance only covers collisions, *and* I've been out of work while it's getting fixed. I've been hurting, but I didn't want you to worry about it."

Concern filled each of my veins as I took in my dad, looking so much older than I'd ever noticed. "But can't you miss a mortgage payment or two?"

"I've missed six. The bank technically only had to give me four, but since I've been good this long, they let it slide. But I'm out of options, Mags. I either lose the house or sell my truck, and with it being in the shop, I don't think I could sell it soon enough to make a difference, then there's the issue of me getting another job since I've been out of work and they had to find another trucker..."

I could feel the ache, the worry gutting him from the inside out. He must have felt all alone, dealing with this while putting on a brave face for me. "Why didn't you say anything?"

He ran his hand through thinning hair. "I didn't want to tell my daughter that her old man's a failure."

It was just that much of a reminder that even though I loved and looked up to my dad, he was still human. Things could come up and take you off the path you thought you were on in just a few months' time.

"How much do you owe to get out of foreclosure?"

His brows furrowed. "Maggie, don't you dare put your life on hold for me. I'm a grown man—I can figure it out."

"I can't let you be homeless, Dad," I said, my voice

breaking. "What other kind of job are you going to get with your back the way it is? Where would you rent?"

"Worst case scenario, I'll sleep in my truck," Dad replied. "Please, don't worry about me."

Frustration bubbled up in my chest. "*Don't worry about you?* Dad, if you would have set your pride aside for a second, you could have told me, and we would have worked out a plan months ago. But instead, you kept it to yourself, and your house, the home I grew up in, is going to be taken away!"

"Mags..."

"Don't," I said, tears falling down my cheeks, because I knew what it would take to fix this. And it meant giving up everything I'd worked so hard for, putting my dreams on hold to keep a roof over my father's head. "How much do you owe to get out of foreclosure?" I repeated.

He looked to the ground.

"Dad!"

His chest heaved as he looked up at me, and he uttered, "Ten thousand dollars, give or take."

My mouth fell open. "Are you kidding me?"

He shook his head. "It's what I owe plus fees."

I stepped back, my hand to my chest.

I knew what it would take to help him, what I'd have to give up.

Dad gave me life.

He raised me.

He'd been there for me and supported me through hair school.

And now it was my turn to help him, no matter how much it hurt.

From the sidewalk, I heard Rhett call, "Mags?"

Dad and I both looked his way, and I wiped at my face. "Yeah?"

"We're about to see Cam and Coop off. You ready?"

I nodded and turned to follow Rhett.

Dad held on to my wrist. "Mags... don't hate me."

I shook my head at him. "I love you, Dad. To the ends of the earth." But it still hurt like hell.

When I reached Rhett, he put his arm around me and kissed the top of my head. "Everything okay?"

My throat felt tight as I said, "I'm not completely sure."

We walked to the steps of the township hall where Dina was passing out sparklers. We each lit them up and cheered as Cam and Cooper walked under the sparks to the pickup waiting for them along the street.

Our friends from Austin had all gone in together to book Cam and Cooper a weekend stay at a cabin outside of Austin as their wedding gift. Selfishly, I wished she would hang around Cottonwood Falls a little longer, leave for her honeymoon next weekend so we could talk this out, but I think this was part of us both growing up.

Her husband, her family had to come before me.

And I needed to learn to stand on my own two feet and make decisions—with or without her.

62

RHETT

AFTER THE WEDDING, Mags and I drove back to her place, and I could tell something was off.

"What did you talk about with your dad?" I asked as we undressed and changed into pajamas.

Maggie slipped a nightgown over her head. "I told him I'd need to stay in my old bedroom for a while."

"You know you can stay with me," I offered. I kind of thought it was a given.

She looked up at me, blinking quickly. "Dad said I couldn't stay with him because his house is in foreclosure."

My jaw dropped. "What?"

She nodded. "Sounds like it was a case of one thing after another and not being able to catch up or humble himself enough to ask for help before things got dire."

"Is he declaring bankruptcy?" I asked.

She wrapped her arms around herself and shrugged. "I don't know." She looked so small, so worried, holding herself like that. "But I can't let him lose his house, not when I have the savings to cover it."

I pulled her in, hugging her. Maggie had the biggest heart. "That's sweet of you. But what about the salon? Didn't you need all your savings for your down payment on the loan?"

"I did. I do," she said.

My stomach sank further. "So it's his house or your salon? Do you think Rhonda would do rent to own or something like that?"

She shook her head against my chest. "It's her retirement plan. She put everything she had into that salon and didn't set any aside for herself. And she needs to get hip surgery. This would delay all that for her. God, I feel awful."

A tightness in my chest started to form. "What are you going to do?"

She stepped back from me, sitting on the edge of the bed. "I think the only thing I can do is ask Rhonda if she'll wait another six months or so for me to buy the shop while I try to come up with the money. And hopefully Dad can pay me back once he's back on his feet."

"And if she doesn't agree?" I asked. "Doesn't it make the joint worse to put off a replacement?"

The blue in her eyes was gray as she took me in, full of unspoken words I probably didn't want to hear.

"What?" I asked her.

Her eyes traced over my face, like she was trying to remember it. "I can't stay here without a job."

"Then I'll buy you the salon," I said as I sat by her. "Fuck the land. I have savings too."

Her eyes were wide. "I wouldn't let you do that,

Rhett. I saw how excited you were about that land. I'd never be the one to take that look away from you."

I leaned my head against hers. I knew we would have struggles come up that we'd have to face in life, but everything had just been going so well. I hadn't imagined that things would change so quickly. "But you can't take yourself away from me either, Maggie."

She held the back of my neck, kissing me softly. "I love you, Rhett Griffen."

"We're gonna figure this out, right?" I asked. "You can't leave me. Not again."

But instead of answering, she kissed me again. And again.

I held on to her, hearing her message without any words.

She didn't know how things would go, so we needed to savor this moment we had with each other. Even if the thought of losing her had my throat tightening in my chest and my eyes stinging with unshed tears, my future unraveling before it even had a chance to begin.

I laid her back on the bed, kissing her and savoring everything about her. The pillowy softness of her lips, the soft scent of her perfume, the way her hair tickled my cheeks as I nipped at her ear, her neck.

The way she held on to my neck and shoulders like if she didn't, she'd simply float away.

I etched into my memory the feel of her full chest under mine, the softness of her stomach contrasting my hard core.

How, every time I swirled my fingers around her clit, she let out a soft whimper.

Her voice touched every part of my soul as she said, "Rhett, I need you closer."

Feeling desperate to fulfill her wishes, I undid my pants and slid them off as I crawled over her on the bed. I didn't bother with a condom, knowing I would be closer with Maggie than I ever had or ever would be with another person.

Her eyes were wide as she looked up at me. "You need a condom."

I shook my head. "It's you, Maggie. It was always you."

She pulled her panties to the side, and I plunged into her hot, tight sex, letting out a choked moan as she whispered my name. She felt so good against my unsheathed cock, wet, warm, ribbed and so much more than I had words to describe.

"Rhett," she breathed.

My name on her tongue.

How many more times would I hear that?

How many times would I hear it in my dreams after she left? My waking nightmare of life without her?

As I picked up my pace, her head rolled back, but I said, "Look at me, Magnolia. Eyes on me."

Our eyes met, and I saw moisture building in hers.

Tears matching mine.

They spilled over my cheeks, falling onto her chest as I put everything I had into the thrusts, into this time we had together.

And when I came inside of her, she cried out my name, taking every drop I had to give, every ounce of love and hope I had in my heart.

And when we finished, I fell to the bed beside her, holding her close as she sobbed into my chest.

Because we both knew we had everything in each other.

And that meant we had everything to lose.

63

MAGNOLIA

I TOLD Rhonda I'd be a little late to work Monday morning and instead drove to the Cottonwood Falls Bank.

I knew I had to do this before I found out what she said, because I was so close to making the selfish choice—the one that would keep me in town with Rhett no matter the cost. But my dad had raised me, alone, after Mom left, putting my needs first even when he was reeling from a broken heart. I had to do this for him, because this town, it wasn't home without him, without a house to go back to.

The teller at the first window welcomed me over. She'd been a few years ahead of me in school, a pretty, curvy blond named Jessica.

"Hi, Maggie," she said. "How can I help you?"

"I'm here to pay down a loan," I said.

She raised her eyebrows. "Oh? I wasn't aware you had a loan here yet."

I whispered now in case anyone in the bank overheard and decided to spread gossip. "My dad's home is going into foreclosure; I want to make sure that doesn't happen."

Her green eyes opened wider. "That is so kind of you, Maggie. I can't share the details of how much that would be, but if you want to make a direct contribution, I can help you with that."

I nodded, thinking back to the number Dad said. "Ten thousand dollars," I said, hoping it would be enough.

She blinked. "Okay." She began working at the computer and said, "I'm assuming you would like that to come from your savings account?"

My heart felt jittery. "That's right." I laid my hands on the laminate countertop, trying to steady myself. "From my savings account."

She looked at me over the computer. "Are you sure about this, Maggie?"

Was I sure?

Yes.

Did it feel good?

Hell fucking no.

But I knew my dad would do the same for me if it ever came down to it. He'd sell everything, give me the shirt off his back if I asked. That's what family did. That's what we did for each other, just the two of us against the world after Mom left.

"Yes, I'm sure," I said.

She printed out a slip and said, "Sign this. I want you to know once this is done, it can't be reversed."

"I know," I whispered.

She looked from me to the computer and slowly typed

several buttons, like she was giving me a chance to back out.

I didn't.

"The transfer is complete. And between the two of us?" She leaned forward, lowering her voice, "Your dad is officially out of foreclosure."

I let out a teary sigh. "Thank you, Jess."

She smiled at me. "You're welcome, Mags."

I walked out of the bank, feeling the weight of what I'd just done. Sitting in my car, I had to take a few minutes to decompress, to tell myself that it would be okay, that I would figure out a way to own the salon and be with Rhett.

Even if it didn't seem possible right now.

Even if all the odds seemed to be stacked against us.

Because the odds had already been stacked against us before—I came back to this town hating and hurting, and Rhett had patiently turned around my hardened heart. I had to believe we could make this work too. Because if I couldn't believe, I'd be unable to move right now, take one step in front of the other.

But first I needed to see my dad.

I drove a few minutes from the bank to my childhood home. And for a moment, I just sat outside, taking it in. The tan hardie board siding, the lilac bushes on either side of the front door, and the lawn that liked to grow through all the cracks in the sidewalk.

It wasn't a mansion by any means. It really wasn't that different from the houses on either side, but this house had always been home. I didn't have a memory in my life where it wasn't a safe place for me to rest my head at night or bring a friend over or just hang out with my family. It housed all the good times, before Mom left, where it was the three of us, one happy family. It was the place where Dad and I recovered, made new memories, just the two of us. And it was the place I could come back to, no matter how far I moved away. This was our windmill.

A commercial came over the radio, and I shut the car off, opening the door and getting out. The walk down the sidewalk felt normal and heavy at the same time. I'd done this a million times before, but always as the child who needed to be rescued. Never as the one who helped my dad.

Maybe this was the lesson I needed to learn from all of this—the fact that I didn't need to be saved. I could figure things out, no matter how hard they got. I could survive the lows and hold out hope for the highs.

I usually walked right into the house, but today felt different, especially seeing his pickup out front. Dad was out of work until his semi got fixed and grappling with the disappointment of not being where he thought he'd be in life. I knocked on the door.

Eileen let out a warning bark. "Come in," he yelled through the door.

I walked inside, noticing his Gibson Trucking hat hanging on the rack at the entrance. He usually wore it all day every day.

I picked it up, holding the bill in my hands. A few steps into the house, I saw my dad sitting in his recliner, watching TV, still in a pair of shorts and an old T-shirt. Unshaven. Depressed.

"Dad?" I said, looking at him.

He turned his head toward me, and I noticed the

redness in his eyes before he looked back to the TV. "I know I need to get up and do something, but I need a day to wallow, okay?"

I looked down at the hat in my hands and then back to my dad. This wasn't him. This wasn't how the Gibsons did life.

I walked to the TV and turned it off. "Get up."

He studied me. "Why? What's the freaking point?"

I shook my head at him. "Do you remember when Mom left and I was losing all my hair and I told you I wanted to do school online? Just stop showing up?"

His jaw tensed.

"You told me that Gibsons don't quit. We might not be the best at something. We might not be the most popular or the most attractive, but we're going to show up, for each other, for our commitments, every goddamned day, because that's who we are, and that's what we do."

He looked down at his lap.

"I know you weren't lying then, and I'm reminding you now. So get out of the chair, take a shower, and put on this hat." I put it against his chest. "It's time to show up."

Tears fell down his cheeks. "I messed up everything."

I shook my head at him, feeling so sorry to see him this low. "Stand up, Dad."

He got up, looking at me. He held his hands out, then dropped them by his sides. "I'm up."

My lips quivered into half a smile, then fell. "Dad, the house is yours."

His eyebrows drew together. "What do you mean?"

"I mean I paid the bill. You're not in foreclosure anymore."

His mouth opened in shock. "Maggie, I told you not to do that."

I blinked quickly, on the verge of tears. "Remember who we are? We show up for each other, Dad, always." He hugged me, and I held on too, because I needed all the strength he could give me. "Now I need you to show up for yourself," I said into his shoulder. "I know there's a solution here; you just need to find it."

"I promise, I will."

We said a tearful goodbye before I had to leave for the salon.

And as I drove to Rhonda's, I tried to remind myself: there's a solution here. I just needed to find it.

64

MAGNOLIA

I WENT TO WORK, determined to talk with Rhonda about my options now that my financial situation had changed, but we were slammed with appointments all day. The hours seemed to drag by, and each time I saw her take an ibuprofen for her hip or cringe after bending to get something, my heart hurt even more.

I wasn't just hurting my dream; I was affecting her life too, and it had a weight the size of Texas settling on my heart.

Even though I usually closed up, I asked her to stay behind in this shop we both loved so much so we could talk.

With the sign turned to "Sorry, we're closed" and the doors locked up, Rhonda asked me, "What would you like to talk about, darling?"

I wrung my hands in front of me, already feeling on the verge of tears. Rhonda was more than a boss—she was family. She gave me my first job in high school, helped me through alopecia, and had given me my first big break.

I didn't want to disappoint her any more than I wanted to leave this town.

"Is everything okay?" Rhonda asked.

I blinked quickly. I had to get through this without crying. "Rhonda, I was wondering if you'd be willing to postpone the sale until I've been here a year."

Her eyebrows drew together. "Oh, honey, you don't need more time to impress me. I've been so amazed by how you've embraced your role here. I was actually going to ask you if you wanted to move the sale up to next month. I truly believe this place will flourish under your care."

Tears stung my eyes. "That's not it."

"What do you mean?"

I glanced around the salon, wishing with all my heart this wasn't the case. "My dad needed my help, financially, and it set me back quite a bit. I won't have the down payment until at least June of next year."

"Oh, Maggie..." she said softly, bringing her fingertips to her chin.

I waited, holding my breath for her answer.

"I wish I could, but my doctor is saying I really need hip replacement surgery." Now she was blinking quickly. "I needed that sale money for my surgery."

I hadn't thought it possible, but I felt even worse now. "Rhonda, I'm so sorry."

She held up her hands, cutting me off. Her eyes were red as she said, "I know you did what you had to do, but I can't afford to wait for you to save the money. I need to find someone else to purchase the salon."

My lips parted.

"Can you call your appointments and let them know you're taking off at the end of the week?"

"Rhonda..."

She shook her head. "I have to figure this out for my own health, see if I can find someone to take your place as soon as possible. I can't afford to have two people working here."

I looked at this woman I loved, her chin held high, her eyes tinged with red, and knew she had no other choice but to be strong, even if I felt like falling apart.

65

RHETT

MAGGIE SAID she would come to my place after work, and as I cooked supper for us, I spent every second praying that she and Rhonda had come to a solution. That everything would be alright.

Please let it be alright.

I put the lid on the pot of simmering green beans and went to set the table. As I carried dishes from the kitchen, I heard the soft purr of a car engine. A glance out the front window told me it was Maggie's car.

I couldn't read her through the windshield, so I waited until she got out of the car, feeling like I couldn't catch my breath.

When she saw me through the window, her lips tugged down at the corners.

That simple action almost brought me to my knees.

On shaking legs, I walked to the door, opening it, and she fell into my arms, already crying. "Rhonda said she couldn't wait."

"Fuck," I breathed, ready to cry right along with her.

"She said I need to have my stuff out of the salon by the end of the week."

Fighting to keep it together, I said, "You know what? We'll open a salon in this damn house. I'll call my brothers and they can help me tear out the dining room and build you a chair and a table and anything you need. I'm sure my boss will forgive me and—"

"Rhett." She looked up at me, wiping her eyes. "I can't do that to Rhonda. If her salon loses business, it affects the sale. She needs it for her hip replacement."

"Well maybe we find out who's buying it next and you see if they'll let you work there?"

She shook her head sadly. "I've always wanted to own my own salon. That's not happening here."

"Then Rutlage," I began.

"Already has four salons and a new one opening next week," she said. "I already looked into that. And the next three towns. I spent all Sunday looking for options that would keep me here. Even a predatory lender wouldn't give me enough to open the salon. If I could put Rhonda's salon on a credit card, I would."

"Let me buy it for you," I said, my hands holding her face. She had to let me do this for her.

She looked up at me. "You planted that tree years ago, knowing you wanted that land to be your own. I wouldn't ask you to do that any more than you'd ask me to give up the salon."

"I wasn't planning on getting it for another eight years!" I argued. "So what if I have to wait a little longer?"

She lifted her chin, just as stubborn as ever. "Goddamn it, Rhett, I told you I'm not taking that away from you."

"Then I'm moving," I said, my jaw tight. "I'm moving wherever you're going. Wherever you think that dream exists for you. You can't take you away from me."

She reached up, wiping away tears that I hadn't known had fallen down my cheeks. "Rhett, I can't let you ruin your life for me." A tear rolled over her cheek. "These months with you have been amazing, but we both know your life is bigger than us. You have family in town who you love, a grandpa who needs to see you every week. Girls who definitely need you to coach them next year, a best friend about to have a baby, and a heart bigger than Texas. I can't take that away from them or this town. But I can't hang around here either, hoping another chance will come along for me to do what I love."

My throat felt tight. "You can't do this."

"I don't see any other options."

I hung my head. "Maggie. Please."

She reached up on her tiptoes and placed a kiss on my cheek. "You lived your life without me once. You've never lived your life without Cottonwood Falls."

"Maggie..."

"I love you, Rhett Griffen."

My heart shattered around her words because they weren't enough to make her stay. "I will always love you, Magnolia Ray Gibson."

66

MAGNOLIA

I DROVE AWAY from Rhett's house, sobbing, feeling like a piece of me was missing, only to be found in that little white house with the sunflowers out front. The farther I got, the more I realized I couldn't leave Rhett behind. Not a second time.

Why was I settling for an outcome that made me miserable?

I couldn't forget who I was. I *had* to find a way to make it work—I had to show up, just like I told my dad to do. There was no other option.

My best friend was here, carrying her first baby. My dad was here, and only getting older. The love of my life had a dream to start a life with me, and I couldn't picture anything more beautiful than experiencing it with him.

There was only one person I knew who might be able to help me without completely upending their life, so I drove.

I drove and I drove.

I drove for two and half hours until I was parked in

front of the pretty brick house with the bright yellow front door. Rhett had told me before that Gage offered to buy each sibling in their family their own land and ranch, but they were all too proud to take him up on it.

I wasn't too proud.

Not anymore.

Not with the love of my life on the line.

I walked up the driveway, past the black Tesla and white minivan, more confident by the step that my dreams really could come true—that I could make this work.

When I got to the front door, I knocked and rang the bell, because when you knew the person you wanted to spend forever with, you didn't have patience for anything standing in the way, not even yourself.

The door opened, and Farrah appeared in a pair of black biker shorts, a loose blue T-shirt, and a ball cap, a worried and horrified expression on her face. "Maggie, are you okay?"

I realized I must look awful, all my makeup cried off my face, my skin blotchy, my eyes red and hair a mess. But I didn't care.

"I need to talk to Gage," I said.

"He's out back with the kids. Is everything okay? Is someone hurt?"

"No one's hurt," I said, walking past her to the back door before I lost my nerve, before this glimmer of hope could be crushed before my eyes. I slid the door open, finding Gage and the kids in all four corners of the yard, passing a baseball between them.

He had his arm pulled back for a throw when he

caught sight of me, and the baseball came flying my way, nailing me right in the head.

I saw stars, wobbling and falling to the ground. There was a rush of noise around me and a splitting pain in my head as I blinked to clear my vision.

"Oh my God, Maggie, are you okay?" Gage asked, kneeling over me. "Back up, kids, give her some space."

They *maybe* moved an inch.

But I looked up at him, pressing my hand to the lump growing on my forehead, determined to get this out. "Gage, can I borrow ten thousand dollars to buy the salon? I have a great business plan."

"Maggie," he said, but I wouldn't let him finish. I had to make my pitch, even if it was while lying here on the ground.

"The salon already does well financially, but I think I can bring in nail care to really up our bottom line. I expect with some careful saving, I could pay you back in a year, maybe even less if I could live with Rhett. And I don't want to give you a sob story because I'm sure you hear them all the time, but I will if I have to because——"

"Maggie."

"I really need the money because my dad's house went into foreclosure and Rhett offered to buy the salon for me, but I can't let him do that because then he can't afford the land and——"

"Oh my God, Maggie, I will pay you ten thousand dollars to shut up. Just let me look at your head."

Now I had big fat tears rolling down my cheeks. "Really?"

He let out a small laugh and nodded. "You're just as

stubborn as Rhett. Now tell me, did you hit your head on the way down?"

I scanned my body, only feeling the big throbbing spot on my forehead. "I don't think so."

"Okay, let's sit you up. Levi, help me out."

The guys got on either side of me, helping me to a sitting position, and soon Farrah was handing me a baggie of ice to put on my forehead.

"That was quick," I said to her.

She chuckled. "When you have three kids, you have to be ready for a few bumps and bruises."

"True," Gage agreed. He held up his hand in front of my face. "Follow my fingers." He waved them back and forth, then up and down.

"Good. Now look at my phone light." He pointed it at me and turned on the flashlight. "Good," he repeated. "Feeling nauseous or anything?"

I shook my head.

"Okay, let's get inside and we can talk about the salon."

AN HOUR LATER, I was leaving Gage and Farrah's house with a check for ten thousand dollars and a bag of ice tied to my forehead with a tea towel. I couldn't believe I was holding that much money in my hands.

I couldn't believe that after all the chaos of this morning, I was going to be able to live happily ever after with Rhett.

Cam was right. I could figure this out. I could make my life happen instead of letting it happen to me.

But then a new fear struck my heart that almost had me swerving off the road.

Last time I had broken up with Rhett, he had a new woman in his bed that night.

What if this sent him spiraling back to what he'd done all those years ago?

The thought made my gut churn, and I had to take deep breaths not to be sick.

Even though it was late, I was planning to go to Rhonda's and beg her to consider me again now that I had the money. Instead, when I got back to Cottonwood Falls, I knew I needed to handle the most important matter.

I took dirt roads to Rhett's house, feeling every opposing emotion at war in my chest, amazed my body could hold so much fear and so much longing at the same time.

Maybe that's what love was—giving all of yourself to someone who could choose to destroy you or comfort you.

Seeing his house at the end of the road, I knew I'd soon find out which one he chose.

But when I pulled up to the front, I realized his truck wasn't in the driveway.

My heart sank, but I stupidly got out of my car anyway, walking to the front door and banging right below that stupid sign. No matter how long I knocked, he didn't answer.

He wasn't home, and my mind had a million fears about where he could be.

I backed up against the door, fighting tears, and slid down to sit. All of a sudden, I was eighteen again, finding the guy I loved with another woman, ready to tell him yes to his marriage proposal because I'd finally gotten over the fear of forever.

And then I saw headlights coming down the road.

My heart, my battered heart, leapt with hope. Hoping it was him and not someone else coming back home.

I strained my eyes to see if it was, and eventually his truck came into view.

I scrambled up from the ground, already walking to meet him in the driveway. He hopped out of the truck, its engine still running, and said, "Maggie. Oh my gosh, are you okay?" He gently touched the lump on my forehead, and I winced.

"What happened?" he asked.

"Gage threw a baseball at my head."

"He WHAT?" Rhett said.

"It doesn't matter." I reached into my pocket, pulling out the folded check for ten thousand dollars. "Gage gave me the money I need to buy the salon. I'm staying. Rhett, I'm staying in Cottonwood Falls!"

He grinned big, picking me up and spinning me around. When he set me down, he said, "That's amazing, but I kind of already beat him to it."

My eyebrows drew together. "*What?*"

"After you left, I went to Rhonda's place and bought the salon."

"You have that much money?" I asked.

"I don't think you realize how much it takes to buy a hundred acres of land."

I let out a tearful laugh. "Rhett, why did you do that?"

He shook his head at me, brushing my hair away from my forehead. "Maggie, I know you thought owning that land was my dream. But it was never about the land.

My real dream was the life I'd get to share with you there."

Overcome with emotion, I fell into his arms, letting him hold me as I cried it out.

"Maggie, it's okay," he breathed, brushing my hair down my back. "We're together now."

I pulled back, wiping my eyes. "I'm so sorry. I think I was just worried that what happened back then would happen again and..."

He shook his head, holding me. "You know I never showed you what was in my garage."

"What do you mean?" I asked.

"Follow me." He reached into his pickup, turning it off, then held my hand as we walked to his garage. He let go of me for a second to slide the door up, and when I saw what was inside, my jaw dropped.

The entire garage was lined with wire art pieces, everything from wall décor to yard decorations and even wind chimes.

"This is what Lola was picking up that day," he explained, following me inside the garage. "When you started rooming with Cam, I saw Dina in the grocery store and she mentioned that she'd taken you both to the thrift store in Austin and how much you loved it. I got this crazy idea that maybe you could have a piece of me in your home even if I couldn't be there. So I made trips once a month to the thrift stores Dina mentioned with new pieces I'd made, hoping you'd find them. Hoping you'd have a piece of me."

Tears rolled down her cheeks. "You did that for me?"

I nodded. "Mags, I meant it when I said it was always you."

67

RHETT

ON TUESDAY, I went to pick Maggie up from the salon, *her* salon. She was spending the week cleaning, reorganizing, and decorating the place that was now called "Hair and Home." She was now selling my wire art and even bringing in a pedicure chair and added a space to do nails. Her mom happily agreed to start coming one day a week, and if there was enough demand for her services, she wanted to move back to Cottonwood Falls too. She came to a Sunday night dinner with Maggie's dad, and I swore there were some sparks between the two of them. Maybe Maggie and I weren't the only couple who would get a second chance.

When I pulled up along the curb, she came running to the truck, looking adorable in her Farley Trucking cap —courtesy of the trucking company where her dad worked now—paint-stained jeans and a white T-shirt. I got out of the pickup to meet her, hugging her tight and dropping a kiss on her pretty pink lips.

After knowing I could lose her, I was never taking a second for granted.

"Good to see you too," she said sweetly, smiling up at me from under her cap.

I grinned. "Ready to see Grandpa?"

She nodded. "Absolutely. Can you get him a regular Coke this time? I promised him last week that we'd smuggle one in."

I narrowed my gaze at her. "Grandpa's not supposed to have regular soda."

"He's eighty-seven," she retorted. "As far as I'm concerned, he could have actual coke if he wants it."

I rolled my eyes. She and Grandpa were both stubborn as mules. "Just this one time."

"Yes." She pulled her arm down in victory, and I reached over to tickle her side.

She squirmed away from me, yelling for me to stop. I did, but just so we could get in the truck and drive away from the salon. We went and grabbed the food from the diner and then drove the rest of the way to the retirement community.

Cam was already waiting by the door to greet us, her small bump visible through her scrubs.

"Look at you bumpin'!" Maggie said. "You're so freaking adorable."

Cam turned to the side, accentuating the small bump. "I feel like I'm cute pregnant now, but I'm going to be big, uncomfortable pregnant soon."

Maggie laughed. "I need to add maternity stuff to my

next visit to the city. Lord knows I already have tons of cute outfits for my future niece or nephew!"

I nodded. "It's taking over the house. Maybe I should put a baby in you for all the clothes we have left over."

Cam and Mags both rolled their eyes at me.

"What?"

Cam answered, "You better put a ring on it first."

I raised my eyebrows at her.

"I know, I know, do as I say, not as I do." She turned and started walking toward the common area where we always ate with Grandpa.

He was waiting for us at a corner table, his cowboy hat resting on the bench next to him. He struggled to get up as we approached, eventually straightening and hugging all three of us. As we sat down, he gave me a crinkle-eyed smile. "Have I mentioned how happy I am this one came back around?"

I chuckled. "You and me both."

Maggie hugged him and then started passing out the takeout containers. "I got you regular Coke," she whispered.

His eyes lit up. "That's it. I'm writing all the grandkids out of my will and putting you in it instead."

She laughed. "My evil plan is working."

I rolled my eyes at her, and Grandpa only chuckled. Then his face grew serious. And he grunted.

I looked up at him, confused by the change in attitude. "What gives?" I asked.

He shook his head. "Too damn bad you two couldn't be living out on the land. We were supposed to close on it today, you know."

"I know." I pointed my gaze toward the table, not

wanting him to see how disappointed I was about that. It was the one fly in the ointment. I had everything I wanted, but I still had to wonder—what next? Would Maggie and I ever be able to afford that land and a new build?

Grandpa said, "You should just take it."

All three of us swiveled our heads, staring at him.

"What?" He raised his hands. "I already have it in the will to go to you when I die. Seems stupid to wait until then. This way I could actually see you enjoy it."

My eyebrows went up. "Grandpa, you don't have to do that. I can save the money."

He narrowed his gaze at me. "You know you're not supposed to argue with an old guy."

Cam held up her French fry as she spoke. "I thought it was 'you're not supposed to argue with a drunk.'"

"Same difference," Grandpa muttered. "Have you seen the people around here?"

Cam covered her mouth as she laughed, and Mags admonished, "Grandpa Griffen."

He gave her the side-eye. "You know it's true." But then he looked at me. "When I look at you, I see myself. Same sense of humor, same determination. Same stubborn pride always getting in the way." All the smoke he'd blown quickly deflated. Because he was right. I had pride in spades.

"You want to do everything yourself, but look around!" Grandpa gestured at the four of us sitting here. "You're never alone, Rhett Griffen. You need to let your family help you, and you can bless them in return by enjoying the blessings they bring to you."

I tilted my head. "I don't feel like I deserve it," I

admitted. I'd messed up so much in life. Working hard made me feel like I'd earned what I had.

"Well, I'm pretty fucking sure you won't look at the lawyer when I'm dead and tell him to give it back to a corpse."

"Grandpa!" I said, half laughing.

Mags put her hand on my leg. "He wants you to be happy. We all do."

Grandpa tapped his nose. "I want you two to start a life together like Jane and I had, and I want to be here to see it all unfold." He brushed his hand over his hair. "With a really good hairs cut of course."

"Haircut," Maggie corrected.

He gave her a look like she was loopy. "You know I have more than one hair on my head, right?"

I chuckled and pointed at Mags. "He has a good point."

Maggie only shook her head at us. "Are you sure about the land, Grandpa Griffen?"

He nodded. "If Rhett doesn't take it, I'm giving it to you."

Her laugh warmed my heart. "You've got yourself a deal."

68

RHETT

Nine Months Later

I GREETED friends and family as they pulled up to our homestead. I wore a tux Maggie had picked out and a magnolia boutonniere, made from flowers on the tree in our new backyard.

Someone patted my shoulder from behind, and I turned to see Cooper holding baby Cadence in his arm. She was our flower girl at three months old, and my nieces Maya and Cora would be walking her down the aisle in a little stroller decorated with our wedding colors —cream and deep green.

"It's time to go," Cooper said.

I nodded, my stomach full of flutters. Still hadn't come up with a more manly description for butterflies—I was still working on my pride.

"You ready?" he asked.

Remembering his words from his wedding day, I said, "Been ready since I first laid eyes on her."

He grinned. "Right answer."

We walked back around the house, and he passed baby Cadence to his mom, who was helping keep the flower girls on track. Then, as guitar music started playing, I held out my arm for my mom and walked her down the aisle with everyone watching.

She looked up at me as we walked and said, "I thought this day might never come."

I laughed. "A gentleman never comes first, Mother."

She hit my arm. "Rhett!"

Everyone around us laughed, even though they hadn't heard my first comment.

The laughter died down as we reached the end of the aisle. I gave her a kiss on the cheek, and then she sat next to Dad and Grandpa Griffen while I continued to the altar made of reclaimed barnwood from the original Griffen homestead.

Music continued as Cooper and Camryn walked down the aisle together, and then Liv and Fletcher, Tyler and Henrietta, and finally Gage and Farrah.

With all my loved ones standing around me, the preacher said, "All rise for the bride."

I felt like everything moved in slow motion as the back door to our home opened, and Maggie stepped out with her dad.

All my breath left my lungs as my eyes connected with hers. Her sky-blue eyes caught every ray the sun had to give. Her cheeks were warm, and her red lips drew my attention, just begging to be kissed.

My eyes slid over her curves, noticing her dress with loose lace sleeves and a flowing tulle gown. It moved and swayed with her every step.

But so much more than her personality and her looks was the woman behind it all.

This woman had enough spark to light the night sky.

She had enough heart to put the ones she loved ahead of herself.

She had enough bravery to forgive and give second chances to people who might not deserve them.

And she had the drive and vision to create a business and a home that were safe havens to everyone who came in. I knew, with her by my side, I would always be home.

I sniffed in a deep, shaky breath and wiped at my eyes because the future with her was so damn beautiful I couldn't hold it in.

I saw her in this beautiful house we'd built, adding art and personal touches to every room. Saw her carrying a child of our own. Saw dance parties in the kitchen, cartoons on Saturday mornings, and nights full of passion where we got to choose each other, over and over again.

So when the preacher asked me that question, it was so damn easy to say, "I do."

❧

AFTER THE CEREMONY but before the reception in our shop building, we were mingling with all the guests. Grandpa came up to me leaning on his cane. "Kid, I'm happy for you."

I grinned at him and gave him a hug. "This wouldn't be here without you, Grandpa."

He clapped my shoulder, and when I stepped back, he said, "It's damn good getting to see this while I'm still here."

My lips lifted, because he was right. Even though he gave this to me, he was getting something as well: the opportunity to see his grandson and his wife start their life together. I didn't need to be so independent, so proud, because we were truly all in this together.

"I love you, Gramps."

He grinned at me. "Love you too."

Grandpa shuffled along, and before someone else could chat with me, Mags got up on her tiptoes and said, "Come to the bedroom. I have a gift for you."

"Anything including the bedroom and you, I'm in," I said, winking after.

Laughing, she shoved me playfully and said, "I'll see you there."

She excused herself from everyone, saying she had to use the restroom, and a few minutes later, I walked up the back steps and into our home. The build had taken eight months, and we both agreed we wanted to get married in the backyard when it was ready.

This home had been the perfect mix of what we both wanted. A wraparound porch, bay windows to sit in and enjoy the pretty countryside. We had a big open kitchen with room for a long table because we knew family would always be welcome here.

But my favorite place was our bedroom. It had room for a king-sized bed, a corner with chairs so we could sit together and watch the sunrise at the east-facing window, and a massive bathroom and closet—which Maggie had already claimed as mostly her own.

When I walked into the room, I found her looking out the window at all our guests below. She turned when she heard my footsteps on the carpet and gave me a soft smile.

I said the first thing that came to mind. "You're beautiful."

Her smile grew. "When I saw you standing at the end of the aisle, I thought, how lucky am I to get to see his face for the rest of my life."

My lips lifted of their own accord. "So I was told there would be a present up here."

"There is." She walked to my nightstand, by the bed where we'd sleep for the first night tonight as man and wife. She picked up a ream of paper with plastic coiling holding it together.

"What's this?" I asked as she walked it to me, her dress sliding over the floor with her steps.

"It's the story of us."

I looked from the pages to her tentative expression. "I didn't know you wrote."

"I don't. I mean, I didn't. But that night we were at The Retreat, you said you'd read the story of us. And one night when I couldn't sleep, I just started writing. The first thing that came to mind when I sat down to write was the day we met." She smiled down at the pages. "You sat by me in the lunchroom, and when I said, 'That seat's saved,' you replied, 'No need to save it anymore. I'm already here.'"

I chuckled at my teen bravado. I'd been so nervous to talk to her back then. "Well how does it end?" I asked.

"Well, at the pool, you said it could end with hot tub sex, but..." She held the book to me. "I hope our story doesn't end, so the last words are... Hello, Happily Ever After."

EPILOGUE
AGATHA

DEIDRE LET OUT a sigh as she fussed over the table of taco fixings. The bride and groom had decided to have a taco bar, and I agreed to help her with it after the ceremony. "Of course Rhett and Maggie would sneak off after the ceremony while we're all waiting to celebrate with them!"

I chuckled. I'd never had a wedding day of my own, but I hoped I would be as in love as Rhett and Maggie looked if I ever did walk the aisle. But then again, as a woman in my mid-forties, I doubted it would ever happen to me. And I was okay with that. I had a good life—the kids were grown and gone, so I had a little extra money in the bank. I liked my job waiting tables at Woody's Diner. It could be so much worse. Had been, in the past.

"Aggie?" Deidre said.

I turned my head. "Sorry, what did I miss?" Sometimes I got lost thinking and didn't remember to pay attention to what was in front of me.

She smiled at me. "I said I need to go check on the

catering. Would you mind telling Rhett and Maggie to speed it up?"

I chuckled. "Sure thing."

That seemed like a bad idea though as I walked into their pretty house. There were nice wood floors on the main level, and they had new looking furniture and pictures of them and their families hanging on the walls. It was so much nicer than the little house I lived in with its constant drips and leaks and settling foundation. It used to be my mama's. The same house I grew up in, and probably the house I'd die in if I was being honest.

I checked around the kitchen and the living rooms, but when I didn't see them, I started upstairs. Except a few stairs up, I saw someone already walking up in a suit.

"Is that you, Rhett?" I asked. I couldn't really tell in the dim lighting.

But the man who turned around was Grayson Madigan.

My heart instantly started beating faster. This man was the definition of a silver fox. Still fit from work on the farm, with a warm, friendly smile and a thick head of gray hair. He said, "Sorry, Jack sent me inside to look for Maggie and Rhett."

I chuckled. "Deidre sent me inside for the same reason."

He shook his head. "Must have ESP they've been together so long."

I nodded secretly wishing I could have the same thing with someone one day. "Do you think they're upstairs?"

A loud moan echoed through the upstairs, and both our cheeks flushed red.

"Maybe we should..." He stepped down the stairs, but

I moved up, trying to get out of his way, and now we were on the staircase, chest to chest.

Parts of me I'd long since forgotten fired back to life this close to his strong chest and the earthy smell of his cologne.

"I—" I swore I saw his eyes flick down, to my chest, my lips.

I had to be dreaming. He was fifteen years older than me. And I was never known for being the most desirable woman in town, a curvy single mom with two kids and hardly two pennies to rub together most of my life.

He seemed to realize we were both still standing there and stepped past me. "Why don't we turn back and say we tried?"

I smiled, barely catching my breath as I gained some space. "That sounds like a plan to me."

EPILOGUE

KNOX

I CAME out of the bathroom to see Dad and Agatha coming downstairs. Dad saw her almost every day at the diner, but as far as I knew, they were only friendly acquaintances. Except the flush on her cheeks told a different story.

What would be the odds that my dad got remarried before I even had a serious girlfriend in Cottonwood Falls?

I tried not to think about that as I walked outside to the makeshift parking lot in the pasture. A couple country kids were waiting for me in their truck, holding a pig between them with a ring of flowers around its neck and a blanket over its back that said CONGRATULATIONS.

"Thank you, gentlemen," I told them, passing them a fifty. "You'll come get it in ten minutes?"

They nodded.

"Follow me."

I picked up the pig, holding the squirming, oinking

thing in my arms, and walked to the shop where the reception was taking place. Rhett and Maggie shared their first dance on the cement floor, eyes only for each other.

They looked so happy together, and it had me thinking, *would that ever happen for me in this small town?* I wasn't so sure.

The song closed to an end, and the kid on my right said, "Now?"

I shook my head out of those thoughts usually brought on by weddings and said, "Now." I bent, letting the pig on the ground, and it instantly darted around ankles of wedding goers.

People shuffled, screamed, and laughed as they realized there was a pig running around the shop building.

I saw Rhett's gaze follow the noise until he spotted the animal, and when he did, a grin spread on his lips. He yelled, "KNOX! I'M GETTING YOU BACK FOR THIS."

Chuckling, I called back, "I'd like to see you try."
***
Start reading Knox's story today in Hello Tease!

Want more Maggie and Rhett? Get this special bonus scene with a dash of spice a year after their wedding day where Maggie finally gets rename "The Stabbin' Wagon."

Get the free bonus story today!

Start reading Hello Heartbreaker today!

AUTHOR'S NOTE

When I was little, my aunt used to let me visit her for a week every summer. As one of four children, it was so fun for me to go and get pampered by myself and feel so cool with my aunt. To me, she was living the life—she had her own house, a successful job, a closet full of beautiful clothes, and great friends. When I started visiting, she was single, then she had a boyfriend, then she had a new boyfriend. Then she got married.

As I grew older and got into high school, we talked a bunch, and one topic we covered extensively was love and relationships. At one point, I can't remember when, she said to me, "The person you marry is going to break your heart, but you love them and you stay with them anyway."

I didn't really understand at the time.

In fact, I thought it was a little crazy.

Wasn't a good marriage supposed to be the pinnacle, a relationship with your soul mate where you had each other's backs, loved each other and lived happily ever after?

That's certainly what I was dreaming of as a young woman.

I wanted soul mate, happily ever after love.

I just didn't understand what that looked like.

Or that, yes, my husband would break my heart. And that I would still love him and be with him after. We would still share a bed. Still go out on dates and talk about our dreams for the future. Still make love and fight and make up again.

It doesn't mean that we weren't "meant to be together" (if that really is a thing), and it doesn't mean that our marriage is horrible.

It means we're human.

We both come from different families, we have different experiences of life, and we have different pain points and triggers and ways of handling things. Those very human experiences make us who we are, but sometimes cause us to wound ourselves and others.

And when we're in a relationship, we get to decide— do we want more of this or less of this in our lives?

In some cases, we decide we want none of it in our lives. We have to cut off a spouse, a boyfriend or girlfriend, a parent, a sibling, because they're not healthy to be around and have no interest in healing a relationship.

Sometimes, we say, sure that's a "five minute" friend. I'll stop and talk to you at the grocery store or text to see if you're okay, but that's it. Five minutes tops.

Sometimes, we realize that's a person we love, we want them in our life, and we have to learn to forgive and accept them for the person they are and the person they can't be.

I think that's one of the hardest things to do in life.

Like Maggie, I have a tendency to wall myself off. After a harder upbringing, I don't want to invite people who hurt me back into my life. And like Maggie, I've had to learn how to keep my heart open to forgiving and loving people who are flawed, just like I am flawed.

But also believe people can change and grow. I know I'm not the person that my husband married. I've been to way too much therapy for that. (lol) And letting go of old hurts to move on to a new future can be really freaking hard.

But I think it's important to remember too that change comes slowly. Rhett and Maggie got to see big changes because they'd been apart for so long. When we live with someone, those changes come so slowly, day by day, that they can be hard to recognize until enough time has passed.

Sometimes, people don't change. Sometimes they can't or aren't willing to. But the amazing thing is that it doesn't matter so much what they do. *You* have the power.

You have the power to forgive.

To hold boundaries.

To keep distance.

To draw close.

To grow and adapt.

And I think that's an amazing place to be.

ACKNOWLEDGMENTS

OH MY GOSH! Rhett's book is done! I've been thinking about his story for a long time, like since Confessions of the Funny Fat Friend. So many amazing people have helped me get this story out into the world!

First, I want to acknowledge and thank my family for supporting my career as a writer. My husband is a full-time dad and part time accountant. I love having his support in so many aspects of life, including my writing business. My boys are always there to give me name ideas and inspiration too.

Team Kelsie is THE BEST! They support me on this writing journey and pick up so many tasks that help me get writing time in! Sally and Heather THANK YOU for being you!

It was so hard to imagine capturing Rhett's personality on a cover but, Najla Qamber and her team knocked it out of the park! I absolutely love both versions of this cover, and I hope you do too!

Tricia Harden is the best editor I could ask for. She is a cheerleader and friend every writer wishes they could have, and I'm so lucky to work with her!

Jordan Truex proofread this story for me! Our first time working together, it was amazing to see how quickly she worked!

Luke Welland and Allyson Voller signed on to narrate this book while I was still writing it, and I loved creating this story knowing the audiobook would be in their capable hands!

To all the readers in Kelsie Hoss's Hussies, I am so thankful for you. You've created an amazing community full of love, support and friendship. Writing this story for you was an absolute joy.

To you, sweet reader, I'm so thankful to have you here. I love that you came for the story and stayed to learn more about how it was created. Your support and your time spent reading means the absolute world to me. Thank you.

ALSO BY KELSIE HOSS

The Confessions Series

Confessions of a High School Guidance Counselor

Confessions of a Smutty Romance Author

Confessions of the Funny Fat Friend

The Hello Series

Hello Billionaire

Hello Doctor

Hello Heartbreaker

Hello Tease

JOIN THE PARTY

Want to talk about Hello Billionaire with Kelsie and other readers? Join Hoss's Hussies today!

Join here: https://www.facebook.com/groups/hossshussies

ABOUT THE AUTHOR

Kelsie Hoss writes sexy romantic comedies with plus size leads. Her favorite dessert is ice cream, her favorite food is chocolate chip pancakes, and... now she's hungry.

You can find her enjoying one of the aforementioned treats, soaking up some sunshine like an emotional house plant, or loving on her three sweet boys.

You can learn more (and even grab some special merch) at kelsiehoss.com.

facebook.com/authorkelsiehoss
instagram.com/kelsiehoss